ALL FOR 1

A DEE SANDERS ADVENTURE

LP SNYDER

CAST OF CHARACTERS

Dee Sanders
Jamal & Angelic Jones
Mike & Keno Williams
Gina Dubulgee
Dr. Younes Arazi
Ahmed Alami
Ike Mann
Elizabeth Adassa
Dr. Hicham El Aynaoui
Diego Schwartz
Col. Santiago Sanchez
Stefanos Sakkari
Eva Toussaint
Sergei Papadopoulos
Karim Ahmed
Carl Withers
Mohammed Abu
Dr. Harlan Roberts

Portugal
Spain
Italy
Rome
Pale
marsala
Palermo
Tunis
Seville
Algiers
Marbella
Tangier
Ceuta
Fez
Morocco
Algeria
Tunisia

Serbia
Bulgaria
Istanbul
Greece
Turkey
Katakolo
Athens
Syria
Limassol
Lebanon
Haifa
Alexandria
Israel
Cairo
Amarna
Egypt Luxor
N
E
S

PROLOGUE

Three thousand years ago

The moon sank in the night sky as Pharaoh Akhenaten scurried about his treasure room. The dawn would break soon and he wanted to finish the task. As he moved around the dais, the stone hanging from his neck sparkled in the changing light. He watched the pattern on the wall for a brief second before moving on.

As the sun climbed over the notch in the far mountain peak and cast its rays into the valley, the Grand temple was the first thing his awakening people would see. The sun brought light and life to the valley. The pharaoh paused and watched the darkness whisk away, and then savored the beauty of his new creation.

Akhenaten had worked through the night, surrounded by the royal guard, counting and recounting his treasure. His new city, Amarna, would be expensive to build. Only the temple was complete. Building the temple and the city was something he had to do. The worship of the Sun God, Aten, and the love of his wife, Nefertiti, had demanded it.

He looked up, and she stood at the door as the room filled with light. "Hurry Akhenaten, the opening ceremony is a full day. We must not be late."

As she held his gaze, he replied, "Yes, we must hurry. There is so little time."

The royal guard scurried from the room and Akhenaten reset the stone and levered the throne into position. The day was about to begin.

PROLOGUE

Three months ago

The boy gazed out to the horizon. There was nothing but shimmering shapes in the distance. It was hot. His sister was kicking sand in the air with her bare feet and watching it drift on the light breeze. She chanted in a singsong voice that got on his nerves.

They'd been traveling all day, and he was tired and bored. He turned and kicked sand at her. "Be quiet. We should enjoy these few minutes before we have to go back to work."

"I am enjoying them," she replied and continued kicking sand and singing.

They had traveled all day from the Red Sea. Their parents were traders and crisscrossed Northern Africa, searching for goods and for customers, putting together supply with demand. They were meager middlemen who traveled from stall to stall, medina to medina. Sometimes they would stop around large groups of tourists. They would sell their wares and offer to take pictures of the tourists on one of their camels. That was profitable, so their parents said.

The children helped however they could. There were many chores, as the family never stopped moving. They could recall crossing from the Red Sea to the Mediterranean and to the Atlantic several times in their young lives.

On this late afternoon, the family was north and a little west of Luxor, Egypt. They had been along the Red Sea Riviera with many tourists and had sold most of their goods. Now they would head west across the desert and replenish their supplies before they began their journey back, from west to east. There would be several stops along the return trip. Many of the medinas were good for tourists.

The boy liked to explore. His little sister followed along. Near to where they camped, and from where they had just been standing, the boy ran across a small footer and the remnants of a wall. He brushed the sand away to determine what he could see. His little sister settled in to help him.

They worked quickly, as soon it would be time to help their mother with the evening preparations.

The boy used his hands at first, but then his leg and foot as he outlined the remaining shape of the structure. His little sister stayed on her knees and continued to scoop the sand away.

The footer went for some distance beyond what remained of the wall. After several minutes, the boy sat on the ruin to rest. It was nearly time to go back to camp.

His sister came up beside him and continued to scoop the sand away. As he sat and watched her, a portion of the floor atop the footer became visible. There was a design on the floor. He didn't recognize it.

As his sister moved along, he went behind her with his hand and continued to brush the sand away, and then traced the design on the floor with his finger.

Where his finger crossed two decorative scallops, the floor beneath flexed. He stopped and pushed down on the tile. It rocked sideways and turned up on one end. There was a small space underneath, and he peered into the darkness of it.

He couldn't see anything, but he felt sure something was or had been there. Why else would there be a hiding place? His body was blocking the sun, so he moved slightly to see if it would help illuminate the interior of the space.

He still couldn't see much, but then he thought he saw a sparkle. Looking harder, he drew his face closer to the hole. Something sparkled again.

Mustering his courage, he thrust his hand into the hole and felt something metal. He squeezed it quickly and pulled his hand out.

Sitting back and holding the item to the sun, he held what looked like a gold chain and a large sparkling stone.

At that moment, his mother yelled for them. He and his sister scurried back to camp.

1

STARTING OVER... AGAIN

Jamal and I caught the plane out of Mexico City and flew back to Seville. We had said goodbye to Elizabeth at the security gate. She'd caught a flight for Key West to meet Ike. They were going to make a nice couple.

It was a long trip, twelve hours non-stop, and we squirmed in our seats, paced the aisles, and talked about where we might travel next. The rest of our group had stayed in Seville, while Jamal and I had flown the golden bell we had found in the Sea of Cortez back to the Mexican authorities. It had been a wild six weeks, tracking the provenance of the bell and avoiding Miguelito Cortez and his henchmen. It had all been for nothing, really. We'd found the shipwreck by accident on a day when it had settled for a short time on a reef. Miguelito had spent his life looking for the ship, chasing a dream that would never come true, and then chasing us. The authorities had known about the bell all along. It should have been simple, but it hadn't been. I was glad it was over.

Jamal and I hoped the rest of our group had come up with something fun to do. Something that was relaxing, enjoyable, slow-paced, and entertaining. Somewhere in the Mediterranean, we could surely find that.

They met us late in the evening at the airport in Seville. Everyone looked tan, fit, and rested. Greeting us noisily, they all chattered at the same time. The only thing Jamal and I clearly understood was that everyone was ready to do something. They were tired of sitting around in Seville.

"Where are we off to, then?" asked Jamal.

"Did you know we could go to North Africa and never leave Spain?" answered Mike.

Giving him an odd look, Dee replied, "How is that?"

"There's a settlement on a peninsula off the Moroccan coast that Spain never relinquished. It's called Ceuta," answered Mike. "We can take a ferry, see North Africa, and never leave Spain; no customs, no border crossing, and no hassles."

Jamal glanced up and spoke, "There ain't never no 'no hassles.'"

Mike held his hands in the air and gestured. Then he spoke. "You just got to relax, see the sites, and enjoy."

They started the next morning, driving the VW Thing they had bought while fleeing from Miguelito Cortez. It had come with no doors or a top when they'd bought it. While Jamal and Dee had been away, Mike had found some stray doors from a parts dealer and had bought a new bikini top so they could stay out of the sun. North Africa promised to be hot, Spanish or not. The doors had been different colors, and Mike had spray painted them all a yellow similar to the original body of the vehicle. The doors had that spray-painted quality, so perhaps the group wouldn't look as touristy as the folks in the new Range Rovers. There was nothing like blending into the surroundings.

Mike drove as they left the city and headed for the coast.

It would take about three hours to get to the city via the A-92 and the A-45.

The ladies wanted to visit the beaches on Costa del Sol and do a little sightseeing. The group would spend the night and catch the ferry first thing in the morning. Based on experience, they decided it wisest to check out of the hotel and take all their possessions, especially their passports.

They drove east across the interior of Spain and then dropped south to the coast. It was a pleasant ride. The sun wasn't too hot, and in an open vehicle, there were plenty of breezes.

Rolling into Marbella, they drove along the coast road and marveled at the size and style of the homes.

"Didn't James Bond live here?" asked Keno.

"The character, or the actor, Sean Connery?" replied Dee.

"Either," she answered.

"I don't know about the character, but the actor lived here for a couple of decades. He made the place popular and then moved away."

"That happens sometimes," added Jamal.

Mike leaned over toward Jamal, "That ever happen to you?"

"No," Jamal replied and then grinned before answering, "I left Atlanta of my own free will. Actually, it was Angelic's doing," he added, trying to make a joke. He turned to look at her, but she, Gina, and Keno were engrossed in the scenery. Their eyes kept swiveling back and forth between the views of the houses and the ocean.

Jamal turned to look at the water. It was a crystal blue and, with the sun reflecting off of it, nearly blinding.

"Probably a nice place to live," he murmured, "for a former spy."

Dee and Mike nodded their agreement.

As they approached the center of town, Dee turned toward the women and asked, "Since it's early afternoon, do you want to check in, grab some lunch, and head for the beach?"

"Absolutely," replied Keno and Gina. There were nods of approval from several others.

"It's time to stop. I'm hungry," Jamal added.

Mike found the hotel on a side street and parked the Thing in a small adjacent lot. They trooped in together and approached the desk, checked in, and got directions to a local restaurant.

The food was rich and filling. They waddled back to the hotel, making fun of one another.

"Shall we roll out to the beach?" asked Dee.

"That'll be the only way we get there," replied Jamal as he and the others laughed.

After walking the short distance to the beach, they set up at an angle so they could see several of the large homes nearby and the clear blue water of the sea.

"Not as humid as Mexico," noted Jamal.

"Yeah, but the sun feels just as hot," replied Mike.

"Would you boys stop whining and have a seat?" called Angelic.

Dee rolled out a towel next to Gina, but she moved further away and toward the others. Dee stayed where he was.

Shortly afterward, Mike and Jamal got up and headed for the water. They called to Dee but he waved them off and rolled over.

The women were left alone.

"Wonder why Dee didn't go with them?" said Angelic.

"Probably studying up on something," answered Gina in a short tone.

Angelic and Keno looked at her with knitted brows.

"I'm sorry," said Gina. "It's just that he gets on my nerves sometimes always having the answers."

Angelic laughed. "He does know a lot, and he isn't afraid to share. It can be overbearing, but I think he means well. He was a great leader on the island. When we were all stranded."

"I agree with Gina," said Keno. "I get tired of it. We're not on the island anymore."

"You guys not compatible now?" asked Angelic. "You seemed so close."

"It's not that. I'm very attracted to him. He just gets on my nerves sometimes with all those facts."

"Just tell him to shut up and sit down, but don't throw him away."

Keno laughed out loud at that one. "Mike and I fuss all the time, since we were married, but that's part of it."

"Jamal and I are the same. You guys are still just new."

———

Sunburned, windblown, and growing weary of staring at enormous yachts, stark blue-bleached skies, and shimmering water, they all fell asleep and stayed too long. Several hours later, they packed up to leave.

Walking back to the rooms, they decided against any further touristing but opted instead for cool showers, an early dinner, and bed. The ferry would leave first thing in the morning.

"We'd better get some sunscreen and use it. This could be a brutal trip," said Angelic.

Gina poked a finger to her arm, and a white spot appeared momentarily and then disappeared.

"We definitely stayed out too long," she murmured.

2

———

THE CROSSING

The next morning, they woke early and met for a breakfast of eggs and fruit, then traveled to the ferry. It was a small, flat ship, almost a barge.

"When I was younger, I traveled up the Outer Banks in North Carolina on a ship similar to this. I could lean out, reach over, and touch the water," said Dee.

"Good thing it's calm," replied Angelic, looking down at the proximity of the gentle waves.

Dee nodded and answered, "I made that same trip a couple of years ago, and the ship had changed. It looked more like an ocean liner, and you were hundreds of feet above the water."

"Not quite so intimate," replied Gina, who had been listening.

Dee smiled at her and nodded his head. Angelic grinned.

The group spent much of the next three hours roaming around the ship, checking the view from various places, and trying to stay in the shade when possible. Keno had bought several large bottles of sunscreen in Marbella, and they all slathered it on throughout the morning.

"The water is the bluest blue I've ever seen. It's almost like pool water, and the sun is hot. It feels like it's shining directly on you, no filter. It's similar to how it felt some days back on the island, but without the same humidity," said Jamal, as he rubbed sunscreen onto his arms. He was referring to the five weeks the group had spent stranded together on a deserted island after the rogue wave and then the storm had separated their lifeboat from the cruise ship where they had first met.

"I don't know how much more of this I can stand," said Keno. It was an older ship, a converted cargo barge, and there wasn't anywhere to sit other than in the vehicle. The Thing was bunched up toward the interior of the pack of cars, and there had been little breeze when they had sat in it for a few moments.

Mike looked at his watch and then toward the shore, now more plainly visible. "We should be there soon."

The shore and the dock were coming up quickly, and the group moved toward their vehicle along with many other passengers who were doing the same.

A few moments later, the ship docked with a firm and noisy jolt, and the cars began to depart. There had been a rocky coastline as they'd approached Ceuta. But as the barge had pulled nearer and around a point that thrust out into the sea, it had arrived in a bustling harbor and faced a busy metropolitan area along the shore.

The group pulled off the ship slowly, turned into traffic, and began a slow creep with the other cars and trucks.

"What do we want to see first? The last ferry leaves at 6 p.m., so that gives us a half day to catch the sites and some lunch," said Jamal.

"Eating's the high point of your day, isn't it?" teased Angelic.

Jamal grinned and replied, "People have to eat, even if they are in some exotic foreign place."

"There is something called the House of Dragons that I'd like to see," said Gina. "I think it's right downtown. It should be somewhere close."

"Should be hard to miss," said Dee.

"Two brothers built it at the turn of last century. It has four large dragons mounted on the pediment of the second floor," replied Gina.

"Is there a story behind it?" asked Dee.

"Not that I've seen," answered Gina. "You usually know all this stuff," she continued with a harsher tone.

Dee glanced at her quickly, but she looked away and didn't meet his eyes.

"I'm not familiar with it. Let's go look." Dee found it on a tour map and directed Mike, who was still driving, to the corner of Kings Square, at the center of downtown.

The house was three stories tall, in a Moorish style, with four large dragons on pedestals centered near the main doorway. From three stories down, they each looked to be the size of a vehicle.

"They must be heavy," noted Mike.

"Actually, those are fiberglass and don't weigh much. The originals were bronze but disappeared in the 1920s," replied Gina.

Dee turned to her and spoke. "How did you get so informed?"

"I researched it," replied Gina. "We shouldn't have to rely on you to know everything."

Mike and Jamal both turned and grinned at him.

"Sorry, I didn't realize I was a know-it-all," answered Dee.

"Just sometimes," whispered Angelic.

"Dude is keeping us informed," replied Mike.

"I don't want one of those dragons falling on me," added Jamal as he stared up at them. "What's next?"

They spent the next couple of hours grabbing lunch at a Moroccan café, viewing the statue of the Pillars of Hercules, and touring the island's historic fortifications along the water and perimeter of the city—also known as the "Royal Walls," which had protected the Portuguese and then the Spanish from opposing forces. Then they drove to the Fortress on top of Monte Hacho, which was thought to be one of the actual or mythological Pillars of Hercules, along with the rock of Gibraltar as the other pillar.

"I never knew this place was here," said Dee.

"What else don't you know?" asked Keno.

"It would seem a great many things."

Jamal was glancing in the distance toward Spain. Mike was looking toward the Atlantic, toward Morocco, and Tangier, the last city before the Atlantic.

Jamal swung his glance toward Dee and the others. "What if we drove over to Tangier and spent the night? There's a lot to see, and it'll be tough in one day; plus, there's the ferry ride back. Let's stay in North Africa."

Gina had been fiddling with her phone, but she looked up at the group. "It should be an hour or a little more to get to Tangier. I'd vote for making the drive. We could catch a ferry from there and go back to Gibraltar if we wanted. I'd like to see Morocco," she added.

Angelic and Keno turned to look at Gina.

"I don't really fancy another boat ride, especially in the dark and sitting basically in the water," said Angelic. Keno nodded her agreement.

Mike turned to Dee. "Let's go look," Dee replied. "We have everything with us. Our passports should get us across the border."

An hour later, they had entered Morocco and were

halfway to Tangier. Gina was looking up lodging and Keno was looking for sites to visit. Off in the distance, Mike, who was still driving, could see the Atlas Mountains.

"I don't know about y'all, but I'd like to see those mountains up close, after we visit the city," he said.

"They look pretty arid," added Jamal. "It's probably high desert. We'll need to take some water and food with us just in case we can't find any."

They pulled into the outskirts of Tangier. Driving slowly down the streets, they noticed a much stronger Moroccan or Arabic feel to the city. The architecture, the people, and the clothing—all felt different.

"It's not like Spain. Even though Ceuta was on the African mainland, it still felt very much like Seville or even Gibraltar," said Gina.

She had found them a place to stay, a small hotel close to the medina, or the center and most historic part of the ancient city.

"Maybe we should check in, eat, rest, and plan for tomorrow?" suggested Dee. "I'm kind of tired. There was a lot of wind and sun from the ferry and from the drive here."

"I like it," replied Angelic.

"I'm in," added Keno.

Mike and Jamal looked and each other and nodded. Mike pulled the Thing into a small lot across the street from the address Gina had given him, and they went inside.

3

—————

THE DESERT BECKONS

The group slept in, woke late, ate breakfast quickly, and marched out to tour the city.

"Let's go walk through the medina first," said Jamal. "Get an idea of the layout and of the people. It should be quick. When we finish that, where can we go?"

Instead of moving quickly, the group wandered through the alleys of the medina for hours. They stopped at small museums, gazed at private homes, searched in small shops, and then wandered into the bazaar, locally known as "the souq," at the heart of the city.

The marketplace was jammed with people and vendors. Rapid-fire chatter in Arabic and other languages swirled around them. But they also heard English, some of it broken but enough to communicate. The women found clothing, scarves, hats, and jewelry.

Keno poked through one of the smaller stalls. An older woman, apparently Moroccan, was minding the place. She was wrapped from head to toe in the light-colored clothing of the desert. Her eyes sparkled at Keno as she touched different objects, picking them up and then returning them to their places.

Fearing that Keno might not make a purchase and having slow sales so far that day, the stall keeper mumbled, "Mujawharat," and pointed at some jewelry Keno had not seen.

Keno glanced up at her and followed the woman's finger. A variety of necklaces, bracelets, rings, and earrings were piled upon the back of a nearby table. Thinking that she hadn't observed many of the local women wearing jewelry, Keno felt like it must be primarily for the tourists. There was leather wrapping on many items, mixed with stones and brightly colored threads or twine. The jewelry was something specifically for visitors to the area. Then she saw it. A big, gaudy thing, an eight-sided teardrop shaped stone on a heavy, gold-colored chain. She picked it up and held it to the light. The stone sparkled.

The stall keeper smiled.

"What is it?" asked Keno.

The stall keeper rattled off something Keno did not understand.

Another woman had entered the stall and stood only a few feet from Keno. She too was wrapped from head to toe, but her clothing was of much finer, brighter material. She looked up when the stall keeper spoke, then turned to Keno.

"She doesn't know what it is. One of her children found it during their travels. She thinks it's obviously—what is the word?—not fake, but costume. She will make you a good price."

Keno smiled at the other shopper and said, "Thank you. What does it cost?"

The shopper turned to the stall keeper. "Alsier?"

The stall keeper paused for a moment, then held up five fingers.

"Five dollars?" asked Keno.

The other shopper shook her head, "Offer her a dollar, and that's a big price."

Keno pulled a dollar out of her pocket and held it up.

The stall keeper smiled and, as she took the dollar, squeezed Keno's hand.

Keno turned to thank the other shopper, but she had wandered off. Keno smiled at the stall keeper and slid the necklace over her head and around her neck. She turned to look for Gina and Angelic.

———

THE STALL KEEPER NODDED, SMILED TO HERSELF AS SHE turned away, and slid the dollar into her pocket. Whatever that thing was, she was glad to be rid of it.

Sometimes at night, when they had been camped in the desert, the stone would glow and gleam in the darkness, like the stars above. She had taken it away from her children when they had showed their find to her. There was something unusual about the stone, something not quite normal. She had hated to throw the thing away. Goods were too scarce. She had wrapped the stone in dark cloth and put it in the bottom of one of the storage bins. Tangier was as far west as they were going. She'd wanted to throw the stone in the ocean, but surely it had value to someone. Put it in the stall in the medina. Sell it to the first person who came along. If they didn't look, point them to the stone. The young tourist girl had snapped the thing up when she'd seen the necklace.

The woman wiped her brow with some relief. There was another thing. In the last few days of their travels there had been another contingent behind them. It was something that didn't happen often.

When she mentioned it to her husband, he brushed it off. "Just another group of Egyptians, crossing," he said.

"But Egyptians rarely cross the dessert. They have no need. They are home."

"Must be something they want," he had answered.

She didn't like the sound of that and was grateful to be rid of the stone.

***

Gina and Angelic were in a stall across the walkway. Keno strolled over and said, "Look what I found."

They turned, and, spotting the large stone, grinned brightly at her.

"Girl, you will be the envy of gaudy jewelry fans around the world," said Angelic.

"It shines like a diamond," added Gina.

They moved together to the next stall, where the men were admiring leather belts. A pile of straw hats just beyond where they stood caught Angelic's eye.

After struggling to make a choice, Angelic examined her new purchase and held it aloft. "You men should get some hats too. You'll probably need them if we go up in the mountains."

Jamal and Dee turned toward her and examined the selection. Mike was still looking across the bazaar. He stared for several minutes.

Jamal finally noticed, turned to him, and spoke. "What are you looking at?"

Mike pointed across the market. "There was a man over there."

"Don't point at people," whispered Keno. "It's not polite anywhere, much less in a foreign country."

Mike dropped his hand. "I was looking across at the fruit market, and there was a man. He was an old, old man in a light-brown cloak with a dark-brown diamond pattern on it.

He wore a turban that was the same blue as the water when we crossed on the ferry. I was scanning the area, and saw him looking at us. So I stopped and looked at him for a second. He glared at me and shook his head."

"Maybe he doesn't like tourists," replied Jamal. "Show him to me."

Mike raised a hand to point again.

"I don't see anything," said Jamal.

"He's gone," replied Mike.

"You said he was old—probably just cranky, thought you were staring at him," answered Jamal.

They turned to the others. No one else had seen the man. They had been looking at the hats and scarves.

"Let's get some lunch," said Angelic. "I'm hungry."

They ate in a courtyard beyond the bazaar, which offered a view of the market. At one point, Mike thought he saw the man in the blue turban again.

"Look, there he is," called Mike.

The others turned, but the man had moved on around the bazaar.

"It's a big place and full of people. It's no wonder you saw him again, or maybe it's another blue turban. Why is it bothering you?" asked Jamal.

"It's not bothering me. I just wanted you to see. There's something about him makes my skin crawl. He looks so old," replied Mike.

As they were finishing their lunch, Dee asked, "Are we about ready to move on to Fez and the mountains? It's a four-hour drive. We'll get there late in the day but before dark. We can find a place to stay on the way."

Shortly after leaving Tangier, they encountered foothills and could see the Atlas Mountains in the distance beyond.

"Are those mountains just in Morocco or are they a chain?" asked Keno.

"They run across North Africa along the Mediterranean to Tunisia and south to the Sahara," replied Dee.

"How did you know that?" asked Angelic.

"I looked at the map," replied Dee.

Angelic glanced at Gina, who smirked at her and then whispered, "Mr. Google Maps."

What vegetation there had been slipped away, and the terrain turned rugged and desert-like. It was a rocky soil with little plant life, unlike the sand of the Sahara. The Thing kicked up a plume of dust as it traveled along the interior roads. They had fueled in Tangier and bought more water, snacks, and sunscreen.

As they ascended into the mountains, on one of several roads, Jamal turned to Mike and asked, "What is it you hope to see?"

Mike was silent for several seconds before he replied. "I don't really know. I saw the mountains in the distance and felt this overwhelming urge to see them up close. I thought we might look and then head back to the coast. Instead of going back to Spain or Gibraltar, maybe we drive along the Mediterranean and see Algiers or Tunis."

"We're just a bunch of tourists, out to have a good time, see the sights, what's the harm," said Dee.

"Could we drive all the way to Egypt?" asked Jamal. "I always wanted to see the pyramids." He turned and looked at Dee.

"I don't know," Dee answered.

"It wasn't on your map?" asked Keno.

"I guess not."

Gina had been playing with her phone, but now she looked up and spoke. "It appears we'd have to drive across Libya and enter Egypt, and the first place of any size we'd get to would be Alexandria. That presumes we drive from here to Algiers and then to Tunis, which would mean circling the Mediterranean on the North African side. It would be several days."

"I'm not too sure I want to drive across Libya. I mean, how safe is that?" asked Keno.

"Maybe along the coast it would be okay," replied Jamal. He looked at Dee.

Shaking his head, Dee replied, "I really don't know. We could go as far as Tunis and then check out the possibility of driving across Libya. If it's a problem, maybe we could catch a plane, a train, or a ferry to Alexandria. It will be several days before we get to Tunis."

"Let's do it," said Jamal. He looked at Mike and spoke again. "All for one…"

Mike looked back at him and replied, "And one for all."

They rode along in silence after that. The wind whipped across them, and the air was gritty with the dust and sand from the rocky soil. The sun baked down, and they huddled together in the seats of the Thing to stay out of the direct light. The air already seemed thinner and the daylight brighter.

"Fez is at the base of the mountains on the far side from Tangier. We'll have to go up, over, and then back down. Do we want to spend a day in Fez, rest up, and look around before we go back into the mountains?" asked Dee.

"I wouldn't mind resting for a day," replied Angelic.

They all turned to look at Mike. "I'm okay with it. I mean, this is a pretty big change of plans from cruising the Mediterranean on board a ship to driving the north shore of Africa in a VW Thing."

They reached Fez late in the afternoon and found their lodging, a campsite. But not like any they had seen or visited before. There were tents, but they featured wooden floors covered with Persian rugs, and electric lights. There was a bath tent and a dinner tent. Those were much larger than the two-person sleeping tents. The group broke up into their respective couples and separated for a time to unpack and clean up for dinner.

It is against Moroccan law for unmarried couples to stay together, so Gina and Dee assumed the position of a married couple. Gina squeezed Dee's hand as they entered the tent and whispered, "Don't you wish?" before releasing his hand and entering the tent alone. Dee followed closely behind her. He started to speak but thought better of it.

They cleaned up in the large bathing tent, which had separate sections for men and women. Then they met in the dining tent. The women had donned their new scarves, long pants, and mid-thigh tops. The men also wore long pants and Moroccan-print shirts, but no headwear.

"Don't do anything with your left hand," whispered Dee as they approached the dining tent. "Don't shake hands, or pat anyone, or touch anything, and don't eat with your left hand."

"What's up with that?" asked Angelic.

"It's some sort of tradition related to hygiene. I don't know how strict it is in a tourist camp, but let's err on the side of caution."

Everyone nodded, and they entered the dining tent. Chairs and mounds of pillows offered plenty of seating. Fans circulated the air overhead. The tables were opulent and hand-carved, and were set with fine china and crystal. The food was rich. There was no alcohol, but very strong coffee and tea. The group sat on the pillows.

4

UP THE MOUNTAIN

It was an enormous meal, multi-course, and when they couldn't eat any more, they hobbled back to their sleeper tents.

"We eat too much. We're going to have to get some exercise," said Keno.

"We'll start tomorrow. We'll climb up the mountain," replied Mike.

"No climbing," added Jamal. "Let's just eat less."

When they awoke the next morning and stepped outside, much of the camp had already been broken down. Jamal called over to Dee, "I didn't know they were temporary? How does this work?"

"I guess tents are easy to move," replied Dee. "I'm not sure."

Gina had followed Dee out of the tent and called to Jamal, "They follow the tourists from location to location. You can make a reservation in any part of the country and they have a compound somewhere in the area, or they move to it. I saw the background when I signed us up and thought it would be fascinating."

Angelic stepped out of her tent and called to Gina, "And you didn't tell us?"

Gina grinned back at her and replied, "I thought I'd let it be a surprise and if you didn't like it, I could disavow any knowledge."

"Pretty clever," replied Jamal.

"That's my girl," added Angelic, and the three of them linked hands and strolled toward Mike and Keno's tent, leaving Dee standing alone.

Shortly afterwards, all six of them were packed and standing beside the VW.

"Do we want to tour the city and then go up into the mountains or see the mountains first?" asked Dee.

Everyone turned to Mike and looked. He stared back for a moment as if thinking and then said, "Let's go up in the mountains first, come back for lunch, then explore the city."

Everyone piled into the Thing, and Mike drove out of town. He rolled up a few streets and climbed into the hills. Shortly, they saw signs announcing the Borj Nord fort and museum.

"That might be cool. We can look back over the city," said Keno.

"I didn't think you liked heights," replied Angelic.

"I don't, but I'll stand back a ways." She put her hand on Mike's arm. "Let's stop."

As they approached the fort, Mike saw the gate and turned at the entrance.

The fort turned out to be mostly ruins with an enclosed metal building that functioned as a museum and gift shop.

The group took the guided tour and, when they reached the summit of the fort, stopped and looked back over Fez. It appeared to be a solid mass. Very few streets were visible. It looked as though someone had built in every available spot, a tangled web of humanity, teeming streets and crowded dwellings. But it was a fabulous view of the city, the valley beyond, and the downrange mountains. Behind them, in the opposite direction, lurked more mountains.

"The Atlas Mountains pop up, on and off, all across North Africa," intoned the guide. "Everywhere you look, their presence is omnipresent." He turned to move on with the tour.

"What peoples have occupied this land?" asked Mike.

The guide stopped and turned back around. Six people had been the limit on each tour, so there was just the group of them.

"Indigenous Berbers, natives of some type, would most likely have been the first identifiable settlers or occupants, followed by Phoenicians, Romans, Vandals, Arab Muslims, and then Berbers again."

"So a lot of different groups passed through here?" asked Jamal.

The guide nodded. "Most of them stayed for a while. It's why you see so many different influences in the architecture, the languages, the clothing. It's widely varied. The Muslims built this fort in the 1500s. They were the longest non-Berber occupation."

"But you say it's back to Berber now?" asked Gina.

"Morocco is a Muslim country, but the rural areas are made up mostly of the Berber tribes. Many of them are Muslim, but they are non-Arabic, as they are indigenous to this area and not the Middle East."

There was silence for a moment.

The guide began again. "If you continue north, there are some tombs—actually ruins—not far from here. They were built around the same time as the fort. Take a look at them. They're fascinating, and the view of the city is equally outstanding. By the way, there's also an old site further north, near the peak in the road, that dates back to prehistory. No one is certain who built it, but every passing civilization has used it, at least briefly, down through time. It's like a dumping ground of history. It's not a park because the government doesn't know how to market it or how to explain it. It's not marked on the maps, so I'll scribble you out some directions. You can see the Mediterranean in the distance to the north and Fez to the south from the summit of the peak, just beyond what's left of the village."

They finished the tour and drove on to the Marinid Tombs. The group quickly hiked around a free-standing arch, the walls of a small ceiling-less building, and another pair of arches with a common wall.

"I guess none of those passing civilizations had much respect for artifacts from the previous generations," said Jamal.

"That and maybe time, or war. Who knows?" replied Dee.

"You guys ready to go on up the mountain?" asked Mike. "I'd like to see the remnants of that village and the view back to Fez and out to the sea."

The group followed the guide's instructions, with Mike driving and Jamal navigating. They pulled off the mountain road and bounced along a secondary road for a little over a mile, then turned onto little more than a path for the last half mile.

"This isn't four-wheel drive, but it's geared so low that we're not having any problems with terrain or traction," said Mike as they pulled to a stop at the ruins and what looked like the end of the path.

They got out and stretched. The remains of the village were mostly crumbling footers and little bits of wall. There were fire pits, and back up against the rocks, what looked like the remnants of a well. The ruins wrapped around beneath the peak of the mountain and extended to the rock point beyond. Still standing close to the car, the group turned and looked down the valley toward Fez. It was a simmering hub of distorted light and concrete.

As the others looked out over the city, Mike wandered toward the rock point at the edge of the mountain and the remnants of the well. He heard a soft moaning. Quickening his pace, he hurried on toward the well and found a cloak covered leg sticking out from the far side. Mike stopped for just a moment. Then he moved slowly closer as the sound of the moaning intensified. He rounded the well from several feet away.

It was an old man in a light-brown cloak with a dark-brown diamond pattern. He wore a blue turban, the color of the Mediterranean. *It's not possible*, thought Mike. *But it sure looks like the man from the bazaar. Maybe that's a common pattern of clothing for people of a certain age.* The man had dark leathery skin, as if he had weathered a long time in the outdoors, but aquiline features. His eyes were such a dark brown they seemed almost black. Mike looked in those eyes, and they were endless in their depth, like looking back in time.

The old man said a word, "Aman!" Mike didn't recognize it and could not even determine the language. The old man whispered, "Help me."

Mike stepped closer, and the man radiated a heat that was palpable through his cloak and despite the cooler temperature. Mike stuck a hand out but stopped before he touched the man.

He must be burning up with fever, thought Mike. He leaned in closer, and the old man beckoned with his hand. Mike dropped to a knee and put his ear near the old man's lips. The man gurgled for a second and then whispered again, "Aman."

Mike turned his face to the old man, grabbed him by the shoulders, and asked, "What is it?"

The man pointed toward the others. Keno had stepped away from the car, and Mike saw a flicker in the old man's eyes when she turned and the stone around her neck caught the sun and sparkled.

As he turned back to Mike, the man's dark and depthless eyes began to lose their light and fade away. It dawned on Mike that they were sitting by a well, and the old man was burning up with fever.

"Let me get you some water," said Mike.

The old man grabbed Mike by the arms and pressed their faces close together. He shook his head at Mike and slipped back against the well.

"Mike, Mike, where are you?" called Jamal, who was heading toward the well with the others close behind.

Mike stood and walked toward them. He stopped a few feet away from them, a visible tremble in his shoulders.

"Mike, are you all right?" called Keno.

He bent over, hands on his knees, and nodded his head. He held up a finger, as he was breathing hard. He pointed to the well. "There's an old man over there. He looked like the guy from the bazaar."

"What?" asked Angelic.

Mike pointed to the well. "There's an old man over there, dying or dead by now."

The group hurried over to the well, but saw no prone figure in the sand.

"Where was he?" asked Dee.

"He was lying on the ground on the side closest to the mountain."

Dee knelt and looked at the dirt, rock, and sand on that side of the well. "There are a lot of tracks here, which is unusual for an abandoned ruin. It's hard to tell who may have been here."

"He was there, just a minute ago." Mike scrambled from

the well out to the point and back. Then he turned and looked toward the vehicle. He saw nothing. "I'm telling you, he was there."

Angelic stepped across and put her hand to his forehead. "I'm just checking your temperature. Maybe a little heat stroke, or fatigue."

Mike let her check but then stepped away. "I'm not sick. He was here."

"We believe you. He just isn't here now," answered Dee.

Keno had been standing to the side, watching intently. "Are you sure you're okay?" she asked Mike.

He nodded. Keno turned to Angelic and looked questioningly. Angelic shrugged and whispered, "We'll keep an eye on him."

There was a momentary pause, each person looking at the others, and then Jamal jumped into the conversation. "I'm hungry. Let's head back to town and grab some lunch. Then we can tour a little."

5

THE MEDINA

They hopped back in the Thing and drove to Fez. Mike parked at the hotel, and the group walked to the medina and stopped at the first open-air restaurant they saw.

After lunch, they fanned out in the medina, formally known as the "Medina of Fes el Bali." It was highly congested and mazelike. No vehicle traffic was allowed. It was hot. Gina's guidebook said it was best to take a tour so you didn't get lost, or to at least have a map. The medina was densely populated with over ninety thousand people, plus the remaining residents of the city.

They wandered from booth to booth and market to market. It was midafternoon and the temperature was climbing. They stopped for water. Another tour group sat in the shade with them.

The guide droned on. "Fez is the oldest city in Africa and it houses the oldest university in the world, founded in 859 AD."

"That was a long time ago," noted Jamal.

"It feels ancient," added Angelic.

Keno and Gina were studying Mike, who was sweating profusely. Dee stood to one side, just behind Mike's shoulder.

"There's a funny smell," said Mike.

Keno sniffed the air.

"I noticed it too," said Angelic.

Holding up her guidebook, Gina added, "It's probably all the tanneries. Haven't you noticed all the leather goods for sale? The factories are all open-air, and the smell is said to be everywhere in the medina."

Mike slumped a little, shook his head, and said, "Good, I thought maybe I was…" He didn't finish the thought, as he tumbled forward before Dee caught him.

Putting a hand to Mike's head, Dee said, "He's burning up. Get him some water and grab one of those stools."

Dee and Jamal got Mike seated with his back propped against the wall of the adjacent building. Mike shivered despite the heat and sweat pouring from his face and body.

Keno was anxiously rubbing her hands, her eyes growing larger.

"Hold still, girl. We'll get him to a doctor," advised Angelic.

Gina brought a bottle of water, and Dee grabbed a thin, soft woven rug from a nearby vendor and wrapped Mike in it.

As he was doing so, an older woman who was passing by —a local, from her features and clothing—came over to them. She was dark-skinned, dark-haired, and dark-eyed; short in stature; and heavyset. She wore a purple scarf, a brightly colored blouse and a long skirt. She wore lots of jewelry. She looked at Mike's face and then took his hands and said, "Your eyes are full of pain. There is something inside of you that is not of you. It will make you ill if it does not kill you. Rid yourself of it. Do what you must." She squeezed his hands and then chanted for a moment.

Mike sat there shivering but thought, *Her chanting, it's not a language that I've heard. It's not English or Spanish, or Arabic—maybe a Berber dialect? It sounded like the Navajo I heard on the reservations around the Grand Canyon when I visited as a child.*

The woman finished and patted Mike on the shoulder, nodded to the others, and turned away to resume her shopping.

The group had seen a couple of pedal cabs, which were bicycles pulling carts with umbrellas above the seats. Jamal ran down the walkway until he saw one of them in the distance and flagged it. The cab arrived at where Mike sat. Jamal and Dee loaded him into the cart and had Keno join Mike.

Dee gave the driver some money and the address of the hotel. "Are there a couple of other cabs nearby?" When the driver nodded, Dee asked, "Can you summon them? We need two more."

The driver spoke into a walkie-talkie and, after a quick response, replied, "Be here soon," and peddled away.

In a couple of minutes, another pedal cab arrived. Dee stepped forward. "Jamal, you and Angelic take this one. Jamal, you can help get Mike out and inside the hotel."

Angelic spoke. "I'll monitor him until we can find a clinic."

They nodded to one another, and Jamal and Angelic jumped into the cab.

"Just you and me again?" asked Gina.

"Yeah, we were probably the least helpful."

"I'd say you're right," replied Gina as she turned and climbed into the third cab. Dee gave the driver the address, and he peddled them away.

———

AT THE HOTEL, JAMAL UNLOADED MIKE AND WALKED HIM TO the room. Angelic took his temperature and wiped him down with wet rags. His fever was raging. Angelic directed Keno to locate a nearby clinic or hospital.

As Dee and Gina got to the room, so did the concierge who had seen them enter the lobby. He informed the group, "There is a nearby private clinic, one of the best in Morocco. Ask for Dr. Arazi. He is the head physician. We have a car out front that can take you there."

Jamal and Dee walked Mike to the entrance, the concierge following along. Dee turned to the man and asked, "Where is the clinic? How far from here?"

"Three blocks down, turn left, two blocks on the right. Get your vehicle and you can follow."

Dee and the concierge loaded Mike into the car, and Keno climbed into the small back seat as Jamal ran to retrieve the Thing. He pulled behind the hotel car as Dee, Gina, and Angelic gathered at the front door. They climbed in quickly, and the hotel car took off.

Racing the few blocks to the clinic, they were in shock over what could have happened to Mike so quickly.

"Why was it only him?" asked Angelic. "We were all together in the same places."

"I was thinking food poisoning," added Gina, "but we all ate the same thing."

Dee and Jamal shared a glance and shook their heads.

The hotel vehicle pulled into the main entrance of the clinic, and Jamal pulled alongside. He and Dee hopped out quickly and assisted Mike from the car. Keno climbed out behind them.

Angelic turned to the driver of the hotel vehicle. "Thank you," she called.

The man grunted and stepped back into the car.

As a group, they approached the front of the clinic. From

a few steps away, the doors swung open. A tall, slender Moroccan man in a white lab coat stepped out and extended an arm. "I am Dr. Arazi."

He led them through the clinic lobby and two workers came from one wing with a gurney. They loaded Mike and led him and Keno back into the wing from which they had come.

"Please wait here," said Dr. Arazi, sweeping his arms out to the plush lobby area. "Help yourself to whatever drinks and snacks you see. I'll update you as soon as I know something. Now it's time for testing. Please be patient."

Approximately an hour later, Dr. Arazi emerged from the wing where the orderlies had taken Mike. He still looked as fresh as when they arrived. Dee and Jamal glanced at one another but neither spoke.

He stopped, looked at the faces of the group, and managed a smile. "I've examined him thoroughly and run a few basic tests. I don't immediately see anything wrong, any cause. But the fever is clearly evident, and the temperature high. So I've scheduled some additional testing. We'll find whatever it is."

6

____

THE WAIT

They sat in the luxurious lobby for another couple of hours and had it all to themselves. The evening had come upon them, and there was no longer anyone at the reception desk. They ate snacks and found drinks. There were plenty more available, but they had reached that stage where snacks no longer filled them up, despite their still being hungry. Feeling somewhat bloated, nervous, and eager to hear more about Mike's condition, Gina, Angelic, and Jamal spread out on separate couches and rested. Dee paced the room, looking out the small windows, watching the night come up and the traffic die down.

Dr. Arazi returned. His lab jacket was unbuttoned now, and he looked a touch disheveled. Keno followed along behind him.

"I'll tell you all where we're at," he said in a solemn, tired voice. He waited for a moment as they collected around him. "After the basic tests, X-rays, and bloodwork from earlier, I ordered tests for COVID and related antibodies, AIDS, seasonal flu, and bronchial-related items. We're also looking at autoimmune testing for multiple sclerosis, rheumatoid arthritis, Lupus, IBD, diabetes, and Guillain-Barré. We don't see any type of infection, so perhaps it's inflammation. Either can cause a fever. There is also the possibility of tuberculosis."

Keno's hand went to her face and her mouth opened, but no sound came out as she staggered backward a step and collapsed onto the couch.

"How can that be?" she murmured. "He's so healthy."

Dr. Arazi stepped forward to where she sat and placed a hand on her shoulder. "Many of these things we are testing for lurk in the body and are caused to emerge by some external factor, or time. Has he been under extraordinary stress or anxiety for a long period? Does anything run in his family? I asked him, and he shook his head no."

Keno looked up at the doctor, her eyes full of tears. His eyes followed her fingers as she grasped the necklace she had bought in Tangier and spun it around. Her shoulders shook slightly.

"We've been traveling the last several months with our friends here." She gestured to the group. "I mean, it has been exciting, a little scary, and difficult at times, but he seemed to enjoy it all. There's nothing genetically from his family that I know. He gave up his career to be with his friends. Perhaps that's affecting him."

The doctor's face softened, and he replied, "There's no guarantee his fever is any of those things I mentioned. Since there isn't an obvious cause, we're basically trying to eliminate things. It could be nothing at all. They are sometimes called 'Fevers of Unknown Origin' or 'FUOs.' They may appear once and never again, or Mike might be subject to them for some period of time. As much as 40 to 50 percent of FUOs never resolve. They just pass."

"Do they ever come back?" whispered Keno.

"Sometimes. It depends on what triggered them. Fatigue,

stress, other illnesses, or depression can all trigger the fever. But then, he may have been bitten by something that we can't determine or even detect. This is a different part of the world for him. Something here that we are accustomed to, or that you and the others are more tolerant of, might have impacted his system. It's difficult to say. But what I can tell you is what has happened so far."

The doctor paused for a moment before he continued. "When you brought him in, his temperature was spiking in the 105 to 106 area. He was chilling, shaking violently, and coughing. It was very much like a viral illness. But there was no evidence of it. Right before we came out here, his temperature dropped and he went into a heavy sweat. That is typically a sign that the fever is breaking. I want to keep him here overnight to see if he continues to recover. He needs the rest, and he will need it tomorrow also, even if the fever doesn't reappear. Resuming activity too closely after a fever usually causes its immediate return."

"Should we try to get him back home?" asked Dee.

The doctor turned and looked pensive for a moment, then replied, "Short answer is no, in my opinion. Let me clarify for you. I am Dr. Younes Arazi. This is my clinic. One of my specialties is infectious diseases. I do not think Mike can get any better care in this part of the world. The clinic is not inexpensive, but we want to help people. I want to know what caused this. I will work to find the answer. On that you can rely.

"We won't get the test results until tomorrow afternoon. You should return to your hotel." He looked at Keno, then reached and squeezed her hands. "You can stay with him if you like, but I expect he will sleep well into the morning. He is exhausted. You might rest more comfortably with your friends nearby."

Keno nodded and rose from the couch. "I think I will go with them. Can I go back and say good night?"

"I'll walk you."

When Keno returned she looked up at the group and spoke, "He was asleep."

"His fever has broken, and he is resting," added Dr. Arazi.

———

THEY ALL GATHERED IN ANGELIC AND JAMAL'S ROOM TO talk.

"Were you back there with him the whole time?" asked Angelic.

"Only for the first few minutes," replied Keno. "Then I was in a separate interior waiting room. I'd just as soon have been out front with all of you."

"Wonder why they didn't let you stay with him?" said Gina.

Keno shook her head. "I don't know if it was a clinic rule or a local custom. They asked me to wait in the adjacent room and I did. I'd really rather go home."

"Maybe he'll be well enough in a few days," replied Dee.

Jamal spoke. "I still can't figure what might have caused it. I don't think it was anything immediate. I mean, we've all been together, eaten together, and none of us are sick. We've not been apart."

"What about the man at the well?" said Gina.

"It may have been a hallucination. His fever might have already started internally," replied Angelic.

"Could it have been anything around the well?" responded Gina. "None of the rest of us were that close except Dee, but he doesn't seem to have it."

Everyone looked to Dee. "I feel fine," he replied.

He noticed Keno spinning the necklace again, as did Angelic and Gina.

"It's good you found that thing," said Angelic, pointing to the necklace. "It gives you something to hold on to."

"It certainly sparkles in the light," added Gina.

Keno stopped twirling it and squeezed the stone tightly. "I need something to hold on to. This all seems so temporary, fleeting, like a dream."

They talked awhile longer and decided it was time for bed.

"Why don't you stay with us rather than being alone?" said Angelic. "We have two full beds, and you can sleep in one of them. We'll be right there if you need anything."

7

RESULTS ARE IN

They assembled at the clinic late the next afternoon. Dr. Arazi had them sent back to Mike's room.

"Good afternoon," the doctor said as the group trooped through the door. "I have some good news, and I have some other news."

"Bad news?" asked Keno quickly. She had called earlier and been told that Mike was still asleep.

Dr. Arazi answered quickly, "No, not bad news, just inconclusive. Let me explain."

Angelic moved closer to Keno. The others noticed and drew in as well.

"I can see that you are dear friends. But there is nothing to be concerned with at the moment. Mike is feeling much better. He was awake earlier. We fed him a light lunch, and he's fallen back to sleep. A fever, especially one as high as he had, can be very debilitating and take a day or two to recover from. He seems to be in good shape, and his temperature is normal. None of the tests have come back with any positive results. Everything has been negative. We are slowly eliminating things. I can release him in the morning. I should have the rest of the test results in by this evening. I honestly do not expect for there to be any findings. Please remain here with him if you like, or you could come back later tonight. We will wake him to check his vitals a little later this afternoon and try to get him on a regular sleep schedule. He appears in almost every way to be a very healthy man."

Keno let out a visible sigh. "Thank you so much, Dr. Arazi," she exclaimed.

He held up a hand, "Don't thank me yet. We don't know what it was, and if we don't find out later today, there becomes a question of whether the fever will return. How often, how long, and for what duration could become issues. It will be difficult for him until it's cured, or it passes."

"Are we safe to travel?" asked Dee.

"In what manner?" replied Dr. Arazi.

"We're driving at the moment."

"Where is your next stop?"

"We were planning on Algiers."

"That's probably two days or one really long day," said Dr. Arazi. "I'd say keep it shorter. Keep him shaded and hydrated, and have some Tylenol handy. It'll help break the fever. Stay in a nice place where he can rest and take it easy. I'll call you when the rest of the tests results arrive. I'm afraid he needs to stay until then. Assuming you leave tomorrow, Oujda would be a good first stop. It's about halfway, still in Morocco but near the Algerian border. You could spend the night and cross in the morning when you are all freshest."

"Thank you," answered Dee.

"Be sure to call me if the fever returns. Perhaps I can recommend a doctor in your area."

The group gathered and left the clinic for the hotel. They'd only been back an hour when Keno's phone rang.

"Hello." She listened quietly for a second and then

turned the phone on speaker. The group gathered around her.

"We had a finding," it was the voice of Dr. Arazi, "but it's not the apparent source of the fever. Mike had a positive test for latent tuberculosis."

"What?" Keno asked.

"At some time in his life, he was exposed to someone with tuberculosis. He doesn't have it right now, but it might develop at some point."

"Could the exposure have been recent, and could that have caused the fever?" asked Gina.

"The exposure could have been at any time. It's not likely that it was recent or the cause of the fever, but that's always possible. It's difficult to tell the time of exposure. I can release him in the morning. Come by tonight; I'm sure he could use some company."

———

RECEPTION SENT THEM ALL STRAIGHT BACK TO MIKE'S ROOM. He was sitting up in bed, watching local television.

Keno walked over and hugged him.

"What you watching, big guy?" asked Jamal.

"Soccer."

"I think they call that football here."

"Yeah, really," Mike replied sarcastically and switched off the television.

"How do you feel?" asked Angelic.

"Much better. I was weak yesterday, but today I'm feeling more normal. The doctor can't seem to tell me what caused the fever."

"Probably some short-term thing you encountered," replied Angelic.

"Why didn't any of the rest of you get it?"

"I don't know. You may have been the closest in proximity. Your immune system might have been compromised. It's hard to say when the testing doesn't find anything."

"You think you'll be ready to roll out in the morning?" asked Dee.

"I'm ready to roll out now."

Keno put her hand to his face. "The doctor says you have to rest one more night or the fever might come back."

"Yeah, he told me that too. So, you'll pick me up in the morning? Where are we off to?"

"We thought we'd stay with your idea and drive on to Algiers," replied Dee.

Mike looked at Jamal and Dee. "Can one of you drive?"

Jamal grinned at Mike and answered, "We'll take it from here."

Mike leaned back against his pillow. "I guess I need to rest. I feel fine. I just don't have any energy."

"The doctor said it may take several days to come back," replied Angelic. "You just need to take it easy."

"We'll stay for a while and then let you rest," added Keno.

8

ON THE ROAD TO ALGIERS

They checked out of the hotel early and picked Mike up at the clinic. He looked rested and ready to go. While checking him out in reception, Dr. Arazi appeared and took Dee aside.

"Be sure to let me know if the fever reappears. If that should happen, it may be necessary to return here or to fly stateside. My concern is how long the fevers may continue to recur. He won't have any energy and won't want to do anything but rest. He needs to be in a comfortable place."

Dee offered his right hand and said, "Thanks for everything, Dr. Arazi." The doctor shook his hand. "I'll be sure to look after him, with Angelic's help, and I will call if the fever reoccurs, wherever we might be."

Jamal drove them out of the city, and they huddled under the canvas top of the Thing. Temperatures were already rising in the early morning. They were taking the A2 to Oujda on the Moroccan border. It would be four or five hours before they'd arrive.

Driving out of the mountains and into the flatlands, they moved closer toward the sea. But the mountains stayed visible behind and beyond them. The vast desert lay to the south, and their path was like threading a needle.

They drove the first hour in silence, watching the surroundings change as they sped past. The soil became rockier and sandier. There was the occasional palm and a little ground cover. But mostly it was flat, empty, and hot. Once they settled into the flat country, their interest waned.

Whipping along the highway in the open vehicle made conversation difficult. Those in the back seat drifted off. It was a good road, and the sparse traffic moved rapidly along. Only by leaning closely together could they speak.

"Do you think he'll be all right?" Jamal asked. Dee, who sat in the passenger seat glanced into the mirror and saw Mike dozing. "Hopefully he'll just be tired for a while and then recover."

Jamal resumed. "I was thinking: tomorrow, after we cross into Algeria, we pick up the A1 and go north. That will take us along the coast instead of through the country. It should be more scenic. I don't think it will take us much longer, and there are small towns where we can stop along the way."

"That sounds like a good idea. I prefer to be closer to the water."

"I think we all do."

Dee nodded and looked at the paper map they had picked up for the trip. "GPS is nice, but I like to see the bigger picture and the details. Plus, if we hit a dead spot, we'll have no coverage. Our route is pretty straightforward, but still."

Jamal grinned at him. "Ever the Boy Scout."

"Yeah, I guess so."

They continued on. The wind blew harder, and, along with the turbulence from the highway, it made conversation impossible, even with the person next to you. It left each of them alone with their thoughts.

We could be on board a cruise ship in luxury. (Gina)
We're a long way from anywhere. (Keno)
I hope Mike doesn't get sick again. (Angelic)
This probably wasn't a good idea. (Dee)
I wish I was home. (Mike)
How much further before we stop? (Jamal)
I wish the wind would quit blowing. (Keno)
This is supposed to be fun. Why doesn't it feel like it? (Gina)

As if Jamal had been overpowered by all the surrounding thoughts, he took a turn south and drove them into Taza, to the Hôtel-Café-Restaurant Pyramides.

"Lunch time," he called out as the vehicle slowed.

Gina pointed toward the restaurant sign.

"That's it. I always said I wanted to see the pyramids," chuckled Jamal.

"Baby, they are still a long way off, but I'm glad you stopped. That seat was getting mighty hard," replied Angelic.

Jamal parked, and they trooped out of the Thing. Everybody stretched and began talking again.

Keno patted Mike on the stomach and asked, "How are you feeling?" Everyone paused to listen.

"I'm good," he said and stretched his shoulders. "I don't have much of an appetite but I'm as parched as that desert. Let's find something to drink."

They strolled inside the hotel lobby and looked for the restaurant entrance. The lobby was in the Moorish style, with a two-story, inlaid tile arch serving as the entrance to the restaurant.

They walked inside and waited to be seated. The decor featured mirrors and lots of tile. Small green palms were scattered around the walls. The lighting was primarily wall sconces that gave the interior a dark but elegant look.

"I believe we are the only non-North Africans here," said Jamal.

"We're a bit off the beaten path, aren't we?" answered Dee.

"We're south of the main road. It's a fair-sized city, but it is a good way from the coast."

"Maybe it's like at home, and we're right off the interstate."

"Right this way," said the host. He was dressed formally and held himself in a stiff posture as he walked. He led them to a round table that would have seated eight. Bowing his head, he said, "Your server will be right with you."

The menu was in Arabic and English. They selected fish with olives, dates, and fruit, along with freshly squeezed orange juice and mint tea to drink.

There were only a few other customers scattered about the room. The air was cool, and the new group of travelers leaned back in their chairs and relaxed.

"I think we're getting more wind than sun," said Angelic looking at her arms. "So, this is about halfway to where we're going?"

Jamal nodded.

They waited for the food to arrive. It was as if the trip so far had sucked the desire to talk right out of them.

They stared at each other, at the tiled and stuccoed walls and the slowly turning overhead ceiling fans, each lost in their own thoughts.

Keno leaned forward, and her necklace caught the light coming through the archway.

"That is beautiful," said Angelic, leaning forward to touch the stone. "And you only paid a dollar?"

"Yes. The woman I bought it from seemed happy to sell it."

———

A SMALL GROUP OF MEN SAT IN A CAMP OUTSIDE OF FEZ AT the base of the Middle Atlas Mountains. They wore long, light-brown jackets faced with a dark-brown diamond pattern and turbans the color of the Mediterranean. Their faces were leathery and brown, as if they had spent their lives and perhaps many others directly in the heat and sand and sun. Eyes were of the darkest brown and looked black without sunlight shining upon them. Gnarled fingers made the men look ancient, but they moved with an unlikely quickness and grace.

"The Berber woman has sold the stone," said one.

"I told you we should have taken it from them while they were still in the desert," replied another.

"It seemed simple enough to walk through the medina and purchase it. The tourist got there before we did."

"And then they were at the clinic of Dr. Arazi."

The first speaker nodded.

"The girl stayed with her friends. There were too many of them for it to be taken quickly and quietly."

"So what do we do now?"

"Follow them. They have done us a great favor by staying in North Africa, driving across the desert or perhaps along the water. We will catch up to them."

"Do you think they have any idea?"

"Not the slightest. It will be easy in the time and place of our choosing. And, even if they should have an idea, it's a long way to Egypt."

AFTER FINISHING THEIR MEAL, THE GROUP ROSE SLUGGISHLY. They had grown accustomed to the air conditioning and did not relish returning to the hot sun, even if the Thing's convertible top would shade them.

Trying to raise their spirits, Jamal called out, "It's only a couple more hours and we'll be there. We have a really nice place to stay? Right?"

Gina glanced up. "It's tent city again. That was all I could find quickly."

The countryside didn't change, but the heat kept rising while they wound their way toward Oujda. Mike slept, and the others nodded on and off.

As they were heading back to the A1, the breeze died slightly, and they could talk.

"Let me know when you want to switch out driving," said Dee.

"I'm good," replied Jamal. "It keeps me awake."

Shortly after that, Dee was also nodding asleep.

Jamal thought as his eyes scanned the horizon, and he glanced frequently in the rearview mirror to see that nothing was coming up from behind.

Some months ago I was running a corporate gym in Atlanta, and now here I am driving across North Africa, a wealthy man from the reward and the money that we found on the island. What could possibly come next?

9

CAMPING IN STYLE

Jamal drove in relative silence for the next couple of hours. The rest of the group napped or stared off into the distance. The sights remained the same. Finally, he saw a sign for Oujda. He nudged Dee.

"What's the location for where we're staying?"

"Let me check." Dee turned and tapped Gina's shoulder. She fluttered her eyes and gave him the address in a groggy voice.

Jamal located the hotel campsite on the west side of town and pulled in shortly afterward.

They made their way out of the Thing, stretching and yawning.

"I need a bath," said Angelic.

"I need a massage," said Jamal, rubbing his shoulders.

"I need to lie down," added Mike.

That brought them all around quickly. Dee and Jamal hustled to the reception area to register.

The set up was the same as in the prior camp. They cleaned up, ate, and retired to their air-conditioned tents.

Before the group separated, Jamal spoke. "The

Algerian border is about thirty minutes from here. We'll cross there and head north to drive along the ocean. Maybe we can go a little slower so we can talk. I don't know how long the crossing will take. Everyone be prepared and be patient."

————

GINA SIGHED AS SHE AND DEE ENTERED THEIR TENT. "I'M grateful for the cool air. I'm not sure driving across North Africa in an open vehicle was such a good idea, especially with Mike's condition."

"I was thinking maybe when we got to Algiers, I'd suggest we catch a cruise ship and ride the rest of the way."

"What will the others want to do? Do you think there'll be a ship?"

"We'll have to see what they want to do. I'll check on a cruise. I was afraid there wasn't any reception along the highway today. There should be a stronger signal closer to the water."

Gina dropped her clothes to the floor. "I'm still pretty hot from the ride." She lay on the double bed naked for a moment. "It'll probably cool off quickly." She grabbed a sheet and pulled it over her.

Dee had been standing looking at her, admiring the view. He lay down beside her on top of the sheet.

"Good night."

"Good night."

————

WHEN THEY AWOKE THE FOLLOWING MORNING, THE REST OF the camp was still in place. As they gathered outside the tents and looked around, Gina spoke. "I think this is one of their permanent locations. We get breakfast this time and can check out at a more leisurely pace."

Well before lunch, they arrived at the Algerian border. There was a short line but an hour later they were on the A2 headed northeast.

Jamal leaned over and said to Dee, "That wasn't too bad."

"Yeah, I think we've been a little lucky. Spain into Morocco was a tourist crossing. I was afraid Algeria might be more of a problem."

Then he pointed at the Thing. "I think it helps to drive more of an open air vehicle like this, even if it is hot. We don't look so touristy. We're just out doing our business. I'm pulling for some ocean breezes."

"I was thinking about that myself. It'll probably take us all day to get to Algiers. We can eat lunch, take a break in Mohammadia, and catch the highway along the water. We'll have to cross the mountains to get back to the sea. You think Mike's up for it? "

"He seems good so far. We just need to keep an eye on him."

———

THE TRIP TO MOHAMMADIA WAS UNEVENTFUL. THE SCENERY didn't waver, nor did their interest in it increase. It was just semi-desert, hot and flat.

"We cross the mountains and head down to the sea. When we get to the peak, you'll be able to see the Mediterranean," announced Jamal when they got back in the vehicle after the short break "We need to keep moving."

As they pulled out of town, Jamal felt a little sway in the vehicle and thought it was road conditions. They continued on and in a few minutes were climbing the mountain that separated them from the sea. Nearing the top, Jamal felt a definite sway in the car and slowed down as he and the others realized something was wrong. They heard a distinct flapping and pulled to the side of the road. They were near the peak of the mountain. Angling toward the city, they looked back into the valley from which they had come.

"I'll jump out and check," offered Dee. "It feels and sounds like a tire."

Jamal nodded his agreement.

Dee walked around the car and looked at the rear tires. When he got to the driver's side, he called out.

"Rear-side driver. Looks bad. I wonder what we hit?"

Jamal got out, and they examined the tire. The others remained in the vehicle for a moment.

"Hop out if you like," called Dee. "There's a bit of a breeze, and you can see the water on the other side of the mountain."

Gina was the only one to get out. "It's crowded back there, and Mike fell asleep right before we stopped."

"I'll get the spare. See if you can find the jack," said Dee while moving toward the front of the vehicle. The spare was lashed across the front hood.

"The jack is in the front trunk, under the tire," replied Jamal, grinning at Dee.

"Well, then, let me do my job first," answered Dee, grinning back.

They got the tire and the jack out and moved to the rear of the car, grateful the flat was on the roadside and not on the shoulder, which dropped off rapidly.

They got started enough to set the jack, when another vehicle came roaring along the road. It was an old Toyota pickup with several men inside and more riding in the bed.

The truck swerved toward them, and both men scrambled to their feet and prepared to spring out of the way. The truck swerved again, but passed so closely that it flung gravel and sand against both men. Making no attempt at slowing down, the truck sped over the mountain.

Jamal, Dee, Gina, and Angelic all stared at one another.

"What was that about?" asked Angelic.

"I guess they weren't paying attention," replied Dee.

"Or maybe they were curious," suggested Gina.

"Not friendly," added Jamal.

They continued working on the wheel. Just as they had their vehicle jacked up and were about to take the old tire off, an ancient green-and-white Citroen chugged up the hill, barely moving. The car wheezed to a stop behind them. It was older and more beat-up than the Thing. The fenders were dented and the top heavily scratched. Paint had faded to the metal in several places. The car sounded as if it was on its dying breath.

A short, dark-skinned man in a full robe and cap hopped out but stood by the side of his car.

He called out, "May I be of assistance? A flat on this mountain is most unfortunate. I've had several. I am familiar with your type of vehicle. May I?"

Jamal and Dee looked at each other as the man moved slowly toward them.

He squatted beside them and took over removing the tire. He rolled the old tire to the side and reached for the spare. As he did, he stood up and took a long look into the back seat of the Thing. Keno was wedged against Mike, who was still sleeping. Angelic sat a little apart from them and watched the man work. He bobbed his head toward her and crouched back to the tire.

"My name is Ahmed Alami, and this is most unfortunate, my friends," the man said. "Have you far to go? You will need a new tire. Perhaps you should return to Mohammadia?"

"We're headed for Algiers on the N11. There are a couple of towns where we can stop. I'd hate to backtrack," replied Jamal.

"I understand," answered the man as he slid the spare in place. He stood again and moved as if to straighten his robe. This time, he stared directly at Keno, and as she turned away from his gaze, the sunlight caught the stone around her neck and made it sparkle. He smiled and dropped back down to tighten the lugs on the spare.

"That should get you along," he said.

"Thank you for the help, Ahmed," said Dee. He held out a bill.

"There is no need for that," the man said, and he waved the money away. "It has been my pleasure." He bowed to them but did not extend a hand. "Whom may I say I had the opportunity to assist today?"

"I am Jamal, and this is Dee."

"Indeed, Jamal is a fine Arabic name, and"—glancing up at Jamal—"you live up to its meaning." He bowed again to Dee and strolled back to his vehicle.

Dee, Gina, and Jamal climbed into the Thing and, after getting settled, pulled away.

Jamal glanced in the mirror to see Ahmad sitting quietly in the battered old Citroen.

"There was something strange about that," said Jamal.

Dee was leaning near Jamal's shoulder, and Gina and Angelic had their heads forward between the seats.

"It seemed odd that he stopped," answered Dee.

"You don't think he was just being helpful?" asked Gina.

"Why?" replied Jamal. "We had it under control. I mean, I appreciate it, but he seemed awfully curious."

"Did you see him stare at Keno and her necklace? At first, I thought perhaps he'd never seen someone with her features, but the second time he looked, he just stared at her necklace," said Angelic.

"You suppose he thought the stone was real?" asked Gina.

"Surely not, but he looked at it hard enough, and what's this business about your name and a meaning?" replied Angelic.

Gina whipped out her phone and looked up the meaning. She smiled broadly at Angelic. "You're going to like this one. The meaning of Jamal, in Arabic, is 'good looking.'" She leaned back, giggling.

"I know that's right," said Jamal.

"Don't let it go to your head," Angelic replied and rapped him on the ear.

Their vehicle had crested the mountain and started toward the sea. The sky and the air were suddenly full of bright-blue reflected light, and the smell of the Mediterranean drifted up to them.

"Now there's something to look at," said Jamal, pointing below them to the water.

10

TIME FOR A CHANGE

They pulled slowly down the road, all awake now.

"I'm ready to get back on a ship," said Gina.

"I agree," replied Angelic. Keno nodded her agreement.

"Ladies," said Jamal, "where's your sense of adventure?"

Angelic patted his shoulder, "It got burned up in the desert and bounced off of these hard seats."

"I'm just worried about Mike. He's slept an awful lot, and it's boiling out here," replied Keno.

"Let's get to Algiers, and we'll look for a cruise," replied Dee, glancing over to Jamal.

Who replied, "Whatever the group wants to do, although I was enjoying the drive. It's several hours yet to Algiers. You'd just as well get comfortable. We seem to have a better breeze, and there looks to be some activity on the water."

A GROUP OF OLDER MEN IN SIMILAR-LOOKING APPAREL SAT around a fire pit at a small camp outside of Mohammadia.

"We should have taken the stone while they were changing the flat tire," said one.

"I directed the men to have a look and to act if they thought it could be done quickly," replied another. "They did not like the location."

"Then Ahmad went by, and he learned more than the others. The girl has the stone and is wearing it. Her husband is sick. She is likely to be distracted."

"Good. They are going to Algiers. We will follow them there. An opportunity will present itself."

———

JAMAL DROVE THEM THE REST OF THE WAY, STOPPING TWICE IN small seaside villages to refuel and to stretch. It was early evening, just after twilight, as they made their way into Algiers. They were staying at the Hotel Aurassi which was on the west side of town near the water.

Mike had been awake the last several hours and admitted that he was hungrier than at lunch, and that he was tired. That was no surprise as they were all tired, wind burned, and dehydrated.

After checking into the hotel, they ate dinner in the hotel restaurant and then went to their rooms for long baths or showers.

The next morning for breakfast, they discussed how to spend the day.

"What's to see?" asked Angelic.

"There are art museums, mosques, temples, palaces, another medina, the beaches—what would you like?" replied Jamal.

"The drive has been fun, but let's look for a cruise. It's so slow, and the scenery is the same," answered Gina. "I really just want to rest a few days."

"I agree with staying here for a day or so. Let Mike get better, look for a cruise," added Keno.

The women looked to the men.

"I'd like to see the art museum," said Jamal.

"I'll look for the cruise while you all rest or sightsee," said Dee.

Mike just nodded.

They split up, with the women and Mike staying around the hotel, Jamal sightseeing, and Dee going to the docks. He planned to look up potential cruises online, but he wanted to see the ships and the harbor in person.

There were a couple of cruises but none that appealed to Dee. One was heading back toward Gibraltar and the other for the French Riviera. The cruises were on smaller ships, and Dee wanted the group to be comfortable. The original plan had been to skirt the Mediterranean and see all the sights. Gibraltar was where they had come from, and the Riviera cut off the western half of the trip. Jamal had wanted to see the pyramids. There wasn't a good answer.

He went back to the hotel in time for dinner and found the women gathered around Mike, who had developed a slight shudder. His temperature was rising. The rooms were a little cool, but Mike was bundled completely in all the blankets the room had on hand. He was beginning to chill and to shake harder. Angelic and Keno were feeding him Tylenol and wiping him down with cold rags.

"Dee, call Dr. Arazi, see what he has to say. I can monitor the fever, and it's likely to run its course, but we should let the doctor know. Perhaps other symptoms will arise," said Angelic.

Dee nodded and made the call.

The clinic answered on the third ring. Dee identified himself and was put on hold. In a few seconds, Dr. Arazi came on the line.

"I feared you would be calling me. How is he?"

"Mike developed chills and a building fever earlier this afternoon. He has had no energy, has been sleeping a lot, and has done nothing but ride in the vehicle."

"Have Angelic help Keno monitor him and track his temperature. Have them try to keep him cool. If his temperature goes above 105 degrees for any amount of time, call me back. There are a couple of clinics you could check him into and then transport him here."

"Okay, thanks. I expect that Keno will want to return to the States. She was already nervous about him staying and us driving. We had decided to get back on a cruise ship, but it may have taken us too long to get back to the water."

"This thing could go on for a while. He needs to be someplace comfortable. He is welcome here, but I understand their desire to return home. I have a former partner, also in infectious diseases, who is based in Miami, at Miami General. His name is Hicham El Aynaoui. I will be happy to call him for you. He is an extremely talented doctor and is knowledgeable with fevers. He'd be happy to help."

"I'll pass that along."

"If this is a developing pattern, it would appear that you have three to four days between bouts. You could schedule the flight the day after this one ends. You might have time to get there before it appears again. Of course, it's a lot closer to come here." He let out a soft sigh. "But I understand, and Hicham could be a big help."

"Thanks again, Dr. Arazi. I'll share all this with them and let you know the decision."

Going back inside, Dee wasn't sure how to tell the others. Blurting it out was probably the simplest and quickest. If there was a way for Mike to get help, it needed to be done. They had been together as a group for much of the past year. Dee hated to see anyone go, but they all needed to be healthy.

Dee went back inside the bedroom. "How's his fever?"

"It seems to be holding right now, around 104 degrees," replied Angelic.

"That's good. Dr. Arazi says to watch closely, and if he gets to 105 degrees and stays there, to call him back. He suggested returning Mike to the clinic. Or, he knows another infectious disease specialist in Miami. He suggested you fly back between bouts, which look like every three or four days."

"I think I'd like that," replied Keno without looking away from Mike. "We'd be closer to home, in our own country, our own language. I think he might rest better, and we could stay there and run tests until the doctor can find out what caused this."

Angelic leaned across and squeezed Keno's hand. "Do what's best for Mike. I have to agree about returning to the States until you get a better idea of what has happened and what needs to be done."

Jamal sat, silently listening to the conversation.

"I can check flights for you, Keno, if you'd like?" said Gina.

Keno turned to her. "That would be great. If this fever is like the last one, it will pass in about eight hours. That would make it the middle of the night. If he could sleep another eight hours after that, maybe we could fly home tomorrow evening? What do you think, Angelic?"

"That seems reasonable. It depends on the flight duration, stopovers, changing planes, things like that. But mostly it depends on how he feels. How much energy he has to expend. Mike can probably sleep most of the way, if it's direct."

Gina researched on her phone. It didn't take long.

"There is an Air Algérie flight out late tomorrow night. It's a seventeen-hour direct flight to Miami. It only flies once a week. Want me to book it?"

"Yes, please," replied Keno.

Dee left the room again, his phone in hand. He dialed and listened to a couple of rings, and when it picked up, a familiar voice said, "Hello."

"Ike, this is Dee."

"Dude, where are you? Is everything okay? How's Gina and Jamal and the others?"

"Yeah, we're fine."

"What's up?"

"We're in Algiers. We drove across from Tangiers."

"Wow, what happened to the cruise ship? You guys spend all that reward money already?"

"No, it was just an idea we had, a change of plans. It was going well, but then Mike contracted some kind of fever. Doctors here can't determine what it is, and it appears to be lingering, recurring. He and Keno are going to be flying into Miami for a doctor that was recommended at Miami General."

"Okay, how can we help?"

"Is Elizabeth still there?"

"Yeah, she's going to stay awhile."

"I was wondering if you could meet them at the airport and see that they get to Miami General. The doctor's name is Hicham El Aynaoui. He'll be expecting you."

"No problem. Happy to help. Get me the details and Elizabeth and I are on it."

Dee went back into the bedroom and looked at Gina. "Are they booked?"

"Yes, leaving tomorrow at 9 p.m. local time and arriving in Miami at 8 a.m. That is the flight time less six time zones. It's a long one."

"Keno," he called. She turned toward him. "Ike and Elizabeth will meet you at the airport and get you to Miami General."

"Thank you," she murmured and turned back to Mike.

Dee stepped out of the room again and dialed once more.

"Arazi Clinic," the doctor's voice came on the line.

"This is Dee. Can you set Mike up with Dr. El Aynaoui? He'll be there sometime after 8 a.m."

"Not a problem. I'll let Hicham know."

"Thank you so much."

11

FRAGMENTED

They took turns sitting with Mike for the rest of the night. Keno and Angelic stayed with him, and the others rotated on the hour.

The fever followed the path it had taken at the clinic. First, Mike shuddered and chilled, then got very cold and covered himself in layers of blankets. This lasted for several hours. He would suddenly get hot as the fever moved toward peaking. Then he would lurch out of the bed and dry heave in the bathroom for several minutes before going back to bed. At that point, he would burn up as the fever peaked. Angelic and Keno would work feverishly to keep him bathed with cold rags and to monitor his temperature. After several more hours, the fever would break and it would drench Mike in sweat. His body would finally relax, and he would fall asleep.

The fever lasted eight hours from the shudder to the sweat. It was three o'clock in the morning when he finally drifted off.

Mike was exhausted, as were Keno and Angelic. Everyone slept until late the following morning.

Rotating watch throughout the next day, everyone stayed close to their rooms and helped as needed. There wasn't much to do. Mike required sleep more than anything else.

Angelic sat down to look over him and then spoke to Keno, who had been on watch. "Get packed, and try to rest a little. We'll take you to the airport and get you on board. Get a nap if you need one."

Keno nodded and moved into the other room.

———

MIKE WOKE UP IN THE LATE AFTERNOON. HE WAS THIRSTY but not hungry.

"Try to eat before you get on the plane," advised Angelic. "On the flight the food won't be good. We'll try to find you the Algerian equivalent of chicken soup."

Mike grinned for the first time since leaving the clinic. "I hope they can figure out what's wrong. I can't take too much more of this. We're going back stateside, is that right?"

Keno nodded at him.

"I got no energy at all. I just want to go back to sleep."

She put her hand to his head to check his temperature. Mike put his head on the pillow shortly afterwards.

Keno returned to the other room to finish packing. Gina hopped up to help her.

"That is so not like him," Keno said. "I'm worried. How long can this last?"

"The doctors will find the cause," Gina assured her. "You'll see. I'll go relieve Angelic."

In a few seconds, Angelic stepped into the room and watched Keno throw the last of their things into the suitcases.

"We really don't have much anymore," she said, looking at Angelic.

"Just the basics."

Keno finished packing, stepped across the room, and hugged Angelic. "Thank you for helping with Mike. That was a long night. I couldn't have done it without you. I'm so scared."

Angelic hugged her back. "You know I'm always willing to help. It'll work out."

Keno took a step back and looked at Angelic, tears in her eyes. She pulled the necklace over her head and handed it to Angelic. "I want you to have this. It's not much, but I think you like it."

Angelic held her hand up. "I can't do that."

"I want you to have it. You can wear it and think of Mike and me."

Angelic paused for a moment and then replied, "Okay, if you insist."

They hugged again and went back into the room with the others.

———

Angelic stayed with Mike, and everyone else went downstairs to the restaurant for a quick dinner. They brought Mike some of the local bread and a soup called chorba frik, which was a meaty vegetable-filled stew.

He ate half of the large bowl and the bread.

"It was good, very filling," he said lying back in the bed. "But that's all I can eat."

"You should rest until we leave for the airport. You'll need your strength," advised Angelic.

Mike closed his eyes and was breathing softly in minutes.

Keno stood beside him and looked to the others, "I'm glad it's a direct flight. I appreciate Ike and Elizabeth meeting us."

As Keno sat with Mike, the others drifted into the living room of the suite and sat on the couches.

"There weren't any longer cruises out of this port," said Dee, "just a couple of shorter things, mostly backtracking where we came from. What do you all want to do?"

"We could stay here a few days and then go back to Spain," said Gina.

"Or we could fly somewhere," added Angelic.

"I'd still like to see the pyramids," replied Jamal, "and I know no one wants to hear this, but I'd like to drive a little further. I know we don't want to cross Libya, but we could go on to Tunis."

"How far is that?" asked Angelic.

"It's the same distance as from Fez to here, about two days driving steady. We can follow the water about halfway, and then we'll have to go cross-country, in and out of the mountains, until we reach Tunis. We can probably catch a larger cruise ship there," replied Dee.

———

At seven o'clock that evening, a big, black, air-conditioned Mercedes cab picked them up outside the front lobby. They all fit into it comfortably. They had decided as a group that driving the Thing in the open-air at night, in a city they didn't know, wasn't a good idea. This way, Mike was inside and they could focus on keeping him comfortable.

The attention embarrassed Mike, who felt pretty good by this time. But he was glad to be going home.

The cab dropped them off, and they made their way to Security with plenty of time.

Sitting in one of the lobby bars, they talked for a few moments.

"Let us know when you arrive," said Gina.

"And keep us posted on what you find," added Angelic.

"Ike and Elizabeth will look for you," said Dee.

Mike took a step back from the group and, addressed all of them. "Thanks for everything. I don't know when or if we'll be back, but it's been an amazing adventure."

"We'd better get through Security," said Keno. She took Mike by the hand and waved at the others as they walked away.

Heading to the cabstand, Jamal spoke. "He's right. It has been amazing— unbelievable, really."

The others nodded as they climbed inside the cab and returned to the motel.

———

Camped on the outskirts of Algiers, the men sat around a small fire and debated a decision they had to make.

"The girl and her husband are leaving for Miami. We will have to follow them. With him sick, they are all very attentive and staying close together," said one man.

"We could just take them all," replied another.

"There's too much chance for problems or publicity. If we can just extract the stone and be on our way, it's much preferable. No one will look for anyone or anything. Upon questioning, the Berber woman said the tourist only paid a dollar for the necklace. She won't miss it or even think about it with her husband sick," replied the leader.

"It would have been nice if they had gone back to Dr. Arazi's clinic," said another of the men.

"Certainly, but now we must follow them to Miami. Who would like to go?" He looked slowly around the circle at his choices and nodded briefly at two of his men.

———

THEY WERE ON THE ROAD THE NEXT MORNING. THERE HAD been no sites in Algiers that Angelic and Gina had wanted to see.

Dee felt a subtle pressure from them to get to Tunis and back on board a cruise ship. He had to admit, driving around the Mediterranean was slow and the scenery was often similar and had become tedious. The landscape had a stark, harsh beauty of its own, but it was a hard trip. The temperature was hot and dry, and it was difficult to talk. He understood the others' desire for comfort. Jamal had said little, except that he wanted to drive. Dee was content to sightsee.

They would travel along the water until they had to turn south and go cross-country the rest of the way to Tunis. They planned to stop for the night when they turned south. On the second day, there would be many different highways to follow, and elevation changes around the mountains, so they wanted a good night's rest and plenty of daylight.

Dee, after studying the paper map, felt that by the time they reached Tunis, Jamal would be ready to wrap up the driving and relax.

It was rugged country even along the water. They didn't stop often or for long. Jamal pressed on, driven by the silence and aura of need that emanated from the women. They were tired of this adventure.

12

THE TURN TO TUNIS

They arrived at Skikda late in the day. It had been a long, hard drive. Windblown and bleary-eyed, they finally found the Hotel Titanic, right on the bay beyond downtown. It was a multistoried, stuccoed building with a tile roof and lots of arches. They checked into a fourth-floor room with a rooftop restaurant above them.

After cleaning up quickly, they went up for a late dinner. The restaurant was nearly empty, and they had a magnificent view out to sea and back into the town.

The sun dazzled as it set to the west of them, and the sky filled with stars, little twinkles of light in the inky darkness. They sat for a long time, mostly silent.

"It's so beautiful after all that desert," said Gina.

"It was nice being along the water, but this is better," added Angelic.

Gina pointed and spoke. "The beach is right down there."

"Could we stay a day?" Angelic asked.

"Can we?" added Gina.

Dee and Jamal looked at one another. "I'm a little tired," said Jamal.

"Yeah," replied Dee. "Since Mike and Keno got in safely, we have a little time." Ike had texted Dee that afternoon when Mike and Keno had arrived. Elizabeth had contacted Dr. El Aynaoui, and his office was expecting them. "Ike said they'd text us with any test findings."

"Let's sleep in and soak up the air conditioning. There's a little balcony in the room that looks right down on the water," said Gina.

Everyone agreed, which meant they could sit a longer and look up at the stars. The night was cooling, and the couples slid closer together as the darkness deepened.

They closed the restaurant and then adjourned to their rooms.

LATE THE NEXT MORNING, DEE AND JAMAL SAT ON THE balcony off of Dee and Gina's room. The couples' rooms were adjacent, and there was a door between the two that they could open and pass back and forth through.

"I could stay awhile," said Dee. "All that riding was beating me down."

"Yeah, the steering vibrates, and I wonder how it will do cross-country?" replied Jamal.

Angelic and Gina had found a little shop in the hotel's lobby, and now they came bursting in with new local-style clothing for them all. "I think it's time for some longer sleeves," said Angelic. "When we start across the mountains perhaps we'll blend in a little better and burn a little less."

They lounged away the day and ate again at the rooftop restaurant. It was busier than before, and they didn't want to take up a table, so after eating, they took a short walk on the beach in front of the hotel.

"It's just so nice to rest. It's beautiful here," said Gina to Dee as they strolled along holding hands.

Jamal and Angelic had turned and were starting back.

"We'll see you in the morning," said Jamal. "If we're going on, we'd better start early."

Dee and Gina waved to the other couple and watched them walk away.

"We don't get to spend much time alone. I'm so tired all I want to do is sleep," said Gina.

"It's been a hard trip," replied Dee.

They walked for a few more minutes, and Dee guided them back to the room.

Dee brushed his teeth, and thought perhaps he and Gina could talk. But when he came back from the bathroom, Gina was sprawled out on the bed, already asleep.

———

As they were leaving at midmorning, Jamal made the comment, "It's a good thing we are over halfway, because I don't know how fast this portion of the trip will be."

Leaving the coast and dropping into a valley, they wound their way through foothills. They climbed the occasional mountain and spent most of the day switching back and forth between valleys. They changed highways six different times.

"This is nice, driving through the mountains after several days along the water," said Angelic.

Jamal shook his head at her. "It's better than all that desert."

"It's roomier too," added Gina. "We can stay out of the

sun easier. Both women were wearing their new longer length clothing.

Late that afternoon, they arrived in Tunis and drove all the way into the city to the area around ancient Carthage, now a suburb of modern-day Tunis.

"I'm up for some ruins," said Jamal. "We studied this area in art history. There's a lot to see."

Angelic and Gina rolled their eyes at one another.

"Didn't you see enough ruins in Mexico, Jam?" asked Angelic.

"This is a completely different society, not the same at all," he replied.

"It's a big city. There'll be great shopping," added Dee.

"And who says we don't want to see cultural sites?" asked Gina.

Dee shrugged. "Hey, we got it all. Let's take our time."

"We're staying at the Four Seasons. The Hotel Titanic was fun, but I need some luxury and some serious spa treatments. Besides, it was in the Carthage area," said Angelic.

The hotel was, in fact, very nice, very new, very modern, and right off the water.

THE FOLLOWING MORNING, THEY MET FOR BREAKFAST. JAMAL had an enormous grin on his face.

Dee and Gina sat down with him and Angelic. Dee looked back and forth between them. Angelic rolled her eyes at Dee and then turned to Jamal.

"Go ahead and tell them," she said to Jamal.

He couldn't stop grinning. "I got a call last night, from Diego."

Dee and Gina looked at him and waited for the rest of

the story. Diego Schwartz had been the curator at the art museum in Seville. He'd been instrumental in helping them with the Castillo painting and determining the provenance of the gold bell they had found in the Sea of Cortez.

Jamal began his story. "The museum found—actually, was contacted by—the heirs of an old French family that had multiple castles in France and Spain, right along that common border. In one castle on the Spanish side that was primarily abandoned, they found two large storerooms in a lower level that held ancient Egyptian artifacts. Diego knew my interest in Egyptian art and history and called to ask if I'd be interested in helping him catalogue the items. I can start as soon as I get there."

Dee and Gina leaned back in their chairs, as did Angelic.

Jamal looked at them for a moment. "It's a real opportunity to establish myself, or at least gain entry into the art world. There'll be a lot of publicity."

"I'm happy for you. It sounds like a real opportunity," replied Dee. "Especially with the publicity you got from finding the Castillo."

"Absolutely," added Gina.

They turned and looked at Angelic, who shrugged her shoulders.

Jamal continued, "I've made reservations for this evening. I'll be there later tonight."

"What are you going to do, Angelic?" asked Gina.

"I'll go support Jam in his dream. I liked Seville. Hopefully, it'll be fun. Maybe I can assist in some fashion."

———

JAMAL AND ANGELIC REPACKED, AND DEE AND GINA RODE with them to the airport. They took a cab again.

Jamal was so excited he had little to say. They could see his mind turning, his eyes bright.

When they got to the airport, Angelic stepped aside with Gina. "I'm sorry to ruin the trip. Everything seems to be falling apart for us. Now we're all broken up and in different places."

Gina clasped Angelic's hands and smiled. "Don't worry about it; bound to happen. There were six of us with different interests and plans. It was a great time. I'm so happy I met everyone."

"So am I. It's been a journey. I know this will make Jam happy."

They stepped back toward the men, and Angelic stopped. She reached in her pocket and pulled out the stone Keno had given her. She hadn't worn it. Somehow it hadn't felt right.

"Keno gave me this for helping her. Now I'm going to give it to you for helping me."

Gina looked up in surprise.

"Please, I'd like for you to have it. It will remind you of all of us when you wear it."

Gina slipped the necklace in her pocket, and they hurried after the men.

13

———

BACK ON THE WATER

Dee and Gina watched Jamal and Angelic disappear beyond the security gates and then made their way to the cab stand.

"I'm going to miss them, all of them," said Gina. She looked up at Dee. "But it could be nice to have some time alone."

Dee nodded his head in agreement. "We've all been together for so long. I keep turning around looking for them."

They rode to the hotel in silence, and when they arrived, their room seemed big and empty. There had been so much chatter and so much energy and intensity over the last couple of days, and now it was all gone.

Dee sat on the couch, looking at his phone, trying to find a cruise. Gina lay on the bed in the next room.

After studying the possibilities, Dee decided on a potential itinerary. He and Gina would take a ferry from Tunis across to Marsala Sicily. From there, they would take the train to Palermo, and from Palermo, they would catch a cruise across the Tyrrhenian Sea to Rome. If Gina was game, they could take the train across Italy to Pescara, and catch another cruise and then sail down the Adriatic Sea to Athens. From there, Dee wanted to travel to Egypt to see the pyramids. Jamal's excitement had rubbed off on him. They had time, and there were many places from which to choose. Or, they could take a short cruise from Tunis to Malta and catch a large cruise line there. Dee preferred a roundabout route and hoped that Gina would too.

"I do think I want to get out of here," she replied. "I'd rather get back on a large cruise ship, but we can do it your way."

Dee went to work making the reservations. But first, he stopped at a small local car lot and sold the Thing for cash. Dee took a last look after he handed the keys over, then smiled and walked away. He confirmed the details of the cruise and started back to the hotel.

Dee wished they had the time to see some of the local ruins—Carthage was a big deal in the ancient world—but the ferry was departing in the morning.

———

Keno sat in the room assigned to Mike. It was a large private room high in the hospital tower. Standing at the window, she had a view across to Biscayne Bay and the immediate Miami area. Elizabeth had gone downstairs to get them something to drink.

Dr. El Aynaoui had been very pleasant and had taken an intense interest in Mike. The testing had begun as soon as Ike had dropped Mike, Keno, and Elizabeth off. Ike had gone to make reservations for them at a nearby hotel.

Keno expected to spend most of her time at the hospital, but it was nice to know she'd have some relief and a place to stay when she got exhausted.

So far, Dr. El Aynaoui had rerun all the tests that Dr.

Arazi had completed, with the same results. The fever had recurred the second day they were at the hospital. Mike was hooked up and being monitored by various types of equipment. All the X-rays, CAT scans, EKGs, MRIs—everything had been repeated. Blood work and COVID and antibody testing had been done, and now blood cultures were being tested.

Dr. El Aynaoui then said they would start individual testing for autoimmune diseases and for tuberculosis. It was a daunting battery of tests. Keno felt they might be there awhile.

———

THE TWO EGYPTIANS HAD RIDDEN IN A CAB TO THE HOSPITAL. They had scrambled out of Algiers and, not being on the same once-a-week direct flight as Mike and Keno, they had to fly to Paris, then London, and then Miami. They were eager to catch up.

The men had changed clothes and now looked like two old Miami Beach tourists. They would have preferred to stay in South Beach, but their surveillance had led them to the same hotel as their quarry. Their English had been the best in the group, and they knew it was why they had been chosen.

———

DEE AND GINA WERE ON THE FERRY EARLY THE FOLLOWING morning. It was a half-day trip followed by another half-day train ride. They would spend the night in Palermo, Sicily.

This was a larger ferry than the one they had ridden from Marbella to Ceuta. They sat, shaded and higher above the water. Even with all the shade they had sought so far on the trip, both had dark golden-brown tans.

Dining in Palermo that evening and realizing they had a small cruise line ship to catch in the morning, they were quick to eat and to rest. Again, Dee wished for more time to enjoy his surroundings in Sicily, but once on board the ship and in Rome, they could be more leisurely. The timing from Tunis had been tight.

The cruise would only be overnight, and they would disembark in Rome for several days. Dee wasn't certain what Gina wanted to see. She had said little while traveling on the ferry and the train.

———

JAMAL AND ANGELIC ARRIVED IN SEVILLE LATE THE SAME evening of their flight. Diego met them at the airport and drove them to the hotel they'd stayed in previously, near the museum.

"Could I be of assistance as well?" asked Angelic.

"I was hoping you would ask," said Diego, smiling brightly. "We could certainly use your help, and I think that will make it easier for both of you."

"Tell us how this happened. What came about?" asked Jamal. "What're Egyptian artifacts doing in an abandoned castle in Spain?"

"I think it was Crusaders, most likely. They were all over the Middle East. It may have been Richard the First who led the Third Crusade, or it might have been the Fourth Crusade. The French were heavily involved in the Third Crusade. The Moors, who were Muslim, held much of southern Spain. It's hard to know."

"How did you or they find these things?" asked Angelic.

"The estate was being liquidated by a French family, as

the heirs had died out over time and not maintained their fortunes. They sold this one castle just across the border in northern Spain. It hadn't been lived in for years and was in disrepair for quite some time. There's a lot of new money that has a great fascination with castles. The family had made a deal with some Hollywood type, and in cleaning the place out, they ran across these underground storage rooms. It was quite by accident. We were fortunate the family discovered the items. It's hard to say what might have happened otherwise. The family wanted the publicity for handing the items over, and any reward that might be available, although that prospect is probably remote."

"Unbelievable," whispered Jamal.

"My job is to catalogue the items for the Spanish National Museum, although the French are also trying to lay claim and the Egyptians want their artifacts back. It's hard to say where the items will end up, but we can enjoy them while we're doing the cataloguing and being a part of the process."

———

For three days, Dee and Gina played the dutiful tourists. They went to the Coliseum, the Pantheon, the Spanish Steps, the Trevi fountain, the Vatican, and the Sistine Chapel. They rode buses, took trains, and walked. Dee couldn't get Gina to slow down. She looked at everything, but he wasn't sure she saw any of it.

She held his hand once or twice, but at night, she tumbled into bed and went straight to sleep. He scheduled the train for the fourth day, and they left for Pescara.

14

———

KEEPING UP

There had been several days of testing. Dr. El Aynaoui had performed extensive tests for MS, lupus, rheumatoid arthritis, tuberculosis, AIDS, and COVID. He had found nothing.

Keno was grateful Mike didn't have any of those things, but each time the doctor said no, she worried more about what Mike might have.

A little fluid on his lungs had shown up in one X-ray. A small dose of antibiotics had taken care of that. Hoping that might resolve the fever, Keno had been sorely disappointed when it had returned two days later.

The hospital had determined that Mike didn't have any tumors, so cancer could be initially ruled out. The doctor was running out of options.

Keno, Ike, and Elizabeth had taken turns at the hospital, each staying four to six hours. Not that Mike needed them there. They just wanted to be supportive and stay informed. On their off hours, they ate or slept at the hotel.

———

THE TWO MEN TOOK TURNS, ONE AT THE HOSPITAL WATCHING the group, the other at the hotel watching the rooms. At night they talked.

"Who are these new people?" asked the one.

"Who cares, as long as they don't get in the way or take the stone," replied the other.

"It makes approaching the couple more difficult."

"We've not yet seen the stone. We must watch them all until we do."

"In Africa, the woman wore it every day."

"We're not in Africa. We'll break into her room, steal the stone, and disappear into the night."

"I hope so."

———

JAMAL AND ANGELIC TRAVELED WITH DIEGO TO THE SPANISH border near the French province of Nouvelle-Aquitaine and the Atlantic Ocean. A convoy of trucks came by ground. The trucks would arrive a day later.

The three of them traveled from Donostia–San Sebastián, on the Bay of Biscay, to the castle.

"You'll like the town, if by chance you don't enjoy the castle and the artifacts," said Diego to Angelic. "It's a world-class resort and shopping experience."

Angelic rolled her eyes at him. "I'll be just fine hanging out with you two. Although I'm glad we have a nice place to stay."

Diego smiled at her.

"What specifically do you think we'll find?" asked Jamal.

Diego scratched his face and shrugged. "I don't know. It depends on what the Crusaders had in mind. Did they see something unusual and bring it back, or did they just grab all the gold, jewels, weapons, or art that they saw? Our findings will depend on where they were, what they found or took, and how well it traveled back to Spain. Also, what might have happened to the items over the ensuing time period? We're talking almost a thousand years from the Third Crusade. "

They reached the castle and parked. Diego led the way through the upper ruins and down into the bowels of the castle. Armed members of the Spanish military stood guard. Jamal eyed them curiously. Angelic stared at the ground.

"Can't be too careful," said Diego. "It would be a shame for these items to disappear now, after all these years."

———

THE TRAIN RIDE ACROSS ITALY WAS SLOW. DEE AND GINA crossed rolling hills and saw mountains in the distance. Traveling up and down the grades, and winding through the valleys, they paralleled the river for a time and looked out upon farmlands and pastures.

"You haven't said much since the others left," said Dee.

"There hasn't been much to say," replied Gina, who was looking out the window.

"Are you unhappy?"

"I'm just kind of sad. We had a good thing, and now they're all gone. It's just you and me. At least they have something that holds them together. They are married, committed to one another. You and me, we have nothing. We're just traveling around seeing the sites—no plans, no dreams, no future."

"We have each other."

"Do we?"

Gina reached in her pocket and pulled out the necklace that Angelic had given her. "Angelic told me that when I put this on, I'd think of all of us and remember." She pulled the chain over her head, and the stone dangled in front of her, resting on her chest. Gina touched it with her fingers, picking it up and slowly spinning the stone around. She turned and resumed looking out the window.

—————

WHEN KENO CAME TO THE HOSPITAL ON HER NEXT SHIFT AND wasn't wearing the stone, the man watching slipped away and went to the hotel.

"She's not wearing it," the one man said to the other. "Let's try something. They are eager for us to retrieve the stone and return home. It is not good for the stone to be so far away."

"What do you have in mind?" replied the other man.

"I'll wait near their room door. You go down a floor and pull the fire alarm. Come up the stairs quickly. When the other couple leaves, we'll check the room and verify. I do not think the stone is here. I would feel it."

The other man nodded. "Good. I'm ready to go home."

—————

JAMAL AND ANGELIC FOLLOWED DIEGO INTO THE FIRST storage room.

"We'll take a quick look and see what we are dealing with," said Diego.

"Did the family go through everything?" asked Jamal.

"They said they found the first room and opened one box. Then went into the second room and did the same. They called the antiquities division immediately. I'm their resident Egyptian expert."

"You're the resident Egyptologist?" exclaimed Jamal.

Diego grinned at him. "What, did you see that in a movie?"

Jamal blushed.

"It's not quite like that, but yes, I have an overview of Egyptian history and expertise in specific time periods. I recognize most eras. Depending on what we find, we may need additional assistance."

Diego walked over to the first box and removed the lid.

———

Keno was sitting beside Mike, holding his hand as he slept, when Dr. El Aynaoui came into the room.

"I have nothing to report," he said. "None of the autoimmune testing had any positive findings. I think Dr. Arazi mentioned the latent TB cells, and I analyzed those thoroughly. He has nothing, except the potential for the disease. As Dr. Arazi also mentioned, sometimes these fevers can't be resolved. They pass in their own time. I would like to keep Mike for a couple more days and see if the next fever occurs—if we can chart any sort of pattern. Perhaps that would tell us something. If not about the cause, perhaps about the cycle of the fever and how much longer it might last."

"Is he going to feel better soon?"

"He's probably going to remain weak and not feel like doing much until it passes. He'll want to sleep a lot, and I'd encourage him to do so. His own immune system may strengthen or rally to help him eliminate the problem, or the fever may just cycle out from having run its course, whatever its cause may have been."

"What should we do?"

"I suggest you stay in the area, if possible. I don't need to keep him here in the hospital as long as you feel comfortable managing him if or when the fever strikes. If you stay in the area, then you can contact me if something goes awry."

"My friends that have been staying with us live in the area—in the Keys, actually. We could probably stay there, or I could rent a place."

"Familiar surroundings and friends would probably help him feel better, faster. You can get here from the Keys, late at night, in a couple of hours by car, or quicker by boat if you have access. Or helicopter, if you need."

"Let me talk to Mike and to our friends and I'll let you know."

———

Dee and Gina arrived in Pescara later that afternoon. They had reservations and were scheduled to embark on one of the major cruise lines later that evening. On the third morning from their departure, they'd be in Athens, Greece.

Dee thought a couple of days on the water would be good for them. They could just cruise and relax.

They boarded and found their state room. Dee hadn't skimped on it. It was upper deck, outside, with its own patio.

Gina walked in, looked around, and stepped out on the patio. When she returned, she took his hand, squeezed it, and gave him a short, soft smile.

"This is nice. Perhaps we can talk more."

———

Jamal and Angelic stood beside Diego as he pulled the first item from the crate. It was wrapped in cloth and tied with a string.

"There may be items from many different eras in these boxes. The family was probably aware of them for some time after their original arrival. They may have shifted the artifacts around and removed, sold, or traded some of them. They may have repackaged them. This material and string don't look that old, maybe early 1800s. If we knew the history of the family, we might see where some of these items were dispersed to, or in which generation they fell through the cracks."

He untied the string and pulled the paper back. It was a tablet on some type of stone. Etched into the stone were two seated figures gazing upward at a large sun, with rays streaming down toward them.

"I'm not sure I recognize that period. Egypt worshipped many gods. One of them was the sun god, 'the Aten' in the old religion. In the new kingdom, they merged it with the god Ra, and it became Amun-Ra. I expect this has something to do with that. I am most familiar with the King Tut era. This looks as if it might be prior to that."

Diego laid the tablet on an adjacent table and unwrapped the next item, a small gold figurine with an animal head.

"That is Anubis, the god of the dead, with the body of a man and the head of a jackal," said Diego.

"Is that gold?" asked Angelic.

"I imagine so. Typically, statutes of this size and type are gold."

"What must that be worth?" asked Jamal.

"Commercially, we could figure it out based on weight. Historically, it's priceless. At auction, still outrageously expensive. But then it would have to be on the black market. You couldn't sell it at open auction."

"Someone would melt that down?" asked Angelic.

"All throughout history, this and many other gold objects like it, that fell in unscrupulous hands often got melted down and repurposed. Some people and some cultures have no respect for the cultures that came before them."

The next object was a golden disk, nearly a foot across, with textured rays that cascaded downward from the top half of the sphere—or upward, if you turned it around.

"It's Aten, the sun god, again. It's looks similar to objects from the time of King Tut but likely just prior."

"So this family must have been very respectful. These two objects alone are worth fortunes," said Angelic.

"Probably the original procurer, whoever stole the sun, and successive generations. But we don't know what they might have disposed of, and you realize that the value might not have been as astronomical to them as it would be today."

"I think it had value to them, but the fact that they possessed it may have meant more to the earlier generations, at least until the items were lost," added Jamal.

"Exactly. Let's see what else we have."

THE OLD TOURIST-LOOKING MAN PULLED THE FIRE ALARM AND sprang surprisingly quickly into the stairwell. He bounded up a flight of stairs and emerged slowly on the next floor. In front of him, standing and peering around a corner, was his partner. The man at the corner heard the sound, turned, and waved him forward.

"They are coming out the door."

"What if they come this way?"

"We will stand by a door and be arguing."

The man at the corner turned to look again before speaking. "They went the other way. Let's go check the room."

15

THE BEAT GOES ON

Later that afternoon on the water, with the Italian coast on the starboard and Croatia, on the port, Dee stood at the rail and watched Gina lie in the sun on the pool deck. Her face looked relaxed for the first time in days.

Dee thought, *I hope this will be good for her, for us. She's not happy, and I'm not completely sure why. I miss our friends too, but we are still together, at least for now.*

Dee glanced about the ship, noting the tourists, the wealth they possessed, and the affluence of the ship. It was far different from the drive across North Africa. There, they had seen many types of people, all levels of wealth and poverty. It was more comfortable here, although it now seemed a little unreal.

Dee settled into a chair on the upper deck where he could stay shaded and still see Gina. She was wearing the blue fringe thong he had first seen her in when they had met, what now felt like so long ago. She still looked amazing.

DIEGO, JAMAL, AND ANGELIC WORKED FOR THE BALANCE OF the first day. They unpacked half dozen boxes in the first room and found more items with the sun motif. But there were also masks, assorted gold trinkets, beads, pottery, and jewelry. To Diego's consternation, there were also a few items from later in time. Late Renaissance, as best he could tell.

As they prepared to leave, Diego spoke, "If all these boxes aren't in fact Egyptian, or primarily Egyptian, we're going to have egg on our face."

"You mean these findings aren't also valuable?" asked Angelic.

"Of course they are. It's just in a different context. The museum really shouldn't have released the Egyptian press notice until we know more of what we have."

"So the sun-related stuff is King Tut's-era?" asked Jamal.

Diego shook his head. "It's similar, but I believe it may be slightly older. As I mentioned, the Egyptians were polytheist: they believed in many gods. Everything we've found so far with a sun motif seems to be strictly regarding the sun and none of the other Egyptian deities. It's strange."

One of the Spanish military officers came into the room. "Director Schwartz, will you be working much longer tonight?"

"No, Col. Sanchez, we'll be leaving shortly. Your men can secure the area."

The officer bowed his head, and left the room.

"Director?" asked Angelic.

"What's up with that?" asked Jamal.

Diego dusted his hands, looked up at them, and smiled. "I am the Director of Antiquities for the Spanish National Museum."

"So that's how you made all this happen," noted Jamal.

"It helped. That man was Col. Santiago Sanchez. He has been my assistant on antiquities issues for many years. I trust him completely with the items' safety. Let us clean up and go to dinner. The rest of the team will be here tomorrow, and we will be busy."

———

AFTER A THOROUGH SEARCH OF THE ROOM, THE MEN FINALLY gave up.

"It's not here. I'm telling you," said the one.

"And she wasn't wearing it, hasn't been wearing it in the time we've been here," replied the other.

"I say we notify the others and go home. Although it might be in her purse?"

"She hasn't carried a purse for several days. We went through it in the room. I believe you are right. It's not here. Call the airport and find us a flight home. I'll let the others know."

He called a clinic in Algiers. The phone rang twice before it was picked up.

"We do not have the stone. It is not here."

"Are you positive?" the voice replied.

"Yes."

"Then return at once, and we will pursue the other tourist couples."

"What if she gave it away or, worse, threw it away?"

The voice from the phone responded, "She wore it constantly from the moment she purchased it. That seems unlikely."

"Perhaps she gave it to one of the others?"

"We have only kept loose tabs on them. They have split up further. One couple is in Spain and the other is on board ship, cruising the Adriatic."

"What should we do?"

"Return here, and I'll send a few of the others to track

each of the couples down and see who has the stone."

———

Ike and Elizabeth went on to the hospital from the hotel. The fire alarm had gone off, and they had exited their room and thought it would be nice to check on Mike and Keno.

Upon arriving at the hospital, they made their way to the room. Mike was dozing, and Keno sat by the window, looking at the city and the bay.

"Hey," Ike called out softly. "How is he doing?"

Keno turned and smiled at the couple. "He's better. Is there something wrong? You're both here."

Elizabeth shook her head. "There was a fire alarm and so we came by to check on you."

Keno rose and walked toward them. "Dr. El Aynaoui has one more test, something called a GlycoCheck. It's a wand with a camera that is stuck under the patient's tongue, and it measures red blood cells and looks at the microvascular system. I'm not really sure of it all. Something about the health of the blood cells, or abnormalities. I'm not sure exactly what it will tell them. He said they will run the test in a day or so."

"Mike can leave after that?" asked Elizabeth.

"That's what I understood."

"Can he go as far as the Keys?" asked Ike.

Keno shook her head. "Dr. El Aynaoui said that would be fine. I feel that if this last test proves nothing or there's not another fever in the next day or so, he'll let us go."

"We have plenty of room. You can stay with us in Key West for as long as you like."

Keno stepped toward him and hugged them. "Thank you so much."

16

HOLD THAT SPOT

On the second day of the cruise, Dee and Gina slept over in the morning. Dee lay on his side facing away from Gina. He felt her turn, and her arms appeared around his shoulders.

"You want to talk now?" she asked.

"Okay."

She paused for a moment. "I miss Mike and Keno and Jamal and Angelic. The last few months have been amazing. It felt like family, not just me being responsible because I had to. I wanted to look after my brothers and sister, but there was no other choice. I felt the weight of it. With our friends, I felt the fun of it, the togetherness. I just don't know if I'm going to feel that anymore. My brothers and sister are grown. I was alone until I met this group. Now they are gone. There's just you and me."

"Yes, things have changed a lot in the time since we all met on the cruise. It has been fun, and it has felt like family. I'm sorry they're gone. But we're together." He paused.

"Roll over and face me."

He turned toward her, and she pulled him close.

"Are we?" she asked.

Dee could only nod.

Gina pulled him into her embrace. "Show me."

————

THE TWO MEN CAUGHT A FLIGHT OUT OF MIAMI THAT evening, returning to Algiers. Sitting in the first-class section in an adjacent two-seat lounge, they spoke privately in Arabic.

"I was told the others are pursing the remaining tourists. Two men will intercept the ones cruising on the Adriatic, and two more will go to Spain for the other couple."

"I understand that two of them are not married. It is disgraceful."

"Perhaps, but it is their custom."

"Are we ready to take the stone when we see it, regardless, or are we still skulking around like thieves in the night?"

The first one smiled. "Skulking for now, at least until we see if either group has the stone."

"I don't like it. We should have taken the stone from the traders that found it and not wasted all this time."

"I don't disagree, but here we are."

"Most of our brothers will not be so patient if the stone is located. We have searched for it for a very long time."

The first man looked at the second one, who had just spoken.

"Our leader will want his orders followed explicitly."

There was a pause, and the second one responded, "Many of our brothers grow weary."

————

By the following morning, the two trucks full of equipment, supplies and other staff had arrived in Donostia–San Sebastián. They met Diego, Jamal, and Angelic at their hotel and drove to the site.

Arriving, they saw the Spanish military units camped to one side of the castle.

Leaning toward Diego, who was driving, Jamal spoke. "I'd guess there won't be any issue with security."

"Believe it or not, we have had attempts in the past by grave robbers or 'artifact hunters,' as I call them. Anything for a quick buck. Egyptian artifacts can be quite valuable, and you can be sure there will be confusion and opposing points of view as to ownership. "

"I'm still amazed the family turned the items over so easily," said Angelic.

Diego smiled at her before speaking. "As far as we know they did, since there is no inventory. Although I've seen no evidence of opened items or partial boxes. Everything so far has conformed to their story. Plus, it would be difficult for them to black-market these items. They wouldn't likely have the expertise or the contacts."

"They'd rather have the publicity?" asked Jamal.

"In certain circles, that has a value."

They pulled in near the castle walls and parked the vehicle, and the two trucks followed alongside. Four young Spaniards jumped out of the cabs and moved to the rear of the trucks.

"What's going to happen?" Jamal asked Diego.

"They will unload some additional tables, photographic equipment, lights, and standardized containers for repacking. They will handle the cataloguing or the separation of items for additional research while you, I, and Angelic open the boxes. They are my cataloguing crew. Each of them has a specific expertise and an overall knowledge, and they support my initial identification or research options if there are various ones to choose from."

While the young assistants began unpacking, Diego led the way to the collection rooms. Reaching the underground level, Diego waved to the guards, who parted to let the three of them enter the first room.

"We'll set up a bit of an assembly line. Since these are recovered items and not part of an archeological site, we won't have to be as precise about removal. In fact, the faster we can get them identified and catalogued and out of here, the better off we'll be."

The first of the assistants arrived with tables. Diego directed them to an adjacent room where they could set up and accumulate the artifacts as Diego and Jamal revealed them.

Diego led Jamal and Angelic back into the room of crates, and they went to work.

———

In Algiers, two groups of two men each made their way to the airport. The first group was flying to Seville, Spain, to pick up the trail of Jamal and Angelic. The second group was going to fly to Athens and then to Katokolo, where they hoped to intercept the cruise ship that Dee and Gina had boarded.

Finding Jamal and Angelic had been simple enough for the men. They had checked outgoing flights. One of their group who had been trailing the couples across the desert had followed the last four of the tourists to the airport and watched only two of them return to their hotel.

Finding the other two tourists, Dee and Gina, had taken more work. By starting at their hotel, the men had gotten lucky. A clerk had identified the couple as having caught a ferry to Sicily. From the ferry landing, there had been some wasted time before they'd determined Dee and Gina had immediately caught a train to Palermo. From Palermo, the men's group leader felt a cruise line seemed most logical and, following up on his thought, the men had located Rome as the tourists' destination.

The men caught up to Dee and Gina during the time they spent in Rome. They then followed them across the country to Pescara and noted the cruise line, the itinerary, and the destination for the ship that Dee and Gina had boarded. After reporting back to Algiers, their work was done, and two other men in the group would intercept the ship at the second overnight stop in Katokolo.

———

AFTER THE LONG MORNING OF GETTING REACQUAINTED, DEE and Gina spent the rest of the day by the pool. They swam periodically and watched the Italian countryside slip past as the afternoon progressed. Their stop that night would be in Brindisi, Italy, the home of Flavia Pennetta, a former US Open Tennis Champion. Dee knew of her, as she and Ike had played mixed doubles in the Australian Open some years before.

They went ashore and strolled the walkways around the harbor. In the early evening, the city was beautiful. The palm tree-lined walks, at nearly sea level, highlighted the ancient architecture, and the beauty of the sunset cast a golden tinge to all they saw. Across the harbor was different. It was an older and dilapidated industrial area which threatened to spoil the view and the evening, but Dee and Gina chose not to allow that.

———

THE MEN FOLLOWING JAMAL AND ANGELIC ARRIVED IN Seville and quickly went to the museum. Their group leader had suggested they start there and inquire about the director.

A chatty woman at the information desk advised the men that Diego Schwartz, the museum curator, was on a job in the Donostia–San Sebástian area of northern Spain and would not be expected back for a week or two. She was fairly bursting with pride.

"He's working on an important archeological find," she told them.

The men thanked her and moved along. Acting quickly, they planned for the next leg of their journey.

17

WHAT ABOUT MIKE

Keno opted to stay the night with Mike. He was feeling better and had gotten talkative.

"I hope we can get out of here soon."

Keno smiled at him before speaking. "Ike and Elizabeth have invited us to Key West. The doctor says it's okay. Hopefully, it will just be another day or so."

"That sounds great. I liked Ike's place, and with just four of us, we'll have a little room. Maybe we can stay awhile. I'm anxious to get out of here, but I don't really feel like doing much."

"You need to rest for quite a while. If we get to be a burden to them, we'll rent a place or stay in one of the resorts."

"That sounds nice, slow things down a bit. We've been busy."

"Yeah," replied Keno, squeezing Mike's hand, "too busy."

———

Ike and Elizabeth left Keno at the hospital, at her insistence. They made their way back to the hotel and stopped at the desk to inquire about the fire alarm.

"There was nothing to it," noted the clerk. "It must have been kids or some kind of prank. We had three engine companies combing the building."

Ike and Elizabeth made their way to the room. When they got inside, Ike plopped down on the bed and asked, "What's for dinner?"

Elizabeth did not answer immediately. She was shuffling around the room, glancing about, and looking in the drawers.

Noticing her, and not getting an answer, Ike spoke again. "Is something wrong?"

"The room looks like it's been picked over."

"What do you mean?"

"Things aren't where they were. Stuff is out of place."

"Is anything missing?"

"I'm checking, but there doesn't seem to be."

Ike picked up the phone and called the front desk. The young woman they had spoken to on the way in answered. "Front desk."

"Yes, this is Ike Mann. I believe we spoke to you a moment ago about the fire drill. Did anyone enter or search the rooms?"

"No sir. When there was no sign of smoke, the fire crews only checked the hallways. Is there a problem?"

"It looks like someone went through our room looking for something, but we haven't identified anything that seems to be gone."

"I'm sorry, sir. That wouldn't have been any of our staff or the fire department. Please let us know if there is anything missing."

"Thank you."

Ike hung up and helped Elizabeth search the rest of the room. "Do you notice anything? What about Keno's stuff?"

Elizabeth turned toward him. "No, I don't think so. Keno had nothing but her clothes. This is so strange."

They searched for a few more minutes to no avail.

Ike looked up and spoke. "Let's get some dinner and let our minds settle. Maybe we'll think of something when we come back."

They walked down Biscayne Boulevard and found a Cuban place that looked interesting. After a quick bite, they returned to the hotel.

"Do you think they'll actually let Mike out?" asked Elizabeth.

"I hope so. He seems ready to go. It'll be nice to have them at the house." He squeezed Elizabeth's hand. "Although I'm sure we'll miss our privacy."

"We can stay in the loft, and they can stay downstairs. We'll just have to be quiet."

"We've not had much luck at that so far."

She squeezed his hand in return. "I'll wear a gag."

———

Dr. El Aynaoui strode into the room and raised a hand to Keno, who was nearly asleep in the chair beside Mike's bed. Mike was asleep.

"We can run the test now. The equipment finally appears to be functioning properly, and I think we can get an accurate reading."

"Right now?" Keno asked.

"Yes, let's get it done. We have personnel on hand." He grinned. "The hospital staff never sleeps."

Keno touched Mike's shoulder, and he stirred.

"Mike, honey." Keno shook his shoulder. "Wake up."

Mike shook his head for a moment, flexed his shoulders, and sat up in the bed.

"Hey Doc, what's happening?"

"One more test and I'll let you out of here."

"Let's do it."

A couple of technicians came and got Mike and rolled him to a small testing lab a couple of floors below his room. Keno followed along behind as Dr. El Aynaoui walked beside Mike and explained the test.

"There is a small camera on a probe that goes under your tongue. It measures cellular health in a series of tests. Each of them is approximately two to three minutes long. There are twenty-four of them."

Mike looked at him incredulously. "Twenty-four?"

"We have to get a good, broad sample to get an accurate reading. The tests are compiled and cross-analyzed for cell health. The results can tell us if you are suffering from a particular cellular breakdown. Often, the findings point toward coronary artery disease. If the blood vessels around the heart muscle are not working the way they should, it can cause chronic chest pain."

"I don't have chronic chest pain."

"True, but you have these fevers which are symptomatic of some irregularity. We have turned up some elevated cholesterol numbers and elevated blood pressure. All of which point toward a possible microvascular issue."

"You got all that from a fever?"

"Not definitively," said Dr. El Aynaoui, smiling and gesturing with his hands. "But we're working through it. Eliminating things as we go. We'll see what happens with this test."

"But you will let me go afterwards? I don't have to wait around?"

"You can go. I don't think it's helpful, you being in the hospital. I want you to get to some comfortable place and rest. Keno tells me your friends are in Key West. That should be nice. We can reach you there. You can fill prescriptions if needed. You can get back here if needed. Biggest thing: you can relax."

The two technicians stood on each side of Mike. They handed him a wand on a cable that connected to a computer screen. The camera on the very tip stuck out like a little eye that could see the world, and it transmitted a signal to the screen wherever the wand was pointed.

The first technician handed it to Mike. "Put this under your tongue."

Mike slipped the wand into his mouth, and the screen came alive with little wiggling images of everything inside. There were air bubbles, microorganisms moving about, cell walls, and whatever else was in there.

"Hold it still," said the second technician.

Mike braced his arm, and the first test began. He tried to hold his hand and head still, but the picture jumped all around.

"Try to hold still," said the first technician.

Mike nodded as slightly as he could, trying to hold still. The movement slowed a little, but a light on the side panel of the image kept indicating movement. Mike finally braced one hand with the other and held the camera still enough that the blue light, indicating testing under way, came on.

He repeated this six times over the next twenty minutes. The camera's image got blurry, and one technician told him to remove the camera from his mouth. He handed Mike a tissue.

"Wipe off the camera, please, and try to swallow more. "

"Every time I swallow, there's movement."

"Just do the best you can."

"Dr. El Aynaoui said this would only take about forty-five minutes. We're over halfway in time and only on test number seven."

"It'll take however long it takes. He needs this to determine your cellular health. This looks like the best opportunity to find an answer to your issues."

"I don't know how much longer I can hold this thing still. I'm already tired."

Hearing that, Keno jumped up. Dr. El Aynaoui had left a few minutes before, and she had been sitting quietly, watching.

"Isn't there some way you can help him or that the camera can be held still?"

"He's rested for a moment. Let's see how he does," replied the technician.

They resumed testing. Mike made it through two more tests, stopping repeatedly to wipe off the camera lenses. His hands were trembling.

"I can't do this anymore."

The technicians did not reply. One of them leaned forward, guided Mike's hand, and placed the camera back under his tongue. The technicians stood beside Mike and held his hands still. They each braced against one of his shoulders. Slowly, they made their way through the remainder of the tests.

Dr. El Aynaoui returned before they finished. Over an hour and a half had passed since they began, when they completed the last test.

After pulling the camera from his mouth, Mike looked up at Dr. El Aynaoui. "You may have to keep me an extra day, just so I can recover from that. It was exhausting."

Dr. El Aynaoui grinned back at him and replied, "You

can rest this evening, and we'll check you out in the morning. I'll be in touch in a few days with the test results. You did well. That's a grueling test. The techs only had to hold you for a little over half the time. Most people don't make it that far."

He smiled, nodded to Keno, and walked away. "See you in the morning," he called.

18

———

SAIL ON

The ship departed that evening after Dee and Gina had returned from their stroll on the wharf at Brindisi. On the second day, they were scheduled to arrive in Katakolo, a small local port on the Greek coast. The third day, they would arrive in Athens.

The following morning, they relaxed and watched the last of the Italian coast pass by and the Greek coast come on display. It was a pleasant, slow, lazy day.

That evening the ship docked at the port of Katakolon. It was a small fishing village, but the second most-visited port in Greece.

Dee and Gina stood on the deck of the ship and looked out at the wharf and the dock area, which was full of shops and restaurants. They had decided not to leave the ship and spent their time watching other passengers and people scurrying around.

Gina saw the men first. They were standing on the dock, looking up at the ship. Two short men—but from that distance, everyone looked short—were watching the deck of the ship and studying the passengers through binoculars.

They wore the light-brown clothing of the desert with that dark-brown diamond pattern, and blue turbans.

"They look like the ones we saw in the medina," said Gina as she poked Dee and pointed at the men.

Dee turned and glanced down to the dock. He saw the light reflected from the end of the binoculars. "Probably just tourists like us. That must be a common form of dress for certain people. We've seen it several times now. It looks to be mostly older men. Maybe it's a generational thing, like short pants, socks, and dress shoes in America."

Gina punched his shoulder. "Be serious. They make me uneasy."

"Old guys in shorts, socks, and dress shoes make me uneasy too."

Gina punched him again.

Dee nodded to her and took out the monocular that he had used on the cruise where they had first met. He extended it and drew down on the two men on the dock.

He lowered the monocular and turned to Gina. "Yeah, they seemed to be looking at us, and they saw me looking at them."

They turned back to look at the dock, but the men were gone.

———

It was the next evening when the ship docked at the Port of Piraeus, the entry point and seaport for Athens since the fourth century B.C. Dee and Gina would not disembark until the following day.

They gathered on the deck after packing the next morning.

"Where are we staying, and how long will we be here?" asked Gina.

"I booked a place near the Acropolis. We'll have to take a taxi. It's about six or seven miles from here. We can stay as long as we like or move on, whatever you want to do."

"I guess there are a few things I'd like to see, maybe spend some time together," she replied while touching his arm softly.

"Agree completely. What would you think about going to Egypt afterwards and seeing the pyramids? Maybe whatever else we can run into while we're there? Would you like to ride a camel?"

She scowled at him. "Don't try to be funny."

Dee shrugged in return. "Just a thought."

They disembarked and caught a cab. It was loud. The windows were down, there was no air conditioning, and it was smelly and hot. The driver cursed at other drivers in what appeared to be several languages, but spoke sweetly to Dee and Gina.

"Is your first time here?"

"Yes," replied Gina. "What must we see?"

The driver held both arms in the air, steering with his knee, and gestured. "See it all. All of world history, it is here. You will learn much if you pay attention."

"Speaking of," said Dee, gesturing toward the steering wheel, and the driver returned his hands and grinned broadly.

"I drive like this all the time. I can take you around the city, quickly."

"I'm sure you can," replied Gina, winking at the driver. "We'll get your number or your card when you drop us off."

They arrived at the hotel, and the driver slammed the vehicle into a parking spot and jumped out to grab their small amount of luggage.

"My name is Stefanos Sakkari, and I am here to serve

you." He waved his arms around himself and then expanded them to indicate the surrounding area.

"Thanks," replied Dee. "We'll be in touch."

Stefanos handed them a ragged, dog-eared business card, then hopped back in his cab and roared away.

They checked into the hotel and, when they got to their room, stepped out onto the balcony, from which they had an amazing view across the Acropolis and into the city beyond.

"This is great. You picked this out?" asked Gina.

"Just from online; I took a guess. We got lucky."

"What do you want to see first?"

"I guess we could start in the immediate area. Do you want to book a tour or just sightsee?"

"Let's get Stefanos to drive us around and get the big picture."

"Seriously, he was crazy, and I'm not sure about his driving skills."

"You, Mike, and Jamal drove us across North Africa. How much worse could this be?"

Dee looked at her, and she smiled in return.

"It'll be fun."

"All right, I'll call him."

Dee called and made arrangements. They ate lunch in one of the hotel restaurants and went back to the room to change for the ride with Stefanos.

He pulled up promptly at 2 p.m. and hopped out to open the doors of the cab.

"I didn't really expect to hear from you," he said as he circled the car to return to his seat. "But, now that I have you, let's have some fun. I'll drive you around the city to get some ideas. Then tonight, I suggest you try the Segway by Night tour."

Gina turned to look at him, her eyes questioning.

"You know those little motorized things with the big

wheels? You stand on them and go around in circles; great fun. I have a cousin, and he organizes a tour around the Acropolis. I'll get a good price for you. But the city, at night, under the lights, it's amazing. You've seen nothing like it. I'll give you a preview of the tour route and point out a few things so you can be further ahead and can enjoy the trip, not have to listen so much. Slip off for a little private fun, maybe?" He grinned and arched his eyebrows at Dee and then Gina.

"Just drive for now," replied Dee.

19

THE SON OF THE SUN

They had been opening boxes all day and were about halfway through the first room. When Angelic reentered the space, having delivered a gold mask to the assistants, Diego waved to her and Jamal.

"Let's set down for a minute. I'm tired," he said.

Jamal looked around the room at all the remaining boxes. "We're not moving that fast."

"No, but discovery takes time, and we haven't stopped since this morning."

Diego was right. The Spanish soldiers had brought them lunch, compliments of Col. Sanchez. They had eaten on their feet and kept working.

There was a long list of items they had unboxed.

"What we've seen so far spans nearly a thousand years of Egyptian history. There are little bits and pieces from so many periods. The Crusaders must have grabbed anything or everything they saw."

"Where do you think they got everything from?" asked Jamal. "All from within Egypt?"

"Doubtful. I mean, the Crusaders were all over the

Middle East and Eastern Europe. These items could have been picked up anywhere along the way, coming or going, probably mostly on the way. They had armies of servants and pack animals and carts. Some of that depends on which crusade they were on, perhaps several of them."

"So this might represent several crusades or a collection of items in some fashion?" asked Angelic.

"Absolutely," replied Diego. "The family had no idea, and there's no telling how long it's been since anyone actually knew or had a good account. One thing that will probably happen is that scholars will be engaged to review period records for any evidence, mentions of these items or lists of them. Someone will try to quantify the background of this collection."

"That could be really long and drawn-out research," said Jamal.

"And tedious," replied Diego. "I wouldn't want any part of it. I'd much rather enjoy the items themselves and assist in the categorizing of them. Something for you to think about, Jamal. What area in the art world do you wish to be involved? Do you want to conduct research, be in the field doing recovery or whatever, or work at a museum as a curator or subject expert? There are many choices, and you will need to decide when this is over."

Jamal was silent, and Angelic stepped into the conversation. "We have seen many beautiful items so far. That gold mask was amazing. It was lifelike."

"Probably modeled on a real or live face. Egyptians were quite the artisans."

"There were fewer of the sun items as we moved along. That first box was full of things that looked related," noted Angelic.

"Yes, I bet we'll see more sun artifacts as we progress. The sun and gold are closely related. There was that depiction of the pharaoh in the chariot under the sun's rays. I'm suspecting that the gold items we've seen so far are from the period just prior to that of King Tut. There was a pharaoh, Akhenaten, who worshipped the sun more exclusively than the other Egyptian gods. I'm guessing those items may have come from his era. It's in the figures and the faces. They aren't quite as evolved or stylized as the later-kingdom art."

"Those first couple of boxes had similar items," added Jamal. "The balance of the items don't seem to be related."

"Could have been as simple as how it was packed, or perhaps a particular knight took an interest in the sun items. But again, I'd bet it had more to do with the gold."

They went back to work. In the second half of the room, they found two more boxes that had gold objects similar to the mask and the mural. But, for the first time, there were also hieroglyphics.

Jamal reached into the second box when they resumed working and pulled out an unrolled scroll. He held it aloft. "Look," he called to Diego.

"Papyrus. You've found an Egyptian scroll. The handles are gold," said Diego as he pointed to where Jamal held the item. Jamal handed it to him.

Diego took it carefully and moved to an adjacent table. He sat the scroll down gently and prepared a portion of the table with a soft cover. Sitting the scroll upon the cover, he touched the papyrus as lightly as possible. "It's remarkably well preserved, still pliable. You see there where it was sealed." Diego pointed to the edge of the document. "It's been broken open at some point in time and stored flat."

"Would storing it flat have made it less brittle?" asked Jamal.

"Possibly, but I think it had more to do with the temperatures. All these items are in good shape. I expect they were always stored in a cooler environment. Perhaps in this very room."

"It is kind of cool in here," noted Angelic, bringing her arms to her shoulders. "As soon as you slow down, you chill."

Diego smiled at her and slowly scanned his finger above the symbols scattered across the material.

"My interpretation isn't very good. I'm more familiar with symbols from the later empire. But I know someone who might be able to read this. It looks like something about one of the pharaohs. His health, perhaps, or maybe his death. When we go back outside and I can get a signal, I'll call her. I suspect she'd like nothing better than to come and have a look."

"Why would they record something about his health?" asked Angelic.

"Many of the pharaohs didn't live long lives or rule for long periods. They were sometimes sickly, and the priests would record their histories for posterity. They ruled for nearly three thousand years. There was a lot to keep up with."

They found nothing else potentially related to the scroll during the remainder of the day. Instead, they found a box of Renaissance art, small paintings and jewelry, knives, crosses, and other artifacts.

"These were collected much later in time," said Diego. "The Crusades were roughly from 1095 AD to 1291 AD. There is a school of thought that says there would have been no Renaissance without the Crusades. One of my crew has a specific expertise from that period. I'll have him sort this box and identify the specifics and history. He'll get a kick out of something non-Egyptian. He didn't really want to make the trip."

"It's odd to think that, as old as these items are," said

Jamal, pointing to the box of Renaissance artifacts, "they don't compare to the Egyptian items we've seen."

"Agreed. Age is relative, as is time. People see time in little blocks and not as one continuum. History doesn't come in bite-sized chunks. It's never-ending. Events layered one upon the other. But, speaking of time, let's wrap up for today. I want to confer with Col. Sanchez for a few moments, and I need to call Professor Toussaint." Diego turned and looked at Jamal and Angelic. "Eve Toussaint is a teacher and professor at the University of Paris. She's a full-blown Egyptologist," added Diego as he turned and grinned at Jamal.

"She'll come here?" asked Angelic

"Absolutely, she will. To many of us, each of our countries' history is just European history. Certainly we are all prejudiced toward our own country, but when there's an important find, everybody wants to be involved."

They found Col. Sanchez at the camp. His men had radioed ahead, and he came out of the command center to meet Diego and the others.

"Colonel," said Diego as he offered a hand. The men shook. "Have there been any issues regarding security?"

"There's nothing so far. It's been all quiet here on-site. I would expect any problems to occur when we begin transport."

"That's why my assistants have been stacking up the recovered items?"

"Yes, I felt it best to accumulate everything and make one trip, heavily secured, rather than several smaller trips. We're somewhat remote, and there are switchbacks on the highway. A robbery would be easier in an ambush upon a small group. It's safer if we all travel together."

"As you see fit, Colonel. I trust your judgement. We'll be leaving for the day and return early tomorrow."

They exited the camp and walked to the rental car.

"Would someone actually attack this site?" asked Angelic.

"Not likely, I don't think. It would most probably be a small group looking to pick off a transport, as the Colonel says," replied Diego. "Something hit-and-run. But I put a lid on public information about what we are finding, which could work either way. People may forget, or they may suspect we've found something significant and valuable. Anyone willing to use brute force in this circumstance would most likely be looking for gold to melt down. More of a radical intent and not that of a historical or art enthusiast."

"I never really thought about that side of it," said Jamal.

"It's like with the bell you found. There were some very nasty people looking for it. It doesn't have to be lost treasure, or even gold. If it's significant in history, somebody is always after it."

"I guess that could impact the field I choose to enter."

"Absolutely. You and your lovely wife don't want any issues."

20

KEEPING UP WITH THE JONESES

In the wilderness outside Algiers was a small campsite with a large fire. The leader of the group of men pursuing the stone stood before the remaining men, still in his work clothes.

"We are having success, brothers," he exclaimed. "Both of the other two couples have been located. Soon we will have the stone."

One man from the crowd around the fire rose. He shuffled his feet for a moment, but his eyes were defiant in the firelight's glow.

"Amir, why have we gone about this so long? Why did we not take the stone when we knew its location? We are so near to our goal. Why do we hesitate? We have been searching for this stone for three thousand years."

"Be patient, my brother. I know your patience runs thin, but we have the stone within our grasp. It will not be long now. The two other couples have been located, one in Spain and one in Greece. Our brothers will make a quick search, secure the stone, and slip away into the night. No one will be the wiser. We may then take our time and enjoy the fruits of our effort and the efforts of all those before us. Our heirs will live like kings once again."

"You talk too much, Amir."

"And you are disrespectful."

"Perhaps, but I am tired of waiting, tired of crossing the sand repeatedly and searching in vain for all the days of my life. Now is our time."

"Yes, it is, and soon you shall see the results of our work. Two of our men are in Spain. They have located the couple at an archeological site. Best of all, it is a cache of Egyptian artifacts taken by the Crusaders. How ironic."

"Could the couple possibly know about the stone, know of its purpose? Could they be searching for clues?"

"I think not. But it would seem likely that they are the ones possessing the stone. They have the curiosity."

"But why them? How did they acquire it from the other couple, who seemed the logical finders and custodians of the stone? The coincidences seem unbelievable."

"And perhaps they are, but after our misstep with the couple in Miami, we also have two men tracking the couple in Greece, in Athens, to be exact. Just so we know their location until we secure the stone."

"I still don't like it."

"There are many things you don't like, my brother. Many things that none of us like, but we have endured across the centuries, and we are near. The stone will be ours once again."

21

———

ON THE ROAD TO KEY WEST

Dr. El Aynaoui arrived early the next morning. Mike had just woken and was chatting with Keno, who had slept on the loveseat beside the bed.

"Are you ready to go? I've gotten your release together."

"I thought getting out of a hospital was at least a half-day thing," noted Keno as she smiled up at the doctor.

"Usually it is, but I stayed late last night and prepared most of the documents. It's supposed to be a really nice day, and I thought you should get down the road toward Key West. Traffic can be heavy if you don't get an early start. In peak traffic, it's about four hours. But if you run it at midnight, you can make it in two."

"You seem to know a lot about Key West," said Keno.

Dr. El Aynaoui smiled back at her. "My wife loves it there. We go down once a quarter and stay at Pier House or the Southernmost House. We spend a long weekend."

"It sounds fun. Look us up if you come down soon. And thank you for everything, Doctor," said Keno.

"It was my pleasure. I'm sorry we found nothing immediately, but we will continue to look."

Mike leaned forward in the bed and held out his hand. Dr. El Aynaoui shook it firmly and squeezed Mike's shoulder. "Get some rest, a lot of it. I'll be in touch in a few days about the last test result."

A half hour later, Mike and Keno were in the lobby. Mike had been discharged and Keno had called Ike and Elizabeth at the hotel, who were arriving shortly. They would start down US 1 for Key West.

Outside, it was a bright sunny day with a high, clear blue sky. They were anxious after several days in the hospital and the strain of the previous week. It felt a long way from North Africa.

Ike swung into the hospital lot in his Mustang convertible, its top down. He rolled to a stop and hopped out. Elizabeth emerged from the passenger side.

"We got a nice day for a drive: sunny, not much wind, and comfortable temperature. But the road noise and wind will make talking difficult if we pick up any speed." He popped the trunk with a key fob and grabbed Mike and Keno's bag to stash in the back with his and Elizabeth's. "I suggest Mike sit up front, only because he'll have more room. The back seat on this car is small. It's about all my kids can do to get in it."

Keno looked up at him and spoke. "You have kids? Did you tell us before?"

Ike shrugged, "I would have thought so, but I may not have. I can be so scatterbrained sometimes. They're with my ex-wife right now."

Mike opened the door and flipped the seat forward. Keno climbed into the back seat from the passenger side. Ike did the same for Elizabeth, and she climbed in behind him.

"Until we get down below Homestead, it'll be trafficky. Once we get past there, things should open up and we can see better and talk. Shout out if there's something you want to stop and visit. Are you hungry? Did you get any breakfast?"

Mike nodded. "They came in and fed us while we were getting things together to check out. It wasn't much. I'll be hungry soon. We can ask the ladies. Did you and Elizabeth get anything?"

"Just continental style. I'll be hungry by the time we get to Key Largo."

They rolled down the highway for the next hour. Mostly, they watched the traffic, the landscape, and all the new development.

Mike leaned over to where Ike could hear him. "It always this busy?"

"Pretty much. This is a weekday, and most of these people work in this area, but on weekends, most of the year, it's worse. The development never seems to stop, nor do new people coming into the area."

Mike glanced out and took another look.

"That's too bad. Keno and I have thought about moving to the Keys. We enjoyed your house so much when we stayed before."

Ike turned to look at him. "I didn't know you guys were looking. I'd stay away from the area just south of Miami all the way to Key Largo. It's really blowing up. But then, so is Key West. I'm there because of the airport. I mean, I like it, but it grows all the time, gets more crowded. The middle keys are still nice, and the area just north of Key West might be worth a look."

They pulled through Homestead, dropping some of the traffic, as the road narrowed. Heading for Key Largo, Ike slowed a bit, and if Elizabeth and Keno leaned forward, they could all talk.

"Are you ladies holding up all right? Need to stretch your legs?"

They were both leaning in close to the front seats, holding their hair.

"I'm good. It's just so nice to be outside, all the blues and greens. The desert was getting me down," replied Keno.

"I'm okay," agreed Elizabeth. "You getting hungry?" she asked Ike.

He grinned at Mike and then at her. "I was thinking a late breakfast, or an early lunch in Key Largo. Maybe look around a little, if you like. Food-wise, we have fish, pizza, Thai, tacos, BBQ—pretty much anything you want, and most of them serve breakfast as well. There're lots of good choices."

The women looked at Mike. He shrugged. "After a couple days in the hospital, I'll try any of it." He looked at Ike. "You decide."

22

AROUND THE ACROPOLIS

Stefanos pulled out of the hotel parking lot and veered into traffic without so much as a look at the oncoming lane.

"How long have you been driving a taxi here?" asked Gina.

Stefanos caught her gaze in the mirror. "A long time, since I was a child, really. I have children of my own now. My son works for the city, and my daughter works for one of the local cruise lines."

"You said something about a cousin," asked Dee.

Stefanos shifted his gaze to Dee. "Yes, I have many cousins, but the one I mentioned has a small touring company. They do the city and around the Acropolis at night, on the Segways. You will enjoy it. I suggest we drive around the area and see a few things this afternoon. It takes about two hours to circle the Acropolis. Then I can recommend several local restaurants for dinner. Afterwards, I'll take you up to Mt. Lycabettus, and you can watch the sunset. It's the best view in Athens of the sunset and the Acropolis."

"We have a pretty amazing view from our hotel room," said Dee.

"The views from the surrounding hotels are magnificent, but the Mount is the highest point in Athens. You can look across the Acropolis, around the city, and out to the Aegean Sea. It is unbelievable. Trust me. I'm Greek. I know these things."

Gina put her hand lightly on Dee's thigh and smiled at him. "Let's go for a ride."

Stefanos made his way through the thick afternoon traffic. Eventually, the Acropolis loomed large above them. "That is the Parthenon," said Stefanos, pointing upward and in front of them. "It's dedicated to the goddess Athena. It is probably the most famous of the temples and the most visited. More people seem to know it. I think there is a replica in America."

"Yes, there is," replied Dee. "It's in my hometown, Nashville, Tennessee. I've visited many times."

Stefanos turned his head and shoulders to look directly at Dee. Gina tapped him on the shoulder after a second, and he turned his attention back to the traffic once again. "What is it like?"

Dee leaned forward. "It's supposed to be a life-size replica, built for an exhibition in 1900. It's cast concrete rather than stone, but the structure and the surrounding grounds are impressive."

"Does it sit on a hill?"

"No, it's in a park downtown."

"The center of town?"

"No, the west side."

"As you say, it's only a replica. Nothing could replace the original," he said as he held one hand aloft and pointed at the structure. "Still, one day, I might like to see this Parthenon of yours."

Dee surprised himself. "Let me know. I'll help you set it up."

"My wife too?"

"Absolutely," replied Dee, and Gina squeezed his hand.

They continued the circle of the Acropolis throughout the afternoon with Stefanos pointing out the Propylaea, the Temple of Athena Nike, and, late in the afternoon, the Erechtheion, as they swung back around the city.

"What sort of food would you like for dinner?" asked Stefanos as they neared the conclusion of their drive.

Dee looked to Gina. "Greek, I suppose," she replied. "Should we do otherwise?" she asked Stefanos.

"Athens is a large city with many ethnicities. You can find good food from many places around the world. I think Greek is a good choice, since you are here. I have an uncle who has a small place, very near your hotel. The food is magnificent, and the prices are good, for more than you can eat. Be sure to try the pastries. I'll call him, get you a good seat. Then I can pick you up afterward and take you to Mt. Lycabettus for the sunset."

Stefanos got on the phone, and when the other party came on, he fired out some instructions in rapid Greek. He listened for a moment, nodding his head, then gave a short answer and ended the call.

"All set. He'll be expecting you in a few minutes, and I requested him to provide you with the house specialty. Don't worry—whatever they call it, it will be magnificent." He turned back to the driving. "I'll pick you up in two hours, and we'll have just enough time to get you to Mt Lycabettus for the sunset."

Stefanos squealed up in front of a small one-story storefront in a row of storefronts and jumped out before the taxi had settled back in place. With a grand flourish, he opened the car door and held an arm out toward the entrance.

The door opened, and a short, round, well-tanned, bald gentleman in an apron and chef's hat held the door for them and waved for them to enter. Stefanos had already returned to the cab and was pulling away.

It was dark inside the small restaurant, with only table candles and the light from the kitchen providing illumination. The man from the door led them to a table in the middle of the back wall that looked out upon the rest of the restaurant. Then he disappeared, without a word, into the kitchen. Perhaps it was the best seat in the house.

The servers, as there were several, brought appetizers, salads, and main courses of fish and lamb with a host of sides, followed by desserts, which were delicious.

Dee asked repeatedly what the items being presented were, but all he ever received in return was a smile.

After having the dishes cleared away, they ordered ouzo. It tasted potent and probably was. They sipped slowly and passed the time until Stefano returned. The man in the apron, they never saw again.

They had just finished their drinks when the door opened and Stefanos appeared. He stepped inside and looked straight at them in the darkness. They must have gotten the seats he had requested for them. He waved, and they stood to leave, feeling a little lightheaded.

Stefano approached them and reached out to steady Gina.

"That ouzo, it can be potent," he deadpanned. "Come along. I'll get you to the Mount for the evening tour. The night air will do you good."

They rode in silence, watching the city slip past as Stefano drove them toward Mt. Lycabettus.

"At this time of day, you will need to take the tram to the

top. There isn't enough time to hike, and it's too much trouble when you can ride." He turned momentarily toward them and grinned. "The thing is, the tram is underground, so there is no view until you reach the top." He paused. "Sometimes, if people don't know that, they get concerned.

Ride the tram to the top, and when you get off, one of my cousin's assistants will guide you around. Once the sun sets, he will ride back down with you, and you can meet Sergei at the bottom to take you to the start of the Segway tour. I'll pick you up at the end of the tour."

"Sergei?" said Dee. "I thought he was your cousin?"

"He is: Sergei Papadopoulos. His mother was Russian and his father Greek."

They arrived at the tram entrance and quickly exited the car. Waving at Stefano, they ran to board the tram.

Stefano sat for a moment, the engine idling. In only a moment, another cab pulled up, and two older men in desert clothing, light brown with dark-brown diamonds and blue turbans, exited the cab. They ran for the tram that was just pulling out.

So that's who it is, thought Stefanos. The cab had been following them all afternoon. He recognized the driver's face and had noticed him at several intersections around the city. He nodded and threw up a hand at the other driver, who only stared at him blankly and then drove away.

Maybe it's a coincidence. They wanted to see the city, the same as my passengers, and this is the best place in town to watch the sunset. But cab drivers almost never follow one another. They're always looking for a way to get ahead. Stefanos was not a fan of coincidences, but for now he had other things to do, like run home to see his wife, before he picked the couple up at the end of the evening tour.

———

THE SUNSET WAS MAGNIFICENT, AS IT SET IN THE WEST AND the lights came up across the Acropolis. The hilltop literally glowed as the light bounced off the stone and wrapped around the columns.

Stefanos was right, thought Dee. There was nothing else like this that he had ever seen before. The one in Nashville didn't compare.

The assistant had said nothing so far, and when they'd spoken to him, the only response had been a shrug of the shoulders. They had located him at the top of the mountain when he had held a sign up for them that said *Dee & Gina*.

As the sun set, he flipped the sign over, and it said *Sergei*. He waved to them to follow, and they boarded the tram to return to the street below.

23

FRENCH TWIST

They returned to the hotel, dined, and retired to their rooms for the evening. The following morning, they meet for breakfast. Diego had only been seated a moment when his cell phone rang.

"Hello." He listened for a moment. "We're in the dining room, left side. I'll look for you." He turned to Jamal and Angelic. "Professor Toussaint has arrived. She'll be here momentarily."

Jamal and Angelic glanced quickly at one another, both anxious to meet the professor.

All three turned at a sound coming from the foyer of the restaurant. A tall, slender blonde woman of indeterminate age swept into the room. She was wearing a nearly floor-length coat and had her hair pulled up and tucked under a wide-brimmed hat. She paused only for a moment, saw Diego, flashed a smile, and strode toward the table. She wore heels and dark-colored leggings below the long coat.

Arriving at the table, she flashed another smile.

"Diego, darling, so nice of you to invite me to your little escapade."

Diego had risen to his feet. Jamal followed suit. Her hand was slightly extended, and Diego clasped it, smiled warmly, and kissed her fingers.

She winked at Angelic.

"It was wonderful that you could come and shed some light on our Egyptian mystery."

"You know I love mysteries. And who are these wonderful people?" she replied, nodding at Jamal and Angelic.

"This is Jamal Jones. He is assisting me with the cataloguing process. He located the Castillo a few months ago."

She nodded at Jamal—Diego had yet to release her hand—and spoke. "That was an impressive find. The painting had been missing for quite some time, hadn't it?"

She glanced to Diego, who nodded at her.

She turned back to Jamal and smiled brightly. "And it was in the museum, wasn't it?" She turned back to Diego. "Right under Diego's nose." She smiled broadly at Diego and turned just enough to wink at Angelic again. Angelic broke into a broad smile.

"And who is this lovely creature?" she asked, pulling her hand away from Diego and indicating Angelic.

Angelic rose and held out her hand before either of the men could speak. "I'm Angelic Jones, Jamal's wife. I'm also assisting in the cataloguing."

"Fashion model?"

"Nurse practitioner—oncology."

"Ah, beacon of light or angel of death."

"Sometimes one, sometimes the other."

The woman took Angelic's hand in both of her hands. "That's wonderful. I'll enjoy the company of such an intelligent and beautiful woman."

Angelic visibly blushed.

Drawing her shoulders back, the woman continued, "I am Professor Eve Toussaint, Egyptologist, and I have come to clarify whatever issues are clouding Diego's cluttered mind." She turned back to Diego and took his hand again. "And of course, to enjoy his company."

With that, she pulled the hat from her head with a flourish and shook out a length of thick grey-blonde hair that fell halfway down her back. When she removed the coat, they could see she wore a long, fitted tunic over the leggings. Gold jewelry adorned her throat, wrists, and fingers.

Angelic was quick to note that there was no wedding ring.

Ms. Toussaint draped her coat and hat over an adjacent table and sat in the empty chair between Diego and Jamal, facing Angelic.

***

They arrived at the site, and Diego led the way to the storage rooms. For several minutes, they reviewed what they had catalogued so far.

Diego showed Professor Toussaint, whom he called Eve, photographs of the items that had been packed.

She glanced about the room. "I'm glad they are all still here, as we may want to examine a few of them."

"Col. Sanchez wants to move them all at once," replied Diego.

"Good. Maybe we can construct a timeline or determine if they are just random items."

Professor Toussaint pored over the photographs of the items Diego had thought might be of the Sun King.

"I think you might be on to something."

"I thought these appeared to be pre-King Tut."

"Yes, they are immediately preceding him, from his father. A pharaoh who named himself Akhenaten after the sun god Aten. He worshipped only the sun, and, of course, gold."

"Jamal found a hieroglyphic that led me to contact you. Would you care to see it?"

"That would be lovely, darling."

As they moved to the next room where the hieroglyphic was stored, Angelic held Jamal back for a moment and whispered in his ear, "Why does she keep calling him 'darling'?"

Jamal shrugged. "Term of endearment?" He turned to follow Diego and the professor.

Angelic paused for just a second and then started after him, muttering to herself, "Term of endearment or term of ridicule?"

Diego showed Eve the hieroglyphic.

She paused for a moment, and then her face lit up in a smile. "What a specimen. It's nearly perfect. And certainly appears authentic."

"What does it say?" asked Jamal.

"In good time, dear boy," Eve replied without looking up. Her eyes continued to scan the parchment, and her smile slowly widened. "This appears to be from early in Akhenaten's reign. He is telling of the greatness of the sun god and the lesser qualities of the other Egyptian gods. He mentions a city that he plans to build, dedicated to the sun god."

"Do you know of this place?" asked Jamal.

"Yes," Eve replied, "the initial mention of it was from the 1700s. It's called Amarna, and it has been excavated periodically since the late 1800s. But a seventeen-year reign is short in the timeline of the pharaohs. Especially since he was eclipsed by his son, and from what we know almost all traces of Akhenaten's thoughts and desires, monuments, and buildings were subsequently destroyed. But there has been a discovery of an entire city, previously covered in sand, near Luxor, dating from the reign of Amenhotep III, that might shed some light on the parameters of Akhenaten's lost city. I suspect that and many other things from that era are what will be determined by those doing the excavation work. Otherwise, I might have to intervene." And she winked at all of them.

24

CONCH REPUBLIC

"All right, then, we'll stop at the Conch House. You can get breakfast or lunch or just about anything else to eat," said Ike to his passengers.

They ate slowly, watching the tourists and soaking up the landscape. They sat for a while afterwards as they relaxed, ready to leave the hustle and haste of Miami behind them, and to welcome the beckoning open air and freedom of the Keys.

Back in the car, Ike asked, "Anywhere you'd like to stop between here and the house?"

"That was great," replied Keno. She looked at Mike, who nodded to her. "Anything you think we might enjoy?" she asked Ike.

Further down the road, their next stop was Georgie's Gator Farm and Airboat Emporium.

After a quick tour of the gators, they boarded for a short airboat ride. Zipping across the water with the wind, the big engine, and the fan blades screaming, they felt their stress being swept away like fog in an early morning breeze.

Stepping back on the dock, they were windblown and laughing.

"That was fabulous," called out Keno, running her hands through her hair. "So much fun." She turned to look at Mike, who was moving a little slowly.

"Was that a bad idea?" she asked.

He grinned at her. "No, it was fun, just a little more movement than I've been used to the past few days."

Ike and Elizabeth, hand in hand, stepped up beside them.

"What'd you think?" Ike asked.

Mike gave him a thumbs-up.

As they strolled toward the car, Ike spoke to the group. "I'm not sure what we do next, but…"

Elizabeth interrupted him. "What was the name of that park you took me to? The one with the beautiful beaches—Big Hondo or something?"

"Bahia Honda State Park," replied Ike.

"Let's take them there. We can walk around, have a picnic or a late lunch or early dinner." She turned to Mike and Keno. "You'll love it. The beach is amazing, and I'm from the Canary Islands. We have our own beautiful beaches."

Keno tugged on Mike's shoulder. "That sounds really fun. Let's go."

They drove for another hour, crossing Seven Mile Bridge at Marathon and rolling south toward Key West.

"Bahia Honda is on Big Pine Key. It's about an hour out of Key West. We can stay as long as you like. I've got a blanket in the trunk. We can picnic."

"I have a request," said Mike.

Everyone looked at him.

"Can we just get some junk food, a drive-in or a drive-through? I'd love a good burger."

"I know a couple of good places to go for a burger," replied Ike while grinning at them all.

A short time later, they pulled into the state park with a couple of bags of now-greasy burgers.

"Putting your system to the test?" asked Elizabeth, looking at Mike and then at the bag of burgers.

"It's the only way to know. Plus, I missed burgers when we were in North Africa."

They strolled out into the park and found a table with an overlook of the water.

"This place is gorgeous," said Keno.

"I really liked it when Ike brought me here a few weeks ago," answered Elizabeth.

They sat for a while in the afternoon sun, not talking much, just enjoying a warm but not hot day. A slight breeze blew in on them, and white puffy clouds passed by, high in the sky.

Ike was the first one to speak. "We'd better head on. Traffic will pick up later in the day. We want some time to get you settled at the house."

"Are you sure it's okay? We can stay in a hotel," said Mike.

"Absolutely not. You're our guests. The house is plenty large enough for two couples," replied Ike.

"Thank you," chipped in Keno. "We enjoyed it so much when we were here before."

———

TRAFFIC PICKED UP, AND IKE REDUCED HIS SPEED AS THEY headed into Key West.

Mike leaned across the seat, and Keno and Elizabeth leaned forward as they saw him do so. "Would there be homes on Big Pine? Something on the water?" Mike asked.

Ike gave him a quick glance. "Oh yeah. Some nice ones. Condos too."

"Maybe we could look in a day or so?"

"Definitely. The only thing I have going on is a friend who'll visit in a day or so. We should have time before he gets here. His name is Karim Ahmed. He's also a retired former professional tennis player. We played doubles several times together. He's passing through Key West the day after tomorrow on his way to a tournament in Mexico. He works security for the players. I asked him some time ago to stop by. He's Egyptian. You'll like him."

"Will we be intruding?" asked Keno.

"No, he's traveling on somebody else's dime. He'll be in the Pier House or somewhere like that. I want to chat with him a bit, and maybe we can all have dinner."

"That would be nice," said Keno. "We didn't quite make it to Egypt before Mike got sick. Maybe he'll have some good stories."

"He's got lots of stories, probably more than you want to hear. He's a talker, always churning things up."

Mike and the women leaned back in their seats as Ike pulled into Key West and slowed to stop in the gridlock.

"House is on the other side of the island. Sit tight."

25

IN PURSUIT

The two men took the train from Seville into the Donostia–San Sebastián area and then rented a car. They scoured the countryside, looking for a castle near the French border. They found it quickly enough when they saw the large contingent of Spanish army troops garrisoned nearby. The men just kept driving.

"This is not a good option for us," said the first one.

"No, the fates are against us," replied the second.

"Not the fates, the soldiers. We need to locate where the tourists are staying. Maybe we can search the room during the day while they are here."

"Wouldn't they be wearing the stone? Can we be sure they are here?"

"Seems unlikely they'd be anywhere else, with all these soldiers. Let's find a spot where we can park and wait. Watch the site until we see someone leave. Then maybe we'll know."

"We could take the binoculars and creep in closer to look."

"Too many soldiers, if it shouldn't be the tourists, we could get held up and miss them somewhere else."

They sat for the rest of the afternoon behind a small rise under the shade of a large tree. They were on the only road from the castle back to the highway. As the evening progressed, the one man became nervous.

"What if this is not them? What if they don't have it? What if they've figured out something about the stone? This is so frustrating."

The other man put a hand to his brother's shoulder. "For thousands of years, we have searched for the stone, lost in the desert. Now we know of its existence, and we know it is in the hands of these people. We are so close. But we must let the next step unfold. All in good time, brother."

"You are such an optimist."

"Until a few weeks ago, we didn't even know if the stone existed. Now we have every reason to be optimistic. We will secure it, and it will serve our purpose."

The men sat quietly for a few moments, but were interrupted when they heard sounds in the distance.

They sprang to alertness and grabbed their binoculars. A vehicle rolled by, putting a slight dust in the air. Still, they could see three people in the car. Unmistakably, these were the tourists from North Africa and the museum director.

They sat for a few moments until the vehicle was well past. They heard no other sounds.

"It would appear the military remains on hand," said the first man.

The other nodded.

"Let's pursue the three we know of first."

The men knew that the road intersected the highway shortly beyond them and that there was only one way into town. They pulled onto the main road and remained a distance behind the first vehicle, keeping them in sight with the binoculars.

"When we get close to the city, we will close the gap, and when there is more traffic, we will follow along until we see where they stay. We can return and set up surveillance. Maybe we get lucky and she wears it to dinner."

"We can't just take it from her."

"No, but we can confirm she has it. I'll feel better knowing where it is for the moment."

The other man nodded but then spoke. "I don't know why we just don't take it."

"We don't need the problems, the publicity. When we unlock our inheritance, we don't want the world to be any wiser. We will become a power unto ourselves."

"It's very humid here. I want to get back to the desert."

A few minutes later, the men turned around and came back to the hotel parking area. They spotted the vehicle they had followed from the castle.

"Perhaps they will leave for dinner?" said the second one.

"Perhaps, but they could eat on-site. If they don't come out shortly, one of us can work our way into the lobby and watch for them. We'll need some different clothes. We are obvious and highly visible in our desert costumes."

"Could that not help us?" asked the second man.

The first man thought for a moment. "Most likely it would just get us in trouble. But that is a good thing to keep in mind. Perhaps our attire could be useful at some point."

"I don't think they are coming. Should we go check in now?"

"We need new clothes first. I saw some shopping just back down the highway. This is a resort area. We will need to dress appropriately."

———

They stopped, purchased and dressed in tourist clothing, and packed their desert garb in the bags the sales attendants had given them. They had brought little clothing with them, and it was all traditionally North African, so they bought two of everything.

Carrying their small personal luggage and the bags from the new purchases, they made their way into the resort and checked in at the desk. The vehicle they had been following was still in the lot.

Walking across the lobby, the first man nudged the second one. "Now your fates are working. Look there."

Just inside the restaurant, the museum director and the two tourists sat at a table.

The first man spoke. "Go make yourself comfortable on that couch, like you are waiting for someone for dinner, which you are. I'll check in, drop the bags, and return. Whatever you do, don't stare at them."

In a few moments, he returned. The second man was sitting on the couch watching a soccer match and glancing around occasionally. As the first man walked up, he could see the director and the tourists still at the table.

"Anything happening?" asked the first man.

"Real Madrid is winning," the second man replied without looking away from the screen.

The first man shrugged at him and chuckled. "Let's get something to eat."

As the man on the couch rose, the standing man saw the three of them get up from the table and start toward the lobby.

"Quickly, stand up beside me and tell me about the game."

"What?"

"Do it!"

The man rose and recited the action he had seen. The

other man followed the couples with his eyes. They turned for the elevators.

"Come on, let's follow them." Both men took off.

The man who had been standing said to the other, "When we get inside, keep telling me about the game. If you run out of details, keep going, make it up. We'll jump on their elevator and get off on the same floor. Just keep walking until we reach the exit."

"What are we doing?"

"Trying to see what rooms they occupy."

They entered the elevator as it was about to close. Jamal held out a hand to stop the doors. The two men nodded to him and then resumed their conversation.

"Floor?" asked Jamal.

The man not talking noticed the light on the elevator panel and said, "Four," the one already lit.

The doors closed, and the elevator lifted slowly upward.

26

______

BY THE LIGHT OF THE MOON

They reached the bottom of the mountain and emerged from the tram. The moon had not yet risen, and an eerie darkness surrounded them. The guide led the way to Sergei, who was standing nearby. Sergei spoke rapidly in Greek, and the guide nodded and disappeared into the night. Sergei waved to them and led the way to the Segway site.

"I thought we were touring the Acropolis?" asked Dee.

"We are," replied Sergei, who had come to a stop in front of them. "But we start here and we finish there." He turned and smiled. "We get there on these." He swung his hand out in a grand gesture and indicated a long row of shiny black Segways.

While they were black and shiny, they were also lined with colored strips of light. Some were blue, some were pink, some were green, and some were yellow.

Dee looked at Sergei and pointed to the Segways. "Does it matter which one we get?"

"Any one you like. Get a helmet that matches." He turned to another customer.

Dee grabbed a blue-lined bike and a helmet with blue

lights in two strips across the top. Gina grabbed them both in pink. They slipped the helmets on, and when they buckled them, the lights on top came on, emitting a soft glow. They laughed at each other as they were about to climb on board.

"Everyone, stand beside your bike," called out Sergei. "Nobody gets on yet. We have to have a little talk about how to operate these things and about safety."

For fifteen minutes, Sergei talked about the bikes, the path they would take, and about staying together and not wandering off. Glancing around, Dee saw that there were about a dozen couples.

Sergei and his guides came by and took two couples at a time and demonstrated the operation of the bike.

When they had finished, Sergei called out, "Everybody mount up."

With helmets on, they stepped up on their Segways, and in only a moment the group was buzzing around like an army of neon-clad ants circling a massive, brightly lit anthill. Even with the moon rising, the glow from the sides of the Segways and the tops of the helmets was mesmerizing.

The group started slowly, allowing everyone to get adjusted and to get comfortable with other riders beside them, in front of them, and behind them. There were several stops as the caravan made its way slowly toward the Acropolis.

Under the streetlights, the colors of the bikes and helmets were less obvious, and no pedestrians paid them any attention.

It was fun, and before very long, both Dee and Gina were turning little circles or starting and stopping rapidly and making the Segways nearly hop like bunnies.

They were headed toward the loop around the Acropolis. At that point, Dee and Gina had agreed they would pay better attention. The group made a couple of other quick stops for points of interest and then rolled up onto the loop road around the Acropolis.

"Turn and look back behind you," called out Sergei.

The view was magnificent. The city stretched out before them, lit up for the night and glowing in the moonlight. Just above them, the Parthenon shone brightly under its own lights. They stood silently for a moment in a little valley of darkness between the two worlds.

"Mount up. On we go," called out Sergei.

They rode around the perimeter, with Sergei stopping periodically to point out one building or location or monument after another.

"Can you keep this straight?" Gina asked Dee on one stop.

"Not from what he's telling us, but I knew a little about it before, so I can kind of keep up."

"You'll have to explain it to me someday," replied Gina as she got back on the Segway.

Sergei wound them around the access road, and they arrived at the far side of the Acropolis.

He dismounted. "I hope you have enjoyed the tour. It was quick, but still three hours. There are walking tours in the daytime. You should be able to take one now and not need the guides. You can use the brochures. They're better than the guides anyway." He laughed. "Thank you again. Please leave your helmets on your bikes."

Dee and Gina dismounted and removed their helmets. They turned at a sound. It was Stefanos.

"Hey there. Big ride, huh? I'm sure you enjoyed it. Ready for some nightlife? I know a club…"

Gina interjected, "I think I'm ready for bed. The day is catching up with me." She looked at Dee. "Okay with you?"

Dee turned to Stefanos. "Can you take us to the hotel?"

Stefanos swept an arm toward the taxi. "Your chariot awaits, my lord and lady."

———

DEE AWOKE THE NEXT MORNING. GINA LAY SLEEPING BESIDE him. He slipped out of the bed in his shorts and went to stand on the balcony to look over the city and out to the sea.

When they had returned the night before, Dee had thought perhaps that Gina might have had something… romantic… in mind. But no, she had showered quickly, and when he had done the same and returned to the room, she had been asleep on the far side of the bed. He wondered what he had done. *Why does she seem so remote at times but then close at others?* From the time they had first gotten together she had maintained a constant and steady physical presence at his side. Now she seemed removed.

"Hey," she called out from the bedroom. "What you looking at?"

"At the city and out to sea."

"You just love the ocean."

He thought perhaps she might call him back to bed. But when he turned to start back inside, she emerged already dressed.

"What are we doing today?" she asked.

Dee smiled at her, but she didn't return the gesture.

He paused for a moment. "How about the unguided tour Sergei mentioned last night? We can explore a little, wander around the Acropolis."

"That'd be nice." She turned and went back inside.

Dee shook his head and sighed. *I have to pay better attention, I'm missing something.*

Dee got dressed and called Stefanos. He and Gina went

downstairs and met him in the parking area, and Stefanos took them to one of the self-guided tour locations.

"Any idea how long you'll stay?" Stefanos asked.

"Not really. Until we get tired," replied Dee.

Stefano nodded. "Maybe try to wrap by lunch? I got a cousin with a great seafood place down on the water."

Gina laughed. "You got a lot of cousins."

"Yes, I do, and they are all here to serve you. Have fun. Call me when you're about to finish."

And off they went. Dee and Gina circled the access road and climbed up onto the Acropolis. They were at a midpoint near the Temple of Athena Nike.

"Let's start here and work toward the Parthenon. We can see how much time it takes."

Gina nodded her agreement. She paused for a moment. There was a light breeze at this height, and it was a clear, blue, cloudless, and beautiful day. She smiled at Dee, but he had turned away.

He reached back and took her hand, and they walked. They slowly circled around each of the structures as they moved toward the Parthenon. Dee noticed Gina spent as much time looking back at the city and out to sea as she did looking at the temples and other structures.

As they finally approached the Parthenon, Dee stopped to admire it from a short distance away.

"Does it look like the one in Nashville?"

Dee paused for a moment. "It's much grander, and there's only part of it surviving. In Nashville, you can walk inside and throughout the building. I wish we could get closer to this one. It's magnificent."

As they stood there looking, Gina tugged on his hand. "Don't turn immediately, but look over to our left side. Near that temple or building across the way."

Dee turned and faced her. "That way?"

She nodded.

Dee paused for a moment and then casually turned toward the interior of the Acropolis. It took a minute, and his gaze floated across the site. Then he saw what he thought she meant.

"Interesting. It looks a little like those two from the boat dock. But that outfit, the long tan jacket with the dark-brown diamond pattern, and the blue turbans, could be generic."

"You think?" she replied.

Dee turned back to her. "I don't really know. Let's walk some more."

They moved quickly along the side of the Parthenon to the far end and then circled halfway around the perimeter of the building.

When Dee paused and again admired the temple, he also scanned the area around himself and Gina. He did not see the men. Turning to Gina, he spoke. "I don't see them. They could have just been tourists."

"I still think there's something creepy about them."

"I don't disagree, but I'm not sure it relates to us."

"Let's hope so, but I'm not positive."

Dee took her hand. "Let's walk some more. We'll see if we notice them again."

For the next couple of hours, they slowly made their way around the site. They didn't see the men again.

Dee glanced at his phone for the time and called Stefano. They were back at the spot where they had started the tour.

In only a few minutes, Stefano arrived, and they got in the taxi.

"Now to the seashore," he said and grinned at them.

Gina lay back in the seat. "I still think those men were watching us."

"Why do you think that?"

"It's just a feeling. When I was dancing, I developed an

instinct for who might be a problem in the crowd. Stalkers, or persistent types, that you just want to avoid. It's an observation that comes from watching them watch you."

"We can keep an eye out for them."

Stefanos, who had been listening, leaned back toward them.

"You talking about some old guys in funny clothes, brown cloth and blue turbans?"

Dee and Gina both looked up at him.

"How did you know?" she asked.

"I saw them get out of a taxi last night right after I dropped you off at Mount Lycabettus. They were in a cab that had followed us around most of the afternoon. I thought little of it. But you say you think they might be following you?"

"We've seen them or someone in similar clothes before, at the dock in Katakolo when we were on board the ship. They appeared to be looking at us or for us. Back in North Africa, we saw that outfit several times."

Stefano replied, "You must be popular. Those men appear to have been following us around the city. Those are desert people. They do not see the fun in anything; very dry sense of humor. I hope you are not in trouble. It could be a coincidence, I suppose."

"Do you see them behind us now?" asked Dee.

"I've been watching since you both started talking. I have seen nothing."

27

THE SUN STONE

"The scroll tells of Akhenaten's plans," explained Professor Toussaint. "Unfortunately, it doesn't elaborate beyond that. History confirms that he had a city built, or that was his intention."

"Professor," said Angelic.

"Do call me Eve."

Angelic nodded. "Eve, did all these gold objects that we've seen come from this pharaoh?"

"We'll have to check them, but Diego says that several of the first things you located all had the sun motif." She turned and spoke again. "Diego, have the soldiers separate those packages out of the group, and we'll accumulate them as we go along with whatever else we find that seems to fit that era. When we're finished unpacking, we can try to construct a timeline, see what it tells us."

Diego stepped away to advise the soldiers.

Eve motioned to Jamal and Angelic with her fingers, drawing them closer.

"Diego is such a fine man, with a keen mind. I can't help

but tease him. I have a reputation to keep up with him. Please don't think poorly of me." She smiled.

Angelic returned the smile.

Jamal chuckled. "It did sort of look like you were riding him, maybe ridiculing him."

"Heavens, no. We've been friends for years. He and I and my deceased husband used to paint the town in Paris. Diego's quite the sophisticate. It was great fun. Oh, here he comes."

"All taken care of, dear," Diego murmured.

"Thank you, darling."

Jamal and Angelic grinned at one another.

Diego turned back toward the remaining boxes and sighed. "Let's get started."

They spent much of the afternoon trying to finish up the crates in the first storage room. Mostly, they found items from the late Egyptian kingdom or from subsequent periods in time. They also found a group of small statues from the Roman era. Diego and Eve indicated the statues appeared to be of the Roman gods, as they recognized Mercury and Neptune. There were a Grecian urn and more small items from the Renaissance.

After approaching the last few boxes in the room, Jamal uncrated another gold mural.

"Eve, Diego, look." He held the gold disc by the edges for them to see.

Eve held her finger above the work and traced slowly along with the design. Depicted was a chariot with the pharaoh at the helm. Gold rays from the sun at the top of the mural flowed down upon the pharaoh and were reflected back in smaller streams. Eight of them came from an object around the pharaoh's neck. He had an arm raised and was grasping the object in his other hand.

"Fascinating," murmured Eve. "He's sometimes called

the 'lost pharaoh,' not just for his lost city but for his short reign and by the historical omission of him by later pharaohs."

"What is that he's holding?" asked Angelic.

"It looks like it's redirecting the sun's rays," added Jamal.

Eve nodded. "It's called the 'Sun Stone' in Egyptian lore, widely referenced in Akhenaten's history but never verified."

"Does this prove its existence?" asked Jamal.

"Not really. Akhenaten could have had the artist depict him in this fashion. Or it could have existed in some form. The stone has never been seen or even documented in later Egyptian history."

She continued, "Legends surrounding it say that the stone had some specific purpose and wasn't just a large jewel or an ornament. The stories vary widely. Undoubtedly, it served some purpose. The reflected light makes me wonder. Is there some message there? Some clue as to how the pharaoh used the stone?"

Diego shrugged. "We'll not likely ever know."

"Certainly not with that attitude, darling." She smiled up at Diego. "Whatever it was, it was important to Akhenaten."

They spent the rest of the day finishing up the last few boxes in the first room. There were no other gold objects thought to be related to Akhenaten, or the "Sun King" as they now called him. Eve found Jamal and Angelic amusing in their ardor for learning more about the story.

"There is no final chapter, people. It's still being written. You are part of that writing. Isn't it exciting?" She took Diego's hand.

"Are we about done for today, darling?"

He kissed her fingers and murmured, "Indeed, we are, with this portion of the day."

They all walked to the car and discussed dinner.

"Surely you can't expect us to eat in the hotel," said Eve.

"I thought it was adequate, didn't you two?" Diego replied while looking at Jamal and Angelic.

"It would depend on your definition of adequate, I suppose," answered Angelic.

"Excellent response, young lady," retorted Eve.

"Jamal?" asked Diego.

"I'll eat wherever the ladies want."

"Another sensible answer," replied Eve.

Diego but his hands together and looked skyward. "But of course."

"Excellent, then. I'll find us a place to dine."

With that settled, they got into the car and made their way back to town.

Arriving as darkness approached, they agreed to clean up quickly in their rooms and meet again in the lobby.

Jamal and Angelic entered their suite, and Jamal plopped on the bed.

"Get up, lazy butt, and get in here with me to get ready," called out Angelic.

Jamal lay back and looked around the room. He knew housekeeping had been there because they had made the bed. But everything else looked a little out of kilter. The luggage was in a different place. Someone had rearranged the items on the dresser top. The trash can was on the other side of the room.

Odd cleaning process, he thought as he got up to go into the bathroom and wash his face.

He walked into the bathroom and noticed Angelic going through the drawers of the sink.

"What are you doing, babe?"

"Things seem out of place from where I left them this morning. But nothing seems to be missing. The housekeepers don't seem very conscientious."

"Yeah, I noticed things moved around in the bedroom."

They wrapped up and met Diego and Eve in the lobby.

"I found this wonderful French restaurant," cooed Eve.

"But of course," replied Diego as he glanced at Jamal and Angelic.

"Don't be a wet blanket, darling."

Diego sighed but did not reply.

As they walked to the car, Angelic asked, "Did you notice anything odd in the housekeeping in your rooms?"

"Everything was just as I left it," replied Diego.

"Untouched," added Eve.

28

DREAM A LITTLE DREAM

They rolled into Ike's driveway and came to a stop. Each of them climbed out and stretched.

"That last dash across town was just about as bad as the rest of the trip," mumbled Keno.

Ike nodded. "Yeah, the town has gotten really busy. I try not to drive in it. About the only time I get more than a few blocks away is if I'm going to the airport. Everything else is nearby."

He stepped toward the trunk of the car to grab the luggage and then pointed toward the house and said, "Come on, and let's get inside."

The overhead fans were turning, and a light cross breeze was wafting through the house. They all collapsed on the two sofas.

"Who wants what to drink?" asked Ike as he jumped to his feet. Looking back at them as he moved toward the kitchen, Ike called over his shoulder, "Four cold beers coming up."

Upon returning, he passed out the beverages and resumed his seat next to Elizabeth.

"You guys can take the downstairs bedroom and Elizabeth and I can take the loft."

"Don't let us put you out," said Keno.

Elizabeth held up a hand. "We moved our stuff before we left for Miami. Mike needs to rest for a few days, and climbing up and down to the loft is not the ticket. That's final."

"You heard it there," added Ike.

Keno and Mike grinned at one another.

"I appreciate it," replied Mike. "I don't really feel like climbing right now. In fact, I might like to lie down for a few minutes. I had a great time coming down the road, but I'm a little worn out."

He and Keno stood up, and Elizabeth jumped off the couch and led the way.

"I know you've been here before but I just want to see if you need anything."

Keno and Mike made their way into the room and Mike sat quickly on the edge of the bed. "This is great, thank you," he said. "A cold beer and a breeze and I'm good." He lay back on the bed.

Keno looked to Elizabeth. "I'll just make sure he's comfortable and be back out to join you and Ike."

Elizabeth nodded and turned from the room.

———

THE THREE OF THEM SAT IN THE LIVING ROOM, CHATTED, HAD another beer each, and relaxed.

Silence had drifted across the group, and Keno had her head laid back on the sofa when her phone rang.

"Hello." She paused. "Dr. El Aynaoui, yes, we made it to Key West. I'm sitting in Ike's living room now." She smiled and nodded at the phone as the doctor spoke. "Dr. El

Aynaoui, let me put you on speakerphone so Ike and Elizabeth can hear."

They heard his voice. "That would be fine. Ike? Elizabeth?"

They shouted out to him.

"I hope you are both well?"

"Very good, Doctor. You have some news for us?" asked Ike.

"Yes, the results of the GlycoCheck came back."

"Good news, we hope?" asked Keno.

"Yes. The GlycoCheck measures the status or health of the microvascular system. You might think of the microvascular system as a big highway system within the body. It delivers and removes oxygen and nutrients to all the cells in your body. The more efficiently it does that, the healthier you are likely to be. If it has been decimated in some fashion, then the person is likely to have or to anticipate health issues. Sometimes the results can give us a clue as to a problem."

"So Mike's good?" asked Ike.

"Yes, for his age. Think of the results as a chart that goes from red to yellow to green. He is at the very top of the green level. That is a good score. It could be higher, but there appeared to be no issues or irregularities. I thought perhaps the fevers might skew the results."

"Is there anything he needs to do?" asked Keno.

"Not really. It appears he's had an active life or been an athlete, but maybe he eats a bit of junk food?"

"That's pretty accurate."

"Tell him to lay off the junk food, particularly as he ages. I can prescribe a supplement to help with the cell strength if you'd like. I can call it in to a pharmacy down there."

"That would be great. Does it tell you anything about the fevers?"

"Unfortunately not. Whatever source he contracted that from remains unknown. Hopefully, it does not return. Contact me immediately if it does. There are lots of sinister viruses loose in the world, many of them unidentified and potentially deadly. Do take care."

"I will keep a close eye on him. Thank you so much. We'll probably be in town here for several weeks. If you and your wife come down, call us."

"Most assuredly, and I thank you for being so gracious." With that, he hung up.

Ike, Elizabeth and Keno sat for a moment looking at one another.

"It's a good thing he's past it, whatever it was," said Ike.

Elizabeth nodded.

"I hope so," sighed Keno.

———

MIKE THOUGHT HE HEARD CONVERSATION IN THE OTHER room, but he wasn't sure. He was in a dream. There were sounds, but they all ran together.

He couldn't see himself, only what was in front of him. There was a woman with short dark hair, wearing only a man's work shirt. Her face was heavily made up, leaving her eyes in an almond-shaped form. Her lips were brightly colored. The shirt was undone in front, and he saw her swivel her hips and turn toward him to reveal a broad expanse of dark, curly pubic hair. She pulled her hands back to her sides, spreading the shirt even wider, and he noticed a gold bracelet on each arm in the shape of a serpent. There was something about her. Mike went to speak.

He called out in the dream and woke himself with a start. Sitting across the room from him on the dresser was a slice of cabbage sitting in half a glass of water.

Keno came running in from the living room. "What's wrong?"

Mike shook his head slowly. "I was having a dream, a strange one. There was a woman. She looked something like you, but it wasn't you. Something… startled me. What is that?" He pointed to the glass of water.

Keno giggled. "I came back in to check on you earlier, and I had gotten a glass of water and a slice of cabbage from a veggie plate Elizabeth had out. She called me when I came in here and I set them down real quick to go see what she wanted. I forgot to come back and get them."

Mike sighed and shook his head.

29

THE OPTIMIST

The men rode up the elevator with Diego, Jamal, and Angelic. Being courteous, they let the three of them off first. Then the men followed the trio down the hall. While the one man prattled on about the Real Madrid game, the other noted the couple was in a room in the middle of the hallway with the director next door to them. The men continued down the hall, and when they reached the exit, they descended to the lower level and caught the elevator on that floor.

"So now what do we do?" asked the one who had been talking about Real Madrid.

"We wait for them to leave tomorrow, and we search the room. I did not see any of them wearing it, and I'd think they would have it with them. I saw no evidence of a chain around any of their necks while we were standing behind them in the elevator."

"What if they wear it tomorrow?"

"We'll try to be in the restaurant before they leave so that we can observe them. If no one is wearing it, we will search the room."

"I hope we find it. I want to go home."

"As do I, but I want to return home knowing I am a wealthy man."

"You are such an optimist."

The next morning at breakfast, the men sat near the open lobby. The group came in and sat to the left of them against the wall. They passed directly by the men. Neither man saw the outward appearance of the stone or of a chain.

"Good, it is in the room," said the one man.

"Who's the optimist now, my brother?"

"I grow weary of this cat-and-mouse game. Let us fetch the stone and go home. It cannot mean anything to them or they would better care for it. They won't even miss it."

"Hopefully you are correct, for once."

After watching Diego, Jamal, Angelic and now another woman leave the restaurant, the men watched their car leave the parking area. They waited several minutes, then rode the elevator to the fourth floor.

Standing outside Jamal and Angelic's room, they stood silently and watched the hallway and the room doors. There was no sign of activity other than the maid's cart a few rooms down. They heard the maid in the room, talking.

One man walked slowly by the maid's cart. There, what he had hoped for and was looking for: a master keycard. He picked it up quickly and pitched it to the other man, who caught it, quickly inserted it in Jamal and Angelic's door, and then flipped it back to the first man, who replaced it on the cart and strolled away.

They entered the room and hung a "No Service" sign on the door. The first man turned back toward the room and held a finger to his lips. Then he pointed to the bathroom, and the second man went to look. The first man remained and checked out the bedroom.

So certain were they of finding the stone that they

weren't really careful about where things were located. When they couldn't find it and changed rooms for each to examine where the other had just looked, they still came up empty.

"We've been in here too long. We've got to go."

"We didn't put things back where we found them."

"Does it matter?"

"They may realize, they may not. It was messy of us."

"They're tourists. What do they know? Let's get out of here."

The men checked the hall, removed the sign, and then slunk down the corridor toward the exit.

———

Sitting in their own room, the two men held a discussion.

"What are we to do now?"

"Perhaps we should try to talk to them?"

"About what? Tell them what we're looking for and why we want it?"

"Maybe we should call Amir?"

"He will not be happy with us."

"Perhaps we could observe them at the castle?"

"With the Spanish army outside? I don't think so."

"What choice do we have? Seek them out or go home empty-handed. I do not want to face Amir's wrath. I want the stone."

"We'll get caught if we go out there."

"Perhaps we should wear our desert clothing?"

"Then we'll most certainly get caught."

"This is a bad idea. Let's go home."

"First, we search them out."

The men drove out to the castle and parked where they had spied upon the trio the first day they had arrived. They exited the car and walked slowly into the woods. Each man had a set of binoculars.

They wandered along, stopping occasionally to look through their field glasses.

Suddenly they were surrounded by Spanish military stepping out from behind trees and standing up in camouflaged uniforms and Ghillie suits.

The one man immediately held his hands in the air. He was so fast that several soldiers drew arms.

"No," shouted out the other man. "We come in peace. What I mean is we are tourists. There were supposed to be some castle ruins around here. We were just trying to find them. We're on vacation, and clearly we're lost. I'm sorry. I don't know what's going on here."

"Neither do I," replied the nearest soldier. "But we're going to go talk to Col. Sanchez. You can tell your story to him."

The men marched along slowly, their hands on their heads, soldiers in front of them and soldiers behind them.

———

Diego's phone beeped. He read the text message and looked up to the others.

"You want to take a break for a minute? The Colonel's men apprehended a couple of tourists stumbling around in the forest. He doesn't think it's serious, but he thought we might enjoy watching the show as he interviews them."

"Heavens, darling, why would I want to watch such a dreadful thing?" replied Professor Toussaint. "I'll continue unloading these boxes."

"I'd kind of like to see it," said Jamal.

"I'll stay and help Eve," said Angelic.

"Wise decision, young lady. I was right about you: smart and beautiful. We can chat."

Diego and Jamal left the room.

———

"DIEGO THINKS JAMAL HAS AN OUTSTANDING FUTURE AS AN art historian, working in whatever field he chooses," Eve said.

"I hope you're right."

"You doubt him?"

"No, not his ability. Maybe his desire to immerse himself in the politics."

"Darling, the whole world is political."

"Yes, it is. But Jam isn't really political. He left the NFL because he wasn't. I think he might be better off working for himself."

"'Jam.' That's such a quaint name."

Angelic laughed. "That's just my nickname for him. He doesn't really like it, and if anyone but me calls him that, he'll tell them."

"I love a man with a backbone. They're so much more challenging. I find that rewarding."

Angelic smiled at Eve. "It is an experience knowing you."

"A good one, I hope. I love to be a role model."

"That you are."

———

AS DIEGO AND JAMAL APPROACHED THE COMMAND CENTER, they saw two middle-aged or older men in resort clothing with their hands on top of their heads. Diego and Jamal took a position behind a group of soldiers.

Col. Sanchez strode back and forth in front of the men. "Who are you?" he asked.

The men remained silent.

"I asked you a question." The Colonel paused. "I'll simply lock you away for eternity. No one will ever know."

"We were just wandering about. We didn't know you were here."

"I asked who you were, not why you are here."

The other man responded, in a calmer tone, "We're Egyptian. We are on vacation. As I told your men, we were sightseeing, and there are supposed to be the ruins of a castle somewhere around here. Apparently we stumbled into a military base."

"Where would you get the idea there were ruins?"

"From a tour book. But we're desert people. These forests all look alike. We're lost."

"That you are. But… I really don't believe you."

"But, but, but..." said the other man.

"See, he babbles," said the Colonel.

The second man spoke again, "He is easily frightened."

"But you are not."

The second man shrugged. "It's just not as visible."

The Colonel laughed.

The soldiers had stepped away, and Diego and Jamal were visible to the two Egyptians.

The man who had babbled tugged the sleeve of the other and nodded with his head toward Diego and Jamal.

The second man did not look, but the Colonel saw the gesture.

"You know those men?"

The second man responded, "No."

"You didn't even look."

"I didn't have to. I don't know anyone here but him," he said, pointing at the man beside him.

"Take them inside. We'll talk again later."

The soldiers took the two men into the command center.

The Colonel walked over to Diego and Jamal. "Ever see those two before?"

Diego shook his head.

The Colonel looked to Jamal.

"I didn't recognize them. I was in North Africa before coming here, but we were just on vacation, touristing around."

The Colonel nodded. "I'll talk to them again. They seem harmless, although the one is quite clever."

30

CRUISING

The restaurant was right on the water. Unlike the one Dee and Gina had eaten in the night before, this one was open and airy and full of light, with a breeze from the sea that stirred the plants that sat around the perimeter of the restaurant floor.

"That was really good, and I didn't eat that much seafood until I met you and we were on the island," said Gina as she crumpled her napkin and slid it on the table.

Dee sat back. "What else would you like to see?" he asked.

"I think that's about it for me, unless there's something else you'd like to see. I think I've had enough hiking. I'm for getting back on the ship and relaxing for a few days. You said something about the pyramids, didn't you?"

"Yeah. The cruise from here to Egypt stops in Cyprus for a day and then sails on to Alexandria. It's a day plus to Cyprus from here, then a day in Cyprus, and then a day to Alexandria. It's a smaller cruise line that only works the eastern Mediterranean. The ship has a pool, plus we can hit the beaches in Cyprus. They are supposed to be stunning."

"I like it. When do we leave?"

"Let me see what I can book." Dee got on his phone. He called Stefano for a pick-up and then looked for the cruise line and its ships' availability.

Dee thought while he made the calls, *There's so much more to see here. I wonder why she wants to keep moving?*

Stefanos dropped them at the hotel, and they told him of their plan. They could board the following day. He agreed to pick them up in the morning, drop them off at the dock, and bid them farewell.

"What do you want to do the rest of the day?" asked Dee.

"I was actually thinking about taking a nap. You?"

"That doesn't sound bad."

"I thought you might like to do a little more sightseeing since I cut us a little short here."

Dee sensed she didn't really want company.

"Yeah, there are a couple of things I might take a quick look at before we go."

"Good. I'll see you for dinner."

———

LATER THAT EVENING, THEY CHATTED.

"Do you want me to call Stefano and see if he has another cousin with a restaurant?" asked Dee.

"Actually, I'd just as soon stay in and eat at the hotel. I am really craving a hamburger."

They dined on cheeseburgers and fries, Grecian style, and they were good.

Afterwards, they walked around the grounds of the hotel briefly and sat on the balcony of their room.

"It is beautiful here. Maybe we can come back someday," said Gina.

"I'd like that," replied Dee, smiling at her, but she didn't respond.

————

THEY MET STEFANO EARLY THE NEXT MORNING, AND HE ferried them to the dock. As they emerged from his cab he spoke. "I—or, I should say, 'my cousins and I'— have really enjoyed having you here and being at your service. I will miss you. Should you ever come back, you have my card. Call me anytime."

"If you ever decide to see Nashville and the other Parthenon, let me know and I'll help you work it out," replied Dee.

"Thank you. My wife would like to see America." He nodded, and then he was gone.

Gina smiled quickly at Dee as they gathered their luggage. "That was nice of you."

On board the ship, they had a starboard cabin with a large exterior window. The ship looked more like a river cruiser than an ocean-going ship. There would only be hundreds of people instead of thousands.

"You say there's a pool?" asked Gina.

"There's a small one on the top deck."

"I think I'll check it out. What are you going to do?"

"I might walk around a bit and then join you at the pool."

Gina nodded and dug in her luggage for her swimsuit and cover-up.

Dee did a quick walkabout of the ship and had a beer in the bar. He sat and thought. *I don't know what to make of her. I thought we were close. I suppose I could ask. I wonder if I should fear the answer.*

He made his way to the pool and, finding her, sat in the

chair beside her. She looked up at him and smiled briefly. "Anything interesting?"

"Not until I sat down just now."

She gave him another quick smile. "Flattery will get you nowhere, didn't you know that? When you say something, it has to have some real meaning." She leaned back in her chair.

Dee thought, *Perhaps I'd better let that remark go and think about it before I reply.* He sat quietly for the rest of the afternoon.

They docked at Limassol Port on Cyprus the next morning. The cruise line offered several excursions for the day. They chose one that delivered them to the beaches of the former resort area of Varosha.

As they lined up for the tour, the director had them sit for a moment.

"Varosha is an abandoned town that once, back in the 1970s, was one of the most popular resorts in the world. Supposedly the most beautiful beaches on Cyprus. There was a civil war with Turkey, and the Turks claimed that part of the island. They shut the resort down, and it has been abandoned ever since. High-rise resort towers, shops, restaurants all stand empty, as if the people got up and walked away. It's an amazing sight and was strictly off limits to everyone for over twenty years. Just recently, the beaches have been reopened, but the town and the buildings are still closed. Access is strictly prohibited. Please stay on the beach and away from them. Questions?"

There were none, and the group disembarked from the ship and boarded the tour bus. They pulled slowly out of the terminal and made their way into the city of Limassol.

Dee glanced about from side to side as they rode.

"What are you looking for?" asked Gina.

"Ike mentioned a friend of his, a retired tennis player, a

Cypriot, who has a teaching academy in Limassol. I was just watching for it on the chance we might pass it by."

Gina nodded and went back to her phone.

"I think maybe when we get set up at the beach, and if I have a good reception, I'll call Keno and check on Mike."

"Yeah, I'd thought maybe we'd have heard from them."

"Hopefully he's all right. I may also call Angelic and see how Jamal is doing in the art world."

"I bet that's quite a change for him," said Dee.

Gina nodded and went back to scrolling on her phone.

31

UNBOXED

Diego and Jamal returned to the storage area. Having unpacked all the crates in the first room, they moved to the second room. Eve and Angelic had already started unpacking two side-by-side boxes. Diego and Jamal started opposite them on two other boxes.

"Find anything interesting?" asked Jamal.

"Only late-kingdom Egyptian so far," replied Eve.

Diego turned, opened a box, and immediately came across a slew of small Renaissance paintings, a variety of oil portraitures.

"I wonder if this is commemorative of the earlier family," murmured Diego.

Eve stepped across and held two miniatures to the light.

"There certainly seems to be a resemblance, or perhaps the painter was only comfortable rendering one face." She handed the miniatures back to Diego.

Jamal grinned at their exchange as he undid the box he was preparing to unload. He stopped short at the first item, another gold mural. The mural depicted the pharaoh and a woman or young child standing beside him on a dais.

"Look at this. Is it the Sun King?"

Diego turned toward him, but Eve set down the item she was handling and walked to Jamal's side.

She placed her hand over his and changed the angle he held the mural, to better reflect the light. "Yes, that does appear to be Akhenaten. And I believe that is his queen, Nefertiti."

"She was his wife?" asked Angelic.

"Yes, darling, and she's far more famous than he."

"And Tut was their son?" queried Jamal.

"That's the lineage."

They stood admiring the mural for a moment.

"Jam, darling, would you mind carrying this over to the side there? We'll keep it out to see what else we might find before it gets packed away."

Jamal looked at Eve, then at Angelic, and back to Eve. With no emotion on his face, Jamal replied, "I'd be happy too."

"That would be marvelous, darling."

As Jamal stepped across the room, Eve turned to watch him and then glanced quickly to Angelic and winked.

As they worked through the afternoon, Angelic seemed deep in thought. Finally, she turned to Eve. "Tell me more about Nefertiti."

Professor Toussaint stopped what she was doing. "Well, she is speculated to have been short, even for her era; to have had extremely dark hair and dark eyes; and to have had a slender, almost boyish, figure. She may be most famous for her bust that is on display at the Neues Museum in Berlin. She had an exquisitely shaped face and refined bone structure. She is represented as being rather pale for an Egyptian woman of that time, and she is often thought to have been a bit of an exhibitionist, as she is often portrayed partially nude. There is another rumor that she ruled for a time after her husband's death and prior to her son's ascension."

"She was a powerful woman."

"Absolutely, one of the earliest and probably one of the most powerful ever. She commanded a nation."

"How do you know all those physical details?" asked Jamal.

"While they have not found her body, examinations of Egyptian art and artifacts have allowed historians and archeologists to determine with some precision what she may have looked like. At the end of the day, there is always a degree of speculation."

Angelic turned to Jamal. "Doesn't that description sound like someone we know?"

Jamal stood motionless, then shrugged.

"Keno: short, dark-haired and dark-eyed, boyish figure, and powerful when she wants to be."

Jamal grinned. "I wouldn't have thought of her figure as boyish. Slender, I could go with."

"You know what I mean."

"Yeah, she has the look, and she can be dominating."

Eve chuckled out loud at that comment. "I need to meet her."

Angelic replied, "You'd like her, and Gina too."

Eve raised her eyebrows in question.

"Gina was the third woman in our group in North Africa, before we came here. There were six of us touring North Africa by jeep."

Eve paused before replying. "It sounds rather dreadful and dusty."

"True, but it was also dynamic and vibrant. We all felt very much alive."

"Well said," replied the professor. "I must meet all these people."

Eve chose Italian for them that night, and they went back to the hotel to clean up. Angelic was brushing her teeth and talking in between. "I need to call Keno and check on Mike. I can tell her the Nefertiti thing. She'll get a kick out of it."

"Yeah, I bet she will. I can see Mike rolling his eyes."

"Be nice."

"I am nice, always, to you."

"Is that your idea of sweet talk?"

"No, just truth."

Angelic finished her brushing and went over and hugged Jamal. "How do you like all this? Just truth?"

He paused for a moment. "It's fun. I'm not sure that I can run around the world unboxing artifacts for a career, but maybe I'll find something I like."

Angelic paused for a moment, watching Jamal prepare for dinner. "If you don't find something you like, you can always move on."

He nodded his head. "I know, but I'm good for now."

32

SHOPPING

Mike woke up in the early evening. The sun had just set, and Ike, Elizabeth, and Keno came in from the deck where they had been watching it melt into the water.

"How about some dinner?" Mike called as he came out of the bedroom, rubbing his eyes.

"He must be feeling better," replied Ike.

"I think my appetite is back even if my energy isn't."

"What would you like?"

"I don't know; something local with cold beer and good food."

"Several to choose from. I'll lead the way."

A half hour later, they were sitting in a little café off of Duval Street. While munching on appetizers, Mike asked the question. "Do you think you could show us some property on Big Pine tomorrow? When is your friend coming?"

"Certainly. Let's get up early and get in front of the traffic, and maybe we can get back by midafternoon. "

"We can stop whenever to accomplish that."

"Do you want a Realtor?"

"Not at this stage. Keno and I have talked about it, and

we think we'd like to live here. We just need to find the right place."

Elizabeth leaned in toward them. "That's great. It'll be nice to have you close."

"What about your friend?"

"He won't be here for another day, and I only need an hour of his time and then we can all do dinner with him."

———

MIKE WOKE THE NEXT MORNING FEELING THE BEST HE HAD since before the first fever. He felt like he was getting well. Now to find a place to live and something to do, maybe charter fishing, buy a boat. He'd been a good lake fisher back home. Keno could be his mate. It would be fun.

He rolled out of the bedroom and smelled breakfast.

Ike stood at the stove. "Morning. You like eggs and bacon?"

"Love them, and I'm hungry."

"I'll put on some more. We can knock it out and get a move on for Big Pine."

Elizabeth and Keno strolled in and sat at the bar.

Ike leaned toward Mike. "Mind grabbing the plates from the cabinet?"

"At your service."

An hour later, they were cruising the roads of Big Pine. There were a couple of large waterside homes available.

"Want to stop?"

Mike looked at Keno. "We want to be comfortable and have some room, but those things are too big, too much to keep up with, and right on the road with no space."

"You won't get a lot of space unless you're prepared to part with some really big money. In which case, you could buy your own island south of Key West down toward the Tortugas."

"That's an idea, but it also sounds like a lot of trouble."

"There are some new condos over on the other side of the island. Let's look at them."

A short drive later and they were there. Even from the outside, they looked small.

"That's too much the other way. I don't want to hear my neighbor's toilet."

Ike nodded. "That's about it for what's available."

"We can head back. We'll keep looking."

A couple of hours later, they were sitting in the Tree Top Café looking down on the lower end of Mallory Square.

"We'll just keep looking, maybe do some actual research, and contact a Realtor."

"About anywhere from Marathon on down to Key West would probably work for you."

"Yeah, we can broaden the search."

"I mentioned those outer islands. I really don't know what they cost."

"In my part of the world, we can lease them," added Elizabeth.

"Would it make much difference in cost?" asked Keno.

"I don't know, but to get to those islands, you have to have a boat and/or a float plane. You get plenty of privacy and all the fish you can eat, but everything else has to be brought in to you. It would be expensive."

"It sounds nice, but we don't want the hassle, do we, babe?"

Keno nodded. "I just want to take it easy. We have enough money."

Back at the house, the couples retired to their separate bedrooms.

Mike laid down, and Keno knew he'd be asleep shortly.

"I think I should call Angelic and Gina and let them know you are all right."

Mike nodded. "Yeah that would be good. I'm curious how they are all doing and how the traveling is coming along. I wonder where they are."

"I don't think they were sure where they were going next."

Keno looked to Mike for an answer, but he was already asleep.

———

OVER IN THE OTHER BEDROOM, ELIZABETH CAST A GLANCE at Ike.

"I'm really surprised about them wanting to move here. I thought from what Dee told you they would all stay together. "

"Things happen, I guess. They have had a pretty busy time of it for most of the past year. Mike and Keno look worn out, dog-tired. It's not really a surprise. They just want some peace and quiet."

"I hope it works out for them."

33

SEARCHING

The two men had been selected to follow the third couple. They had located them in Katakolo, or least they had seen them from the dock.

"How far do we have to follow them?" asked the one man.

"Until we see the stone or hear that the other couple has it," replied his companion.

"These two don't ever slow down, from Rome to Athens and now to Egypt. At least we get to go home."

"We need an answer by the time we get there."

"I don't think they have the stone. I think it's in Spain with the other couple."

"You may be right, but we need to be sure. Their ship will dock in Cyprus. Let us try to speak with them."

"Okay, but I'm tired of this and I think it's a waste of time. How do you plan to do that?"

The men chartered a boat to Cyprus and made good time, arriving well ahead of the cruise ship. Wanting to look around the island for a day before the couple landed, they hoped to find a place for an intimate conversation with them.

The men disembarked in Limassol and began their search.

34

BEACHED AND BAFFLED

The bus arrived at the unloading area near the beach. The barricades were still in place at the boundary of Varosha. Sheet metal, barbed wire, metal stakes, and crossbars all marked the edge of the property.

A guide led the tourists beside the fence and down to the water's edge, where they entered the beach area.

They could rent chairs and umbrellas, but everything else, they carried with them. Gina had the towels and sunscreen and Dee had the water and snacks. They planned to spend the day. The bus would run back to the ship at noon and again late in the afternoon.

Dee and Gina made their way along the sand. Even this early, the beach was crowded. The sea was a deep, rich blue that melted into a lighter blue sky. Not a cloud anywhere. Bright, clean sand underfoot and a long tide break out to the water all made for beautiful viewing. Chairs and umbrellas were stuck everywhere.

They arrived at the rental shack and stood in line, as a lengthy crowd was already waiting. They glanced around the beach, looking at options. Chairs were filling up fast.

Finally, after they'd made their way to the front, the vendor showed them the remaining spots. Several were far down the beach.

"If people don't stay all day, do chairs come back open?" asked Dee.

The vendor nodded. "You just have to keep an eye on them."

Gina pointed to a chair on the chart. "What about that one?"

The vendor looked. "Not as much demand. It's close to the back of the beach, and the buildings sometimes shade the spot in the late afternoon."

"Some shade late in the day might not be a bad idea," said Dee.

Gina, normally a sun worshipper, agreed. "Plus, it's closer to the pickup point, and we won't have to move."

"The view is actually pretty good from back there. You can see everything," added the vendor.

"We'll take it," replied Dee.

They strolled back to their chairs and deposited everything, then ran down to the water and got wet. It felt wonderful. The water was warm, and the waves slight, but the sand and the sun felt good on their skin.

Back in their chairs and under the umbrella, they slathered up with sunscreen for the long day ahead.

It was a beautiful setting as long as they didn't look over their shoulders at the deserted city behind them. They could have been anywhere in the world.

They swam a while, snacked awhile, napped awhile, then did it all again. They talked little, but they grew comfortable.

In the early afternoon, the beach had cleared somewhat, and they talked about moving closer to the water or closer to the gate back to the bus but decided against it.

Gina reached under the chair and pulled out her bag

with the sunscreen. She skimmed a little on her shoulders and said to Dee, "Let's get back in the water."

They stayed for a long time, romping in the surf and splashing water at one another. At one point, Dee swept Gina up in his arms and turned her in circles into the oncoming waves. They laughed, and she clung to him tightly. He felt it was the happiest they'd been in the last couple of weeks.

They were laughing and chatting when he brought her back ashore, and they started for their chairs.

About halfway to the chairs, they saw a young boy standing beside their belongings. He looked down the shore, and when he saw them, he grabbed Gina's bag and ran toward the fence.

They both broke into a run.

"Stop," shouted Dee.

The boy only ran faster. He got to the fence, wormed his way through it, and started into the deserted city.

Dee, who had on water shoes, continued running after the boy. Gina, who had been barefooted after the first few minutes on the beach, stopped to slip into her shoes and then started after Dee.

Dee slipped under the fence at the same spot as the boy, who was now hopping up the steps of the nearest building. Dee glanced up enough to see that it had probably been a hotel or a condo once upon a time.

He picked up the pace, trying to keep the boy in sight. Gina saw Dee hustling up the steps and followed him.

The boy reached the top of the steps and ran across an open balcony, then jumped from that side. Dee raced to the edge of the balcony and saw a pile of rubble below where the boy had jumped. The boy picked himself up and brushed himself off as he resumed running down the street into the midst of the abandoned town.

Dee thought, *Oh well*, and over the balcony he went. Dee crouched as he landed, then rolled to his shoulder, over to his back, and off the pile of rubble. He shook himself off and resumed chasing the boy.

Gina got to the rail, saw what had happened, and doubled back to the stairs. She sprinted down them and ran around the building and after the other two.

Dee was gaining on the boy when he swerved again and ran across the lot of an empty gas station. Halfway around the abandoned pumps, he made a perpendicular cut and ran back across the street and further into the town. The maneuver bought him a couple of seconds, as Dee still had to go around the pumps and then change direction.

Gina saw it all and kept running straight, nearly catching up to Dee.

The boy disappeared around another corner, and Dee sped up to keep the boy in sight. When Dee rounded the corner, there was no sign of the boy.

Gina closed in behind him. "Where did he go?"

Dee leaned forward catching his breath. "I don't know. I turned the corner. He was gone."

They both stood where they were for a moment, breathing hard.

Gina brought her hand to her face. "That bag had all our stuff: passports, money, and keys to the suite… What are we…"

There was a sound, and they looked up and to their right.

Two men in desert garb stood on the roof of a one-story structure. There was a guardrail around the roof, as if it had been a deck. These looked like the men from the dock in Katakolo and from the Acropolis.

"Perhaps you are looking for this," said one man. The

other man swung the bag over the banister and above the ground.

Dee and Gina looked up.

"Yes, that belongs to us," replied Dee.

"And you shall have it again when you answer our question."

"What?" said Dee and "Question," added Gina.

"It is a simple question and requires only a simple answer."

Dee and Gina looked at each other and back to the men.

"Where is the stone?"

"What stone?" replied Dee.

"The Sun Stone."

Dee looked back at them while Gina continued to look at him.

"I don't know what you are talking about?" said Dee.

"Perhaps your friends in Spain have it."

Worry flashed through Dee's mind. They knew about Jamal and Angelic, or so it seemed.

"I don't think so. None of us have a 'Sun Stone.' Never heard of it before."

"Your lack of knowledge does not preclude your possession."

"That might be true, but we don't have any stone, and neither do our friends."

In the distance, there were police sirens, drawing rapidly nearer.

The two men looked at one another and spoke softly. Dee couldn't make out their conversation.

The man holding the bag dropped it to the ground below. Gina ran for the bag, and when Dee looked to her for a moment and then looked back up, the men were gone.

Dee ran toward the house and circled around the side but did not see the men.

The sirens grew louder.

"We've got to get back to the beach. Run," called out Dee.

He and Gina ran even faster this time than before. They had the advantage of knowing where they were going and the motivation of not getting caught in a war zone in a foreign land.

They made it to the fence as the sirens were on the far side of the building behind them. They wiggled under the fence and ran to their chairs and sat. Then they turned back toward the fence as if rising from the chairs. Combat-clad police or military ran toward the fence, guns out.

Gina stood up and waved.

"What's going on, guys?" she asked.

They stood silently for a moment and stared at her. She had little on. She hadn't bothered with the cover-up, and she stood there and let them look.

Finally, one of them spoke. "There was a disturbance. It was reported that there were intruders in the city. Did you see anything?"

Gina smiled and shook her head. "We've been here all day and not seen anything but this beautiful beach."

Dee had risen and stood beside her. "Nothing at all, officers. Maybe a kid playing a prank?"

"It could be a deadly prank," the officer replied, then turned and walked back toward the street. His men followed him, leaving Gina and Dee standing there silently.

35

HISTORY LESSON

The next morning, the team went back to the castle, determined to make a dent in room two. There were still many boxes, and Col. Sanchez was getting antsy about all the items sitting around unpacked on the tables.

Eve was determined to attempt a timeline of the Sun King objects, both for her own curiosity and for Jamal and Angelic's.

They arrived in the room, and each of them started on a separate box.

Eve spoke first. "Look," she called as she unrolled a three-panel tapestry. "It's linen, and remarkably well preserved."

There was the face of the pharaoh, in profile, on one panel; the face of his queen, Nefertiti, on the second panel; and the two of them together on the third screen.

"It's like a triptych family portrait," murmured Angelic.

"Indeed," added Diego.

Jamal just stood and stared.

"I don't think there's anything like this in existence," said Eve. "There are renderings of this pharaoh or the queen individually or in a scene like on the dais that we saw earlier, but these are amazing. They're in such close profile and with intricate detail."

Jamal continued to study the tapestry. Diego and Angelic stepped closer.

"This is a good representation of very early portraiture. As you can see from Nefertiti's face, she very much resembles the bust on display in Berlin. Her characterization is consistent," continued Eve. "She either looked that way or that is how the artist saw her."

They were interrupted by a knock on the door. One of the soldiers was standing and fidgeting just outside the room.

"Col. Sanchez would like to relay a message to you," the soldier said.

"Please, go ahead," replied Diego.

"He wanted you to know that he has decided to let the two captives go if you have no objection."

"I presume that is acceptable, if he is comfortable?" Diego glanced to Jamal, who shrugged. "He can dispense with them as he sees fit," answered Diego.

The soldier nodded before speaking. "The Colonel spoke to them again, and while he is suspicious of them, he doesn't think their intrusion has to do with this operation. He'll release them and put a tail on them to see what they do, where they go."

Diego nodded. "Please keep us posted. Thank you."

The soldier turned and walked away.

Eve placed the tapestry on a nearby table and resumed working, as did the others. In only a few moments, she spoke again. "Come and look at this."

She was holding a manuscript.

"What is it?" asked Jamal.

"Any guesses, Diego?" asked Eve coyly, looking up and smiling at him.

"A manuscript of note, perhaps? It doesn't look like a Gutenberg Bible. Maybe a diary or a journal of the family?"

"Very good. It is in fact a journal and gives us some backstory from the original Crusaders. It's from the fifteenth century, 1403 AD, and appears to be a written log or history of the family, the castle owners. The story tells of their forefathers, two brothers that fought in the Third Crusade under Richard the Lionhearted, or Richard I, and returned with many golden objects related to a specific time in Egyptian history. It says that the brothers had many stories of the travels, battles, looting, and wealth that lay along the path of the Crusade. These stories were passed down from generation to generation. It goes on to say that early in the thirteen century, 1210 AD, nearly twenty years after returning from the Crusade, several family members, including one of the brothers, undertook a trip to locate and research more information about the objects. They found the site where the objects originated but little other information. Later in that century another trip was made, but it also found little. A grandson of one man who made the second trip made a third trip in the fourteenth century, early 1300s, in search of information, but by this time, they had even lost track of the site. The writer of the log, from the fifteenth century, documented his family's persistence in pursuing what the original Crusaders had described: a room of treasure, lost to time, and a special stone that was the key."

"That doesn't really make sense," said Diego.

Eve looked up at him, eyebrows raised.

"The Third Crusade didn't get any closer to Egypt than Jerusalem. It was the Seventh Crusade where Egypt was attacked by the French King Louis IX."

"I can only tell you what it says. Maybe the knights made a side trip, or maybe they took the items from someone else who had taken them. It doesn't say. Maybe they were on the Seventh Crusade as well."

"They'd have been too old by the time of the Seventh, if they were really on the Third Crusade."

Eve shrugged. "What can I tell you, darling? Would you like to hear the rest of the story?"

"Please continue," piped in Angelic. Jamal grinned at her broadly and thought, *That's the way to keep the bickering on track.*

"After the third trip was unsuccessful, and nearly two hundred years after the crusade, the family lost interest or died off. I'm not sure. Successive generations lost track of the information or didn't care. They clearly didn't know what items were in storage, as what we've seen so far would have been priceless even in their day."

She paused.

"You got that from the log?" asked Jamal.

"No, darling." Eve smiled at them and winked. "I got it from supposition, as many historians do." Then she laughed. "You should see the looks on your faces."

"Yes," said Angelic, smiling, "But that seems like a logical explanation."

"Logical assuming we have all the facts, which is doubtful. Diego makes a good point: how did they get these artifacts when the Third Crusade was nowhere near Egypt? I suspect there is a great deal of missing, incomplete, or inaccurate information."

They spent the rest of the day opening and unpacking more late Egyptian period artifacts and many Greek and Roman relics.

As they walked to the car, Jamal spoke. "We were on a roll this morning, but then we found nothing else. I'm disappointed."

"You mean all those other artifacts didn't interest you?" asked Diego.

"Yeah, they did, but I seem to be most fascinated by the Sun King and his era of time."

"Perhaps working with me in the future might provide you an opportunity for further work in that area," said Eve. "I'm sure the two of you would love Paris, and I'd enjoy the company."

"You'd have something Jam could do?" asked Angelic.

"But of course, darling. There is always a way, if that's what he wants."

"It sounds interesting. I'll think about it," replied Jamal.

Eve smiled at him sweetly.

***

Back in their room after dinner—Greek, at Eve's suggestion—Jamal and Angelic sat on their balcony and looked toward the town.

"Would you really want to concentrate on that period of Egyptian history?" asked Angelic.

"I don't know for sure, but I seem drawn to it. Like there's something there that I should know. Wouldn't you like to live in Paris?"

Angelic looked down at her hands and smiled before looking back up. "Of course I would, as long as you're happy."

Jamal leaned closer and hugged her. "Let's see what happens."

Angelic sat up. "Oh, I should call Keno and see how Mike is doing." She looked at her watch. It was 9 p.m. "It should be midafternoon in Florida. Surely I could reach them."

Jamal nodded. "If Mike's okay, I'd like to speak with him."

Angelic dialed the number for Keno's phone. The phone rang for several seconds, and then Keno came on the line.

Angelic had selected the speakerphone, and she and Jamal both heard Keno exclaim, "Angelic!"

"Hey girl, can you talk?"

"Of course. How are you guys?"

Angelic glanced to Jamal. "We're fine. We're in Spain near the French border."

"What?" Keno exclaimed.

"Diego called Jamal and asked if he'd like to help catalogue some Egyptian artifacts that were donated to the national museum. We're on location on the Bay of Biscay, working out of an old castle."

"Living the dream, are you? Where are Dee and Gina?"

"We're working on it. We left Dee and Gina in Tunis. Not sure where they are. Listen, how is Mike? You guys still in Miami?"

"You aren't the only ones that have moved. But he's fine. The fevers have passed. The doctors could never tell him what caused them. They just stopped. We're down at Ike and Elizabeth's in Key West."

"That's wonderful news, and I loved Ike's house and that whole area."

"Yeah, we do too. In fact, we're looking at property. We may stay here."

Angelic and Jamal glanced at one another.

"It's a beautiful place," said Jamal. "Is Mike around?"

"Let me get him."

They heard movement that suggested Keno must have been going from room to room.

"Yo," Mike responded in a booming voice.

"You sound good," replied Jamal.

"Yeah, I'm getting better. I still get tired pretty quickly, and not a lot of energy."

"I bet you're still keeping Ike hopping."

"He's been a great help, as has Elizabeth. What are you doing?"

"Cataloguing Egyptian and Renaissance art."

"Man, that is you."

"I like it. By the way, we ran across an Egyptian tapestry of a pharaoh and his queen, and the pharaoh was in profile, but he looked just like you. The queen, Nefertiti, looked just like Keno."

As he spoke, Jamal realized he'd just put that together in his mind. He'd known something about the couple was familiar, but the connection hadn't occurred to him until that moment.

36

THE RACE

The next morning, Mike and Keno took it easy. They stayed in bed and lounged around the bedroom. When they finally emerged, Elizabeth was sitting on one sofa working on her laptop.

"Morning," she called out.

"Hey," replied Keno. "Sorry we're so late—just exhausted, and I think maybe as the stress passes, we've got nothing else to go on right now."

Elizabeth looked at them. "That's why you're here, to rest. Want some breakfast?"

"We don't want to be a problem," replied Keno.

"Nonsense, I have some bacon left over. How about a BLT for the moment?"

Keno looked to Mike, who was grinning. "That'd be great," he replied. "Where's Ike?"

"He went to meet Karim for brunch. We're supposed to have dinner with him. All of us. He insisted," replied Elizabeth. "I think you'll like him. He's funny."

"Not to be nosy, but any idea what Ike is talking about or what he's thinking?" asked Mike.

"Not nosy at all. I'm uncertain he knows what he wants, but he's just interested in something on the professional tennis tour. He's looking at different tour-level or related jobs. He might work for a couple of years. He's not sure what to do with himself now that he has retired from playing, and he doesn't want to be too busy for his kids. He made some money on tour, but he's still fairly young. Karim is in tour security, which would be steady work and have somewhat of a consistent schedule. He could pick tournaments to work. Ike got a couple of offers to coach, but he doesn't really want to do that."

"Sounds like he has choices. Always a good thing."

"Agreed, although I think he enjoys hanging out here in Key West the best."

"Who wouldn't?" replied Keno. Then, looking to Mike, she added, "We're looking forward to it."

Elizabeth smiled at her. "Let me get those sandwiches."

Ike returned a couple of hours later. Everyone was sitting on the back deck, catching a little sun or shade as they felt the urge.

"Hey, everybody."

"How'd it go, bro?"

"Good. Karim is a great friend. He offered me a job. I'll probably take it, and I can start when I'm ready."

"That's awesome," said Keno.

"Happy for you, babe," added Elizabeth.

Ike stepped across and hugged her. "I'm excited, but for now, I can hang out with you guys."

EARLY THAT EVENING, THEY MET KARIM AT THE HOT TIN Roof Restaurant on Duval Street at the edge of the water.

They were seated open-air and could tell immediately that they were going to have a great view of the sunset.

Karim was waiting for them, and he rose as they approached.

Ike introduced him. "This is Karim Ahmed: Egyptian by birth, world traveler, and retired top-twenty tennis player. Karim, you've met Elizabeth, and these fine people are Mike and Keno Williams."

"Very pleased to meet you. Friends of Ike's, you are friends of mine." He smiled and gestured to the seats. "Have a seat, and let's enjoy."

They made small talk and ordered. The food was good, and everyone was full by the time they stopped eating.

"Karim," said Ike. "Tell them a tour story."

Karim looked to Mike, Keno, and Elizabeth. "Is there something you'd like to hear about?"

No one spoke for a moment, then Keno popped up with, "Tell us the most unusual thing that ever happened you."

Karim nodded. "Something that I could tell..." He laughed. "I have it."

The group leaned in around the table to hear.

"I was playing in a tournament in one of those oil-rich desert kingdoms, and we had a sandstorm that disrupted play for a day early in the week. That forced the semifinals and finals to be played on the last day of the tournament, on Sunday. Well, Saturday night, another storm came in, and it lasted for three days, from Sunday to Tuesday. So everything had to be played on Wednesday of the following week. That caused the four of us players in the semis to miss the next tournament the following week. In a gesture of good faith, the organizers of the tournament awarded all four of us the amount of the winning prize money."

"What?" asked Mike.

Karim smiled at him. "The organizers paid each of the four of us in dollars as if we had won the tournament."

"Wow," said Keno. "That was nice."

"Yes, it was, but there's more." He smiled at them all again. "The tour officials only gave us the points for our rankings depending on how we did. Semi points or final points or winner points. But we each got paid the winner purse. But the best part was that I won my semi and made it to the final. I lost in three sets, but it was one of the few finals of my career. I reached my highest ranking, and I nearly earned the money they paid me." He laughed. "It's one of my best memories, other than playing Davis Cup for my country."

"You're Egyptian, you said?" asked Keno.

He nodded.

"We were going to see the pyramids before Mike got sick. Are they worth it?" she asked.

"Very much so. The Valley of the Kings is unlike anything you have ever seen. Take the cruise down the Nile and be amazed. I'm from the area around Luxor, and I grew up with it. But I'm still in awe every time I go back there."

"It sounds awesome," said Ike.

"It was a great place to live. So many things to see, so much time and history, so many legends and stories."

"Tell us one," said Mike.

Karim shook his head for a second and then smiled. "This is one of my favorite stories from childhood.

"There was a legend of one of the early pharaohs who built his own city in the desert beyond Luxor, which was called Thebes at the time. In this city, the pharaoh had a temple with a secret room. Not all that unusual in Egypt or for a pharaoh. But the fascinating part was that the secret room—full of treasure, of course—could only be opened with a special stone at a certain time.

"For the first few years of the pharaoh's reign, before he built this temple, he held a race, a competition for any of his people who wanted to take part. It was called the 'Race across the Sahara,' and its course went across the desert from Lower Egypt to the Moroccan coast. There was a trade route out of Cairo in the north that followed the Mediterranean, and several trade routes that ran north and south, but the race course was across the sand, out where the desert meets the sky. The competitors had to survive from one trade route to the next to get to the Atlantic.

"Their goal was to get to an ancient Moroccan port, now called Essaouira, but which has had many names over time. The important thing about the port area was that it was the only place they could find a certain phosphorescent shell. The shell glows when light shines upon it. It reflects the light. This was going to be important to the pharaoh in his secret room. The shells were later used by the Romans to make the purple dye that they used for their senatorial robes."

"It was a great use of natural resources," offered Keno.

Karim nodded. "Indeed." Then he continued. "Anyway, the winner of the race got some special dispensation. Basically, anyone that got back with the shells was rewarded, although many died in the attempt to cross the desert. The pharaoh collected all these shells, and when he built his secret room, he lined the walls with them so that when the room was open, the incoming light refracted and illuminated the space. The shells were considered a part of his ritual, along with this singular, special stone, called the Sun Stone, that would open the room or show the way to the room."

"That's a wild story," said Elizabeth.

"Yes, but great for bedtime," said Karim with a nod.

"What happened to it?" asked Keno.

"The city was lost under the sand for thousands of years. The dunes shift constantly in the wind, particularly in that area. After the pharaoh's death, the city was abandoned, and the new pharaoh returned to Thebes. The story was only thought to be a legend until a couple of hundred years ago when some ruins of the city were found. Excavation revealed that there is a temple, but there's nothing in it other than a raised dais and what may have been a throne. It's an elaborately carved stone thing."

"Nobody found the treasure?" asked Ike.

"Not that anyone's aware of, and no one has ever seen or confirmed the existence of the Sun Stone. The idea has mostly been reduced to myth."

"But still a fun story," said Elizabeth.

Karim smiled. "I always thought so as a child."

37

THE NEXT STEP

The men had arrived in Cyprus the day before the couple. They had scouted the island for locations to search the couple out and address them. They favored a location next to a beach. The men had hoped the couple would disembark, unlike what they had done in Katakolo. With a full day in Cyprus, it had seemed likely the couple would get off the boat.

The men watched had the port from a nearby rooftop and seen the couple board the bus for the beach. They had checked the cruise lines website for local excursions and, based on the time of departure, had deduced that the beach at Varosha was the choice. They followed behind in a cab at a safe distance.

When Dee and Gina arrived at the beach, the men had stood at the entrance and watched them trudge across the sand. Having them select an umbrella toward the back of the beach and near the abandoned city had worked out even better than the men anticipated.

It was a simple matter to hire a local boy to grab the woman's purse and bring it to them. They paid him when they got the purse. They kept the boy in sight after he stole the purse in order to prevent him from stealing anything. Fortunately for the men, Dee had given chase, and the boy had been too busy running to even stop until he had flung the purse at the men, grabbed the money from their hands, and continued running down the street.

The meeting with the couple hadn't gone well. When the boy had tossed them the purse, they had quickly searched it. There had been many things inside—passports, room keys, some money, jewelry—but no stone.

"I don't think they have it," said one man.

"Still, we must ask them. Maybe she has it on her," replied the other.

"I'd think we'd have seen it. She has so little on."

The other man had no reply for that. "Let's question them."

When Dee and Gina had been questioned about the stone, the men had felt that the couple genuinely did not know what they were being asked. The men had planned to come down from the rooftop and return the purse, as a gesture of good faith, and then ask again about the stone, describing it if necessary, even if only to gauge the couple's reaction.

But the police sirens had made that unwise. The men had fled and hidden in one of the adjacent buildings. From their vantage point, the men had seen that the police had caught sight of someone running and had pursued them.

A short time later when the police passed the building the men were hiding inside, and had no captives, the men were silently grateful that the couple had gotten away.

The two men exited the abandoned resort carefully, watching for police or military. After catching a cab, they made their way back to a hotel near the port in Limassol.

Now they were in a predicament.

"How can we return to Egypt with no answer?" asked the one man. When the other did not respond, he continued, "We could contact Amir?"

"No," replied the second man. "He would be most unhappy with us. I do not wish to incur his wrath."

"What must we do then?" resumed the first man, his voice growing more pleading.

"They are on their way to Alexandria. We will go on before them, as we did here. Then we will try again to determine if they have the stone."

"Don't you think the couple in France are the most likely to have the stone?"

"It would seem more reasonable, although this couple is headed for Egypt."

"Maybe we could check with the team of men in France?"

"If they had found it, Amir would have let us know."

"No doubt he would have, but maybe they could tell us something. What do they think about the couple there having the stone?"

The second man thought it over. "I could call and ask. Otherwise, we'll have to be very creative to get close to the couple again, now that they've seen us." He pulled out his cell phone, found the pre-selected button, and punched it.

In only a few moments, the call was answered. "Hello."

He wasted no time with preliminaries. "We are in Cyprus with the one couple. We have not located the stone. Have you had any success, or even seen the stone?"

"We're driving back to Paris now. This couple does not appear to have it. We were caught by the Spanish military police near the site where the couple is cataloguing the Egyptian artifacts. We searched their room and came up with nothing. We haven't seen them wearing it. Our cover was blown, we had to leave. You've not seen anything?"

"These two won't stay still long enough for us to get a good look. We had one encounter, and they didn't have the stone on them. We'll try again."

The phone disconnected on the other end.

The second man in Cyprus looked over to the first man and shook his head. "They don't have it, nor have they seen it, and they have basically been run out of the country."

"This doesn't look good," replied the first man. "Maybe none of them have it anymore. Maybe they threw it away, or gave it away, or left it somewhere. What if we can't find it?"

The second man reached out and slapped the first man across the side of his face. "Never say that. If it's not with any of the others, it is with this couple. We just haven't seen it yet, but we will. Now get busy and get us to Alexandria as soon as possible. Let me think how we'll handle these tourists."

38

BACK TO THE BOAT

Dee and Gina packed up their stuff and walked slowly toward the beach gate to catch the bus. They were still astonished by what had happened.

"What do you think they were talking about?" Gina asked.

"I got no idea," replied Dee. "It bothers me they seemed to know about Jamal and Angelic. We should call and check on them."

Gina nodded. "As soon as we get back to the room, I'll call. I'm just so glad we didn't lose everything. That was stupid of me to leave my bag on the chair."

"We got comfortable and inattentive, but it seems obvious those men set it up for us to see the boy so we'd chase him and have to talk to them."

"If those were the guys we saw on the dock and again on the Acropolis, they've been following us for a while. What could they possibly be talking about? We've not seen any stone this whole trip, since we left Spain."

"I don't know. It's really bizarre."

They caught the bus and rode back to the ship with the

remaining passengers. Upon making their way on board, they went to their cabin and stripped down to take showers.

After a quick dinner in one of the ship's restaurants, they went back to the room to call Angelic and Jamal. There was only an hour's difference in the time zones, so Dee and Gina hoped they could catch the couple after their dinner.

Gina dialed Angelic's number and waited for several rings. Just when she thought the voicemail would answer, Angelic breathed a hasty, "Hello."

"Hey girl, you're out of breath," Gina responded.

"Gina, I was running in from the balcony. Didn't know I didn't have my phone. I was just telling Jam I needed to call you. How y'all doing?"

"We're good."

"Where are you?"

"We're In Cyprus, on a cruise."

"Cool."

"How are you and Jamal?"

"We are having so much fun. Diego brought this French professor lady friend of his in to help identify things, and boy, does she know her stuff. But I think she has a crush on Diego."

"Wow. He's married, isn't he? Where are you exactly, Seville?"

"Yes, he is married, but no, we're up on the French-Spanish border at the ruins of an old castle. The Spanish military is here standing guard. We're cataloguing all kinds of fascinating stuff. The Egyptian things are amazing. That's where the lady has been really helpful."

Dee waved at Gina and pointed to his ear. She acknowledged. "Hey, let me put you on the speaker. Dee wants to hear."

"Okay, I'll wave at Jamal. He'll want to be part of this."

There was a chorus of hellos.

"You guys made it to the pyramids yet?" asked Jamal.

Gina looked to Dee, and he responded, "We're in Cyprus. Next stop is Alexandria and then Cairo. We're getting close."

"Wish I was there. But we have seen some really interesting stuff. There's a ruin called Amarna that you should go to see if you get a chance."

"What's special about it?" asked Gina.

"We've found several gold murals of this pharaoh who supposedly built that city, and he has this stone around his neck that redirects the sun's light. The professor called it the 'Sun Stone.'"

Dee and Gina looked at one another.

"But there's more. The pharaoh, at least in profile, looks just like Mike, and his queen looks like Keno. It's an amazing resemblance."

"This Sun Stone you mentioned—what is it?" asked Dee.

"Not really sure. The professor says it had some special meaning to the pharaoh, but she wasn't sure beyond that."

"That's really odd," replied Dee. "We had two Egyptians, I guess they were, stop us on the beach today and ask us about having a 'Sun Stone.' We did not know what they were talking about."

Jamal was silent for a moment. "Did they look like those guys we saw in North Africa?"

"Similar. Same type of clothes. In fact, we saw them on the cruise from Italy at the first Grecian port where we stopped and again on the Acropolis. We thought little of it until they questioned us."

"That is odd. The military guarding the castle picked up two guys snooping around the site that claimed to be lost tourists. They were dressed like tourists, but they looked Egyptian. When they saw Diego and me, they acted like they recognized us."

Angelic turned and looked hard at Jamal.

He continued, "I didn't think much about it at the time but… I don't know."

Dee replied, "That fits. When the men questioned us about the stone, they asked if we thought our friends in Spain had it. I'm now going to assume that was you."

"What's the connection?" asked Angelic.

"Something they seem to think we have," replied Dee.

"Do you suppose they followed Mike and Keno as well?" asked Angelic.

"Miami is a long way, and Mike was hospitalized. I wouldn't think so," replied Jamal.

"We just talked to them, and they didn't mention it," added Angelic.

"Maybe it has something to do with your artifacts," said Dee.

"We have seen nothing like that, a stone, but we'll keep an eye out and let you know," replied Jamal.

"This is all so strange," said Angelic. "Why would they think we had something like that?"

"Don't know," replied Dee. "But be careful. Let's stay more in touch."

"Agreed," replied Jamal.

"We miss you guys," said Angelic.

"We miss you too!" It was the first time Gina had jumped back into the conversation. Dee turned to look at her, and she smiled.

After they hung up the phone, Dee turned to Gina. "I miss them too, all of them."

She took his hand and led him into the bedroom. "I'm tired. Let's go to bed."

———

In Spain, Angelic stood next to Jamal on their balcony and said, "I wish they were here. We had so much fun."

Jamal looked back at her, "I wish so too."

————

Back in Cyprus, Dee had gone into the bathroom to brush his teeth.

Gina pulled out her suitcase, reached into one of the flap pockets, and pulled out the necklace that Angelic had given her and that she knew Keno had given Angelic. She held it up to the light, and the reflection sparkled around the room in flashes that danced off the walls and mirror. They had paid one dollar for it in a flea market.

Surely this can't be what they were looking for, she thought.

39

MINING FOR GOLD

They were back at the storeroom in the castle early the next morning. Having found a routine, they got up, ate breakfast at the resort, and then drove to work. Diego and Eve sat in the car's front with Jamal and Angelic in the back.

When they got back to work unpacking more boxes, Jamal addressed Diego and Eve. "We were on the phone last night with some friends of ours that were traveling with us in North Africa. He caught some kind of fever in Morocco, and they flew back to Miami from Algiers."

"Is he all right?" asked Eve.

"The doctors never determined the cause of the fevers after a lot of extensive testing. The fevers just stopped. He and his wife are recuperating in Key West with a couple of other friends of ours. The reason I brought him up was that when we were on the phone with them last night, I realized that his profile is very much the same as the pharaoh's, and his wife is very similar-looking to Nefertiti."

"That's odd," said Diego.

"Yeah, I agree, and I didn't quite realize it until we were

talking to them last night. I just knew the pharaoh and the queen looked familiar."

"Facial shapes are often similar across time," added Eve. "It seems that certain-looking people attract one another no matter the place or time." Eve looked over at Diego and smiled.

They worked through the morning, finding no other objects related to the Sun King, then broke for lunch and resumed work in the early afternoon.

Angelic started a new box, and as soon as she opened it, called out to the others, "Look, I think it's more scrolls, more hieroglyphics or portraits."

Eve came over and examined the items that Angelic had uncovered. She again noted their excellent condition. "I think the steady temperature and relative lack of humidity in these rooms has played a big factor in the condition of many of these items."

"I always thought castles were dark and damp," noted Jamal.

"They can be," replied Eve, "but you note how temperate these rooms seem to be and how dry. I think it depends on the construction and location of the castle, or the room in this case."

Jamal nodded.

"I think Eve's correct," said Diego. "I've seen storage rooms in castles that looked like swamps, with everything up on pallets. It varies widely."

Eve took all the scrolls from Angelic. There were three of them. She walked across to the table, where she slowly opened the first one and spread it out. There was better light at the table than where Angelic had been standing.

She perused the first scroll for a few moments. "Diego, come over here."

He sat the item he was holding down and stepped beside

Eve. "I thought perhaps you might like a little space while you evaluated and interpreted."

"Nonsense, darling, I enjoy having you nearby." She pointed at the symbols with her finger. "What do you make of that series of characters?"

Diego leaned forward and studied them for a moment. "I'm not sure—it's not my era—but it looks like he might be talking about his religion."

"That's what I thought as well. It isn't quite clear to me, but the pharaoh seems to be documenting his thoughts on changes in religion. I can make out the part where he wants to elevate the sun god, Aten, as the primary deity, apparently at the expense of the other Egyptian gods." She looked up at the others. "Egypt was a polytheistic society—they believed in multiple gods—so this was quite a radical idea at the time."

Diego pointed to another character. "That one I'm not sure of, but I think maybe he's saying something about demeaning or desecrating the other gods."

"I wasn't clear either, but I agree that looks and sounds reasonable." She pointed to a series of other characters. "Here I believe he is talking about new monuments or construction of new temples to his chosen deity." She scanned the scroll a little further and looked up at the others again. "And here he seems to talk about building a city that will face the east, toward the sunrise, at a new location where the sunrise between the mountains will highlight the temple first. It's an interesting attempt by him to restructure the people's beliefs."

"So the temple's placement would be the first thing the sun light strikes each morning when the sun rises?" asked Jamal.

Eve nodded. "It's quite dramatic."

"That would take years to build, wouldn't it? And you

said he had a short reign. Does that mean the city wasn't completed, or what happened?" asked Angelic.

"Yes, it would take years. I suspect they built much of the surrounding city from baked mud blocks, available in the short term, while the temple was traditional stone. I expect he was in a hurry to get started and thought he'd replace the mud eventually. I think that's why there is so little left of Amarna other than the temple."

"Amazing," said Jamal.

"Yes, it is," added Diego.

Eve smiled at all three of them. "He was an odd fellow for his time, or so it seems. We just don't know all the facts and circumstances." She rolled the scroll back. "Let's look at the next one."

The others gathered around her closely, making no pretense of unpacking any other boxes.

Eve carefully unrolled the second scroll and studied it for a few moments. "This one is much shorter, as you can see, and easier to read. This is praise for his queen, Nefertiti. It's their love story and his adoration of her. He indicated he was willing to lay down his life for her."

"That's kind of rare, isn't it?" asked Angelic.

"Absolutely. Pharaohs were supposed to be descendants of the gods. It was no small thing for one of them to talk about sacrificing their life."

"What else does it say?" asked Jamal.

There were a few characters left, and Eve paused over them for a moment. "This last section says that the pharaoh sees his queen as his equal and that he feels she could rule for him if necessary."

"Why would he say that?" asked Diego.

Eve shook her head. "That's most unusual—not just the sentiment, but why would he document that? He had a short reign, but there are typically male successors."

"Could it be this was early in his reign and he and the queen had no heirs?" asked Angelic.

Eve looked up at her and smiled. "Very good. I expect that's exactly it. But still, his observation that she could rule is most unusual."

"Yes, but everything about this guy is unusual," said Diego.

Eve looked up at Diego and smiled.

"You got that right," added Jamal.

Eve rerolled the second scroll and picked up the third and held it aloft. "Any guesses what we might find here?"

Jamal and Angelic shook their heads.

"You are so dramatic," sighed Diego.

"But of course, darling, don't you love a little suspense in your life? Some excitement?"

He smiled at her. "And what does it say?"

Eve made a grand production of unrolling the scroll and studying the characters for several moments. "Diego, take a look. This one is also most unusual."

Diego stepped across beside Eve and reviewed the scroll. "Something about him being sick?"

"Could that be why he mentioned the queen ruling?" asked Angelic.

"Yes, I suppose it could." Eve looked at the scroll again, moving her lips as she scanned but making no sound. "I read it as something about his chest and sweats or something?"

"Fevers, maybe," said Jamal. "And heart issues?"

"Or stomach," added Diego.

"That's so bizarre," said Angelic. "Those are the same issues Mike had."

"Mike?" asked Eve.

"He was the one I mentioned this morning who looked a bit like the pharaoh. He had unexplained fevers and some heart issues—blood pressure, actually," replied Jamal.

"That is strange," answered Eve.

"Did the pharaohs often document their health?" asked Angelic.

Eve paused for a moment. "Scribes often chronicled things about the pharaoh's health and life after their death, but not usually before. In Akhenaten's case, subsequent pharaohs largely eradicated his memory, so there's no record."

"That's a lot to digest," said Diego.

Eve turned to look at him. "There is so little information regarding Akhenaten. These finds are invaluable. Perhaps we can piece more together about his reign."

Walking to the car that evening, Jamal lamented, "I was really hoping we'd find more scrolls or something that told us more about the Sun King."

"We still have a half room to go, darling, and we already know so much more than we did," replied Eve.

"And we know the family was interested from the ledger you found earlier," added Angelic.

"Absolutely they were. I would be surprised if we don't find a few more things."

40

ANOTHER DAY IN PARADISE

After dinner that night, as Ike and Elizabeth led the way back from the restaurant, they talked among themselves on the walk to the house.

"That was an amazing story Karim told," said Keno.

"Which one?" replied Elizabeth.

"Both of them," said Mike.

Ike laughed at them. "That was one of his calmer tour stories. He was quite the ladies' man. But the childhood story about the pharaoh was fascinating."

"It must be amazing to grow up in a history-rich area like that. To look out your window and see a monument from thousands of years ago."

"I'm sure it was," replied Ike. "But Karim was from a wealthy family. They traveled a lot. He was educated in Switzerland. You heard him say something about when he goes back there, which didn't used to be that often."

"But still," answered Elizabeth. "An amazing childhood memory."

They reached the house and separated to their own rooms.

———

"Tell me about the job," said Elizabeth as she and Ike made their way to the loft.

"It's tournament security, wherever they need me. Escorting players, VIP escort, and perimeter security—whatever they need."

"Will you be happy with that?"

"I don't know, but Karim will be a great employer, and the schedule is specific, so I can get back here to the kids and you."

Elizabeth hugged him. "Let's go to bed."

"You got that gag?" Ike replied.

Elizabeth punched him on the shoulder.

———

Keno and Mike were in their bedroom. "I'm not really tired," said Keno.

"Me either. How about a short walk? I'm not tired, but I don't know how much energy I have."

They heard murmuring from the loft and decided not to disturb Ike and Elizabeth.

Mike and Keno headed out the door, hand in hand. It was fully dark, and the moon shone above the streetlights. People were still milling about and zooming past on mopeds or bicycles.

Keno squeezed Mike's hand. "I love this place. I think I'd be happy here. You?"

Mike squeezed her hand in return and nodded.

As they strolled around the area, nightlife was in full swing on Duval. They made a short circuit and started back toward Ike's house.

"Let's walk down beyond the house to the end of the street," suggested Keno.

"Something you want to see?" asked Mike.

"Just what's down there."

They strolled past Ike's and the three houses beyond, and with only two remaining, they saw a curious sign in a yard. *Coming Soon*, it read.

They stopped, looked at the house, looked at each other, and nodded in unison.

41

IN TRANSIT

The two men made arrangements to catch an overnight ferry from Cyprus to Alexandria. They had no information on where the couple would be going, and were leery now of what Amir would say or do to them if they could not come up with an answer.

The one man called Amir while the other located the ferry.

"We are on our way from Cyprus now," the man said.

"You have the stone?" replied Amir.

"No, we are still in pursuit. We encountered the couple in Varosha and were making progress when we were interrupted by the police. We all fled, and we lost them in the confusion. I still feel confident we will get the stone."

"I do not share your confidence at this moment, but at least they are returning to Egypt. Perhaps they have the stone and some idea of its value and meaning."

"How could that be?"

"Why else would they come here? I'll fly in from Algiers."

"Perhaps they are just tourists."

"I saw them with the stone. I know they have it."

"We'll keep looking. Hopefully gain some news soon."

There was silence for a moment, and then Amir spoke again. "I'll bring the other men together in Luxor. The pair from Spain are returning."

There was no response from the man in Cyprus, who didn't feel like he wanted to share that he had spoken to the pair in Spain.

"They were caught and kicked out of the country. I'll deal with them when they arrive."

"Yes, Amir. We'll be in touch soon with good news."

"I hope so, for your sake."

42

LAND OF THE PHARAOHS

Dee came back into the room, and Gina quickly stuffed the necklace into her suitcase. She wasn't sure why she did it, but she liked the necklace and didn't want to give it up. It was just costume jewelry. That's all it could be.

"We depart later tonight for Alexandria and should be there midmorning tomorrow," said Dee.

"So we're going to see the pyramids?"

Dee replied, "Yeah, I thought it might be fun." He looked at Gina, and she nodded for him to continue. "We'll take a cab or rent a car from Alexandria to Cairo. In Cairo, we'll take the sleeper train to Luxor."

"How long will all that take?"

"The cab from Alexandria to Cairo is about two and a half or three hours, and the train ride to Luxor is overnight. We leave out of the Ramses Railway Station in Cairo in the evening and arrive early the next morning in Luxor. We'll catch a riverboat there for the tour."

"We're not going to any sites in Alexandria or Cairo?"

"Well, there are pyramids, actually, in Cairo. I wasn't sure how long you'd want to stay. We can start with them. I was aiming us toward the Valley of the Kings, which is one of the big sites with lots of different locations to visit, but they are tombs rather than pyramids. Many are carved into rock. The tour is by riverboat. It goes from Luxor to Aswan and back. It takes nine days total, five days to Aswan and four back to Luxor. I thought that might be more fun."

Gina replied, "I do like traveling on the water. How big is the riverboat?"

"Smaller than this one, probably close to the size of a river tour, maybe a couple hundred people. There are smaller sizes, but I thought you might be happiest on a larger ship. Do you want to see some other sites along the way? It's probably more hiking, which I didn't think you liked."

"I don't mind a little, and we've come this far. The pyramids were the object of the trip, weren't they?"

"Originally, they were one thing Jamal wanted to see. Also, I think the site he mentioned on the phone, Amarna, is near Luxor."

"Can't we do both?"

"Definitely."

Dee went to sleep that night feeling better than he had in a while. This was the first thing Gina had reacted positively to in quite some time. He wondered if it was him or if she just missed their friends. Either way, he hoped things with her would get better.

At midmorning, they docked in Alexandria. It was a slow departure from the ship. Despite its smaller size, there were many long lines and delays compared to their earlier cruises. It was early afternoon before Dee could get them a cab for Cairo.

Three hours later, windblown and thirsty, the cab's air conditioning had malfunctioned. The driver dropped them at the door of the St. Regis Cairo.

"Just curious," said Gina. "Why did we take a cab?"

"It was actually the cheapest way to get here, and the quickest."

"Did that consider the broken air conditioning?" Gina teased.

"He didn't advertise that on the brochure."

"What is on the brochure?" Gina asked as they made their way to the check-in counter.

"They have an all-day tour starting tomorrow morning from the hotel to the pyramids at Giza and the Sphinx. I thought we could take that in and then spend the next day resting up. That night, we'll catch the train. The station is about a mile from here. When we wake up the following morning we'll be in Luxor. We can sightsee, maybe go to Amarna and let Jamal know what we see there, then catch the river cruise down the Nile."

"It sounds romantic."

Dee smiled.

They made their way across the massive and ornate lobby, admiring the scale and opulence of the surroundings.

"How did you pick this place?" asked Gina.

"Saw it online and thought it would be nice for us."

Gina nodded as they entered the elevators, and they rose to their room's floor.

Entering the suite, they made their way to the balcony and looked out upon the city.

"We are so far up in the building, but the city stretches out forever before us," whispered Gina.

"Yeah, it does. Cairo has been around for a very long time. The hotel has a handful of five-star restaurants. Let's get cleaned up and go to dinner, maybe stroll the premises afterwards."

Three hours later, they were clean, had eaten a luxurious dinner, and were walking around the hotel. There were shops, and they stopped and purchased a few items for the all-day tour the following morning, including hats, walking shoes, and full length clothes.

Returning to the room, they sat on the balcony and looked over the city.

Both of them were quiet for a time and then Dee spoke. "I miss having the others with us."

Gina turned to him, nodded, and smiled. "So do I. I wish we were all together again."

———

THEY BOARDED THE BUS THE NEXT MORNING FOR THEIR TREK and rode the short distance to the Giza site. There they joined other groups and began the long slog around the area. Throughout the day, Dee kept an eye out for the two men that had accosted them in Cyprus. While there were many Egyptians about, most of the tourists appeared to be from other locations. Dee saw no one he thought might be suspicious or who appeared to be watching them.

Late in the afternoon, Gina turned and said to Dee, "I haven't seen those men or anyone who looks like them, have you?"

Dee grinned before responding, "I didn't realize you were keeping an eye out for them."

"Just like you are," she replied.

Back in the bus late that afternoon, she added, "That was amazing. The size of those things was unbelievable. How tiny they made you feel while shuffling around at the base and staring up at them. I'm glad we came but also glad we are on board the ship for the rest of the tour. A couple of days of that and I'd need a break."

43

FAMILY HISTORY

The next morning, the archeological team was back at work. The number of remaining unopened boxes in the castle's store room was dwindling.

Eve, halfway through a box, was tired of unloading Renaissance art objects. They had found nothing else about the Sun King. *Why did I volunteer for this?* she thought, and then she looked over at Diego.

Digging further into the box, she saw something that made her pulse flutter. It was a small volume, not thick enough to be a book or even a journal. It looked more like a few random notes someone had collected.

Eve tentatively picked it up and held the volume in her hands. It looked to be sixteenth or seventeenth century. She looked up at the others and started to address them but bit her tongue. Eve wanted to savor this moment—if it was a moment?

Slowly opening the binder, she found several loose sheets inside. She read the first one.

It was dated 1612 AD, early in the seventeenth century. Someone in the family had known about the Egyptian

Crusade objects and the earlier documented recounting of events. The writer said that after studying the records and the objects on hand, he had traveled to Cairo with one mural and one scroll. There, he had consulted a known Egyptologist who returned to Spain with him and reviewed all the items.

The notes Eve reviewed indicated that there was an entire series of documents and findings from the Egyptologist. She again looked up at the others. They had seen nothing like that, and the binder she held contained only a few sheets. The promise of more to come teased her, but the lack of its presence frustrated her considerably. The sheet she reviewed indicated that the Sun Stone was somehow related to the throne and not just the throne room as they'd thought earlier.

Eve glanced around the room. They were running out of boxes. Could someone in the family, the writer, have removed the findings, thinking to keep them in a safer place? It was possible. Or her group could still find the Egyptologist's speculations in the remaining boxes.

Diego noticed Eve pondering.

"Eve, is everything all right?" he asked.

She looked toward him and turned on her biggest smile. "Lovely, darling. Come over here, all of you. Let me show you what I've found."

She recounted what she'd just read and went on to speculate. "Apparently, someone in the family knew of these items and their whereabouts. However, this may be the final entry from the family. Of course we have a couple more boxes, but these notes have a tone of frustration and finality to them. The writer states that the knowledge and the treasure is likely 'lost to the past.' Sometime after this writing, the family's interest must have faded, and the objects on hand were eventually forgotten."

"That's like four hundred years later, isn't it? I mean, from the Crusade?" asked Angelic.

Eve nodded.

"And quite a few generations, given the time," added Diego.

"They must have had a real strong sense of the possibility of the room and the treasure," said Jamal.

"No doubt," replied Eve. "There wasn't a lot of common knowledge about Egypt when this was written, and the speculation about the wealth of the pharaohs would have been staggering."

"The family kept the idea alive for hundreds of years," said Jamal.

"An amount of untold wealth could keep people thinking about it forever," replied Diego.

After several more minutes of discussion, they went back to work on the remaining boxes. They broke for lunch and, while they were eating, one of Col. Sanchez's men came into the room. "Do you have a few minutes, Director Schwartz?"

Diego looked up.

"The Colonel would like to share some information with you. All of you are welcome."

Diego looked around the group. Everyone put down what they were eating and followed Diego, who was being led by the soldier, to the command center.

Outside in the fresh air, they all stretched and relaxed in the afternoon sun as they walked across the compound.

Once inside, the Colonel had them all sit in a makeshift conference room. The soldier who had escorted them closed the door behind him, leaving them alone with the Colonel.

The Colonel stood up and nodded to everyone.

"I trust you are nearly finished?" he inquired.

"Yes, it shouldn't be more than another day or so, depending upon what we find," replied Diego.

"That's good, as you have uncovered quite a significant find. The politicians and the museums should be happy."

"I would expect so," replied Diego, who then smiled before speaking again. "Just doing our job, our duty, to history and to our country."

"Well said, Director. I see how you have progressed so far."

Eve smiled at the Colonel, who nodded back at her despite himself. He leaned against the table and crossed his arms. "What I really wanted to talk about were those men we found lurking around the other day." He paused for a moment, looking into each of their faces. "I had my men follow them back to town, then to the closest airport, where they flew out for Cairo, Egypt."

He rubbed his hands together. "I'm concerned about what their objective here may have been. Are you sure none of you recognized them?"

Jamal spoke up. "We saw some similar-looking men in North Africa, but that was before Diego called, and I'm not saying they were the same men. But that's all we know."

Eve and Angelic nodded in agreement.

The Colonel looked to Diego and spoke. "It seems possible to me that these men had an extreme interest in what you are doing. Could they be from the Egyptian government or any over group?"

Diego responded, "Like, perhaps, artifact hunters or collectors?"

"Possibly. They just seemed evasive and uncomfortable."

"We released little information about the artifacts after the initial press release regarding the find."

"Yes, and from a security standpoint, I appreciate that. You don't think someone could have sent them to spy or infiltrate your recovery and identification process?"

"It's certainly possible, but I'd leave that to you and your men, Colonel. We are looking at a significant historical find and a potential wealth in knowledge and resources, so yes, it's possible."

The Colonel paused for a moment. "I'm going to strengthen the guard here, and as we ship the items, I will call for additional reinforcements."

"Sounds wise, Colonel," replied Diego.

"Thank you." He paused. "I've held you up long enough. Please continue with your work."

Walking back toward their workroom, Eve made a suggestion. "It's so nice, why don't we wrap up for today and go back to town, do something different?"

"The Colonel is gearing up for the move. We've only kept the Sun King items unpacked. We should finish tomorrow. Let's go to town," replied Diego.

They returned to the room, finished their lunches, stored the items they had under way, and told the guard they would be leaving for the day.

44

LIVING THE DREAM

"We saw something last night," said Keno as she clasped her hands together, a bright smile upon her face.

Ike and Elizabeth were a little taken aback. Had they not noticed something, gotten too loud in their pre-sleep excitement?

Elizabeth put her hand out to take Keno's hand. Keno clutched it quickly and squeezed.

"Mike and I saw a house last night that we want to buy." She couldn't stand it any longer. "It's three doors down the street."

Ike rubbed his eyes. "What? That's the old Henderson place. Has it gone up for sale?"

"There's a sign that says *Coming Soon*," explained Mike.

"Wow, I knew they had talked about selling, but I didn't think they were ready," replied Ike. "You'd better get on the phone quickly. It won't last long."

"What realty company?" asked Elizabeth.

"Key West Realty," answered Mike.

"I know one of them." Ike picked up his phone but

stopped before he dialed. "You're sure about this? You don't want to look around the island here or further north?"

Mike and Keno looked at one another. "Unless it's a real dog or you don't want us this close, we'll take it and work out the price based on the condition," replied Mike.

"It may need a little work or have something you want to personalize, but it should be in pretty good shape," replied Ike. He pressed the button to send the call and turned the phone on speaker.

The number rang twice and picked up. They heard a squeaky male voice. "Ike? Is that you?"

"Hey, Carl. Yes, it is me. How you doing? Busy? Good. I have some friends staying with me, and they'd like to look at and potentially buy the Henderson house."

There was a pause. "They there with you?" the group heard through the speaker.

"Yes," they all rang out.

"Hey there, I'm Carl Withers," he replied. "The house isn't on the market yet. We just put the sign up late yesterday afternoon. But if you folks are serious, since the Henderson's know Ike, I could probably get you a look."

"What are they asking for it?" called out Mike.

Carl hesitated just a second. "Seven hundred fifty," he replied.

"Let's look if we can," answered Mike.

"I'll call you back shortly."

Mike and Ike shook hands. "Hey there, neighbor," said Ike. Mike just grinned.

The women hugged one another.

Only a few minutes later, the phone rang. It was Carl. "I can meet you down there in a few minutes if now is a good time?"

"We can start that way," replied Ike.

"Give me a five-minute head start, and I'll meet you there."

The Henderson's stayed just long enough to say hello and then went on a short walk. Carl led the four of them through the house. It was not very different from Ike's place.

"They built most of the houses on this street around the same time with similar floor plans. They're still new enough that people haven't started buying and rebuilding or leveling them and rebuilding," explained Carl.

"Are the building codes pretty strict here?" asked Mike.

"There's hurricane code and some other restrictions, but a remodel isn't that difficult."

"I was a builder in the St. Louis area before I retired. I can probably manage most of what I want."

Carl nodded. "Then you know how it is about locals, and materials, and the permit process, and how difficult it can be if you don't approach it properly."

Mike grinned at him. "Yeah, I know what you are talking about. I can manage it with their help."

Carl smiled. "Then you shouldn't have any problems."

They heard a "Hello" ring out.

"We're back here," replied Carl.

The Henderson's entered the kitchen and again nodded to everyone.

"Mr. Henderson," said Mike. "How much are you asking?"

Mr. Henderson looked at Mrs. Henderson. "We're starting at seven hundred fifty, but—"

Mike interrupted him. "We'll take it."

The Henderson's looked at one another again, then turned back to Mike.

"Just like that?" said Mr. Henderson.

"Just like that," replied Mike and stuck out his hand.

Mr. Henderson grabbed it quickly and pumped it up and down several times.

"Where are you folks going to go?" asked Keno.

"We're going back to Kansas," replied Mrs. Henderson.

45

MARSHALLING THE FORCES

The ferry docked in Alexandria, and the men departed looking for cheap local accommodation. They needed to come up with a plan. The couple would dock later that morning, and Amir would be in close contact. They were glad to be home. They did not enjoy traveling away from the desert. Only there did they feel truly comfortable.

The one man's phone rang. He went to answer it.

"We are back in Cairo. Where are you?" said the voice.

"We are in Alexandria. The couple will be here shortly."

"They are our last chance to find the stone. Can we assist you?"

"What did Amir tell you to do?"

"He advised all of us to return to Luxor."

"Can you delay him?"

"For a short time, perhaps—a flight delay, or a missed flight—but not long."

"The couple's cruise terminates in Alexandria. We do not know where they are going. Could you remain in Cairo? If we could get some idea of their arrival and they were coming your way, there would be more of us to pursue them."

———

AMIR, AS HIS MEN KNEW HIM, WAS STILL IN ALGIERS BUT preparing to return to Egypt. He hadn't yet decided where he would base his surveillance operation.

Obviously, his men had not gotten the job done. They should have recovered the stone by now. Amir knew the tourists had it. He imagined he could feel the presence of the stone. His men had confirmed with the seller in the medina that the tourists had bought the stone. The men had been too slow. They should have taken the stone from the Bedouin traders as they'd moved across the desert. Amir was lucky that the woman and her children had stopped to trade with one of his men's families and that the children had pulled the stone out to play with it. The woman had quickly put the stone away and scolded the children. But the man had seen it, although he wasn't positive that it was the Sun Stone. When he had described it to Amir, who had thought he would lose his mind in frustration upon hearing the details, Amir had ordered the men to pursue the family across the desert. They hadn't been sure how to acquire the stone quietly until they had realized the Bedouins were heading for the medinas on their return trade route. They would simply offer to buy it. But the tourists had bought the stone first, for a dollar.

Then he had seen that woman wearing it after his men had followed the tourists along the coast. Their encounter with the old man at the well had been fortuitous. He was one of their society's oldest brothers who had passed away shortly after the encounter. He'd had the ancient fever. The man had gone to the caves at the abandoned site to die. The fever was a concern for Amir. Many of the oldest brothers had contracted it over time, and he remembered stories from his youth. Men that died from it had spent great deals of time among the ruins searching for the stone. Amir had let others perform that work. The tourist had gotten too close to the dying man.

But the tourists must have the stone. Their search was down to the last couple, unless his men had missed the stone's presence with the others. With this couple coming to Egypt, it made sense they had the stone and were going to search for the treasure. Amir would put a stop to that. What would be the best way? He obviously couldn't count on his men, but his additional personal efforts might well net him a larger share when all was said and done. He had wanted to keep this a quiet, uneventful acquisition of the stone, but even he was growing impatient. Amir didn't want to resort to force, but…

He would fly into Luxor, as the couple would have to come there to search Amarna. He would wait for them there unless he could locate them sooner. That would be preferable. Then it occurred to Amir: perhaps he alone could acquire the stone. They had searched for it for so long, and it was his duty, as head of the society, to guide the people in this search. The wealth should be untold, but even the society didn't know how the stone guided the way to the treasure. He would likely need his men's help. After all, his ancient brothers were known for not leaving treasure unprotected. There would be booby traps, and someone could be hurt or killed. Amir didn't plan on it being him.

———

THE TWO MEN IN ALEXANDRIA STAKED OUT THE DOCK AND waited for the tourist couple to arrive. They had learned to find a location and stay out of sight. They observed the couple catch a cab, and they did the same. After a short time on the road, they determined the couple's ultimate location appeared to be Cairo, and probably the pyramids.

The one man got on his phone and called his contacts in Cairo. "They are coming your way," he said into the phone. "I don't know the location yet, but I'm guessing they will tour the pyramids; otherwise, they would have gone on to Luxor. Set up surveillance at Giza and see if she is wearing the stone."

He hung up the phone and turned to his companion. "Even if we lose them in traffic, we should pick them up again in Giza."

The other man started to speak but was interrupted by the driver. "I am with the same company as the cab we are following. I can track him through my dispatch. Do not worry. We will not lose them."

The first man nodded. "Thank you." He thought, *I must tip this man well.*

They followed the cab with the tourists all the way into downtown Cairo and to the St. Regis Cairo hotel.

The driver of the cab with the two men spoke again as he rolled slowly by the building a few minutes later. "These people have expensive tastes. Would you like me to let you out?"

"No, brother, please take us to nearby affordable accommodation."

"I know just the place," the driver replied, and he pulled slowly away.

Several hours later, the two men had checked into an appropriate accommodation, acquired some clothing more suitable to the city, and purchased hats. They hated hats, but they would wear them here. They could hide beneath a hat. A café across the boulevard from the hotel would provide them a spot for viewing the activities of the day unnoticed.

They saw nothing throughout the evening and imagined

that the couple had remained in the hotel. In the morning would be the key. Would they board a tour bus, and which one?

The following morning, a bus pulled up early for the all-day tour of Giza. Each of the men had positioned himself at an angle so he could watch people emerge from the hotel. About midway in the crowd, the one man saw the couple. He waved to the other man, who nodded and pulled out his phone.

"They are heading your way." He told the men at the pyramid site. "We couldn't see them well enough to tell if she was wearing the stone. Stay alert and let us know."

He hung the phone up and walked to the table the men had been sharing before the bus arrived.

The two men in Giza positioned themselves at the tour center and posed as guides. They watched the tourists, specifically the passengers from the buses, get on and off throughout the day. They spotted the couple departing the St. Regis bus and were quick to note that the woman was not wearing the stone. They were again flooded with disappointment. But they held their places and observed. When the couple boarded the bus in the late afternoon, looking tired and dusty, the woman was still not wearing the stone.

46

CATCHING UP

"We have to make a train ride tonight before we get on the boat," said Dee as the bus pulled out from the Giza site.

Gina turned to look at him.

"We need to go clean up, pack up, and check out. We catch the overnight train at Ramses station, which will have us in Luxor in the morning, where we'll catch the boat." Dee wasn't sure how she was going to react to that, though he knew he had told her the plan earlier.

Instead, she surprised him. "Cool," she said. "That'll be fun, but I suppose we'll sleep through most of it."

"I suppose," he replied.

When they returned to the hotel, they showered quickly, packed, and checked out. Grabbing a cab in front of the hotel, Dee noticed a scuffling at the café across the street but couldn't tell what was happening. A few minutes later, the cab deposited them at the train station a little over a mile away.

They entered the station, checked in, and boarded the train. After finding their room and unloading their bags, they searched for the dining car.

They sat down, and while perusing the menu, Dee spoke. "Now that we've seen the pyramids and are on our way to the Valley of the Kings, maybe we should call Jamal and Angelic and let them know what we've seen—and also Mike and Keno just to check on them and see how they are doing."

"That would be great. I've been meaning to call Keno, but we've bounced around so much the last few days. Let's do that."

47

SCROLLING

When they got back to the resort from the castle, the team changed and walked down to the bay for a stroll along the water before dinner. It was a deep beach, and they could walk four across.

Diego was the furthest from the water, then Eve, then Jamal, and finally Angelic, who drifted in and out of water to the tops of her ankles. They were all linked arm in arm.

"This is so nice," said Eve. "We've been locked away in that dreary dungeon for days now. It's nice to get out."

Jamal turned to look at her. "Haven't you enjoyed all our discoveries? You marveled at the information they revealed."

"Of course, dear boy! But you must make time for life, for sunshine, for companionship. Those items have been hidden for hundreds of years. Another day or two will not matter. I could feel myself wilting. We needed to recharge."

"We are about done too." Angelic leaned in and giggled.

"Yes, there's that," replied Eve, turning to smile at her and Jamal. "Diego was getting tired. I could see it in his eyes," she added, tugging on Diego's arm.

He leaned toward the others and waved a hand. "What perception she has."

"He's right, you know," added Eve. "I see and I perceive." Then, turning to Jamal, she added, "Are you sure you will be happy in this field? I'd love to have you both come to Paris and work for me, but I'm not sure you'd be happy. Are you?"

Angelic looked at Jamal. "I'll leave that up to Jam. I'm happy being with him wherever he happens to be."

Eve squeezed Jamal's arm. "You're a lucky man."

He nodded and squeezed Angelic's fingers.

They walked for a few moments in silence. Then Diego spoke. "We should finish tomorrow. We can return to Seville to finish the cataloguing and distribution of the items, dependent upon political considerations and direction, of course."

"You won't need me, darling. I'll return to Paris. You can call if you have questions."

Angelic glanced down the line of faces and could see that Diego looked disappointed.

Diego looked to Jamal and Angelic.

"I want to see the project through to the end if you have a need for me," said Jamal.

"Most definitely," replied Diego. "In fact, I plan to hire you if Angelic doesn't drag you off to Paris."

After dinner, Angelic and Jamal sat on their balcony watching the bay beyond them as the light of the day slipped away.

"You seem sad, Jam. Do you want to go to work for either of them?"

He was still for a moment. "I don't know. Right now, I just want to finish the job and see what happens."

Angelic squeezed his hand.

———

THE FOLLOWING MORNING, EACH OF THEM TOOK A FINAL BOX. When completed, they would be through all the items.

Jamal removed a Roman vase and set it aside. He looked back in the box and found a scroll, a thick one. He called out, "Everybody, come and look. We have another scroll."

"What time period?" asked Diego.

"Sorry, I haven't checked. I just saw it."

Eve appeared by his side. "Let's see what you have found, darling."

Eve removed the scroll and, stepping to the table, unrolled it carefully. It was long and held the largest number of characters of any they had found so far.

She studied the scroll for several minutes while the others gathered around her. Eve looked up after a moment and saw Angelic watching her intently.

"What does it say?" Angelic whispered.

Eve cleared her throat. "Well, it's rather confusing." She pointed to one set of characters. "Here, the pharaoh talks about some sort of contest, a race across the Sahara, where his people cross the desert to the far shore—being the Atlantic—in search of something that glows, a rock or stone or maybe a shell. They must cross the sand, out where the desert meets the sky. Something about trade routes."

"There would have been no trade route that far south," said Diego.

"Agreed," answered Eve. She pointed. "They will be rewarded for returning with this special stone or shell. It seems here"—she pointed to more characters—"the pharaoh plans some sort of chamber in which the stones or shells will be used."

"Something that he's building?" asked Jamal.

"Part of his new city, perhaps?" added Diego.

"His temple?" asked Angelic.

"Yes," replied Eve. She pointed to the final set of symbols. "There, he mentions the room in the temple, the throne room, his family quarters, the queen's private quarters, maybe a treasury. It doesn't say for sure, or I'm not seeing it or interpreting it properly. This seems rather archaic, even for that time period."

"Could he have been trying to conceal something?" asked Diego.

"Very probably," replied Eve. "The pyramids and the tombs are all full of tunnels, passageways, and secret rooms."

"So, could this Sun Stone have something to do with this room he's building?" asked Jamal.

48

———

CLOSING THE DEAL

They made their way back to Ike's house. Carl had told them he'd draw up a contract and get back in touch. Since both parties were only a few doors apart, he'd come back later that day and get all the signatures.

"I'm happy for you guys," said Ike.

"It'll be great having you next door," added Elizabeth.

"I'm so excited," replied Keno. "We've traveled for much of the past year, and I'm ready to be in one place. Although I miss my friends."

"They liked it here, as I recall," replied Ike. "Have them come and see you."

"That's a great idea," said Mike. "It would be nice if we could all be together."

49

KEEPING UP

The one man on duty at the café saw the couple with their luggage coming out the door of the hotel in the late afternoon. He was shocked. They'd just spent the day in the hot sun sightseeing the pyramids, and here they were on the move. The other men he was with had gone to their rooms to clean up for dinner. They were all tired after the long day.

Not taking his eyes off the couple now, the man would only admit to himself and never to the others, he hadn't been paying good attention before he'd looked up and saw them. The man knocked over the table beside him as he rose hurriedly and made for the exit to grab a taxi.

"Follow that cab," the man exclaimed hastily as he jumped into the back seat and pointed at the vehicle that was pulling away with the couple.

He quickly called the other men. "They are on the move," he shouted.

"Who? What?" was the reply.

"The tourists. They have checked out of the hotel and are in a cab heading somewhere—"

The man's driver interjected. "I expect they are headed to the train station."

The man in the back seat shouted in to the phone, "It may be the train station."

"Follow them," came the response.

"Follow them, on the train? I have nothing with me."

"Buy what you need. Do not lose them. We'll follow along. You can tell us where they are going."

"It could be anywhere."

"Possibly, but on an evening train, it's probably overnight, probably to Luxor. Let us know as soon as possible. We'll check out of the hotel and bring your things."

The cab with the couple was slowing down at the train station.

"I must go. I will let you know."

The man jumped from the taxi and ran into the station. He caught sight of the tourist couple and slowed his pace. There were several people between him and them as he followed along behind. The couple approached the Watania Sleeper Trains desk. He knew that was an overnight train which only went to Luxor.

The station was a noisy place, and that worked in the man's favor as he dialed his companions and told them the destination. He then waited quietly across the walkway for the couple to leave.

After they had passed him by, the man hastily entered the office, purchased a ticket of his own, and made his way to the gate.

He settled into his own compartment and considered how to manage with only the clothes on his back. He was still wearing his "tour guide" uniform from earlier in the day, having drawn the short straw for the first watch on the couple when they had returned from Giza.

He took off the jacket and the hat and unbuttoned the

shirt at the neck. *It will have to do,* he thought. *At least they haven't seen me before.* He had come from Spain, where he and his partner had been following the other couple and the artifacts.

The man was hungry and went to the dining car. As he walked in from one end, he saw the couple at a table on the far end. The man sat down quickly.

The server approached.

The man spoke. "I hope this is all right? I was tired, and I just wanted to sit, but I would like to eat."

The server smiled and handed him a menu.

"I'll give you a moment, sir." And the server walked away.

The man stared at the menu, quickly deciding what he wanted. Then he continued to peruse the menu while watching the couple. He wondered, *What do they really know about the stone? How did they learn about it? Did the Bedouin woman tell them something? Did she even know? She had been protective of the stone but then sold it for nothing.*

None of this made any sense, but here the couple was, headed straight for Amarna and the treasure.

But do they in fact have the stone? Could this still be some kind of fluke? Could they just be tourists?

No, there are too many coincidences. They have to know something.

50

GETTING UP TO SPEED

Dee and Gina finished eating and went back to their compartment. The dining car had filled up, and they were glad their sleeper was near the door they had entered. It only took them a moment to stand up, exit the dining car, and go to their room.

Once there, they got comfortable and prepared to call the others.

"I had a thought," said Gina.

Dee looked up at her.

"What if we made a three-way call? Got everybody on the line at the same time? We could all share."

"That'd be great. What are the time zones again?"

"Jamal and Angelic are only an hour difference. Mike and Keno are six hours earlier. So it's 9 p.m. to us, 8 p.m. to Jamal, and 3 p.m. to Mike. Maybe we can catch everybody?"

"Let's try it."

Gina dialed Angelic. The phone rang twice and picked up.

"Hey girl, what are you and Dee doing? Anything you can talk about?" Angelic asked, and she laughed.

"We're just back from dinner, thank you, and we still have our clothes on," replied Gina.

"Tell Dee that Jamal says he's slipping."

"I didn't say that," they heard Jamal's voice ring out. "We're just back from dinner too."

Gina continued, "We were thinking of maybe trying to dial in Keno and Mike as well. Get everybody on the line and catch up. What do you think?"

"That's a great idea," Angelic replied.

"Let me put you on hold and I'll call."

Gina clicked a button on her phone and then dialed Keno. It only rang once before they heard Keno come on the line, her voice excited. "Hello. Gina, is that you?"

"Yeah, it's Dee and me. Is Mike nearby?"

"He's right here."

"Hold on a minute." Gina clicked a button. "Can everybody hear me?"

There were multiple voices as Angelic, Jamal, Keno, and Mike all began talking.

Dee broke through the chatter first. "Mike, how are you feeling?"

"Not bad. Still kind of weak. Low energy, but excited."

"Excited?"

"Yeah, but I'll let Keno tell it."

Keno came on in a high-pitched, voice. "We bought a house three doors down from Ike. We want you all to come and see us. Stay as long as you like."

"Wow!" replied Gina.

"What brought that on?" asked Angelic.

"We like it here," Keno gushed. "This is where we want to live long-term. Mike needs to rest. This is a great place for it. What are you guys doing?"

There was silence for a moment. Then Dee spoke. "Jamal, you go first."

"Okay," he replied. "We're about to finish up at the castle in northern Spain and return to Seville. We got everything unpacked and catalogued. They have offered me two jobs, one in Paris with Professor Toussaint and the other in Seville with Diego."

"Which one you taking?" asked Mike.

"Don't know yet. I need to finish this job while I think about it."

"We have found some really fascinating stuff," added Angelic.

"Like what?" asked Gina.

"A couple of days ago, we found this solid gold mural that had the pharaoh—we call him the 'Sun King'—and he had something around his neck, and the rays from the sun at the top of the mural were coming down and being redirected back out through whatever he was holding up from around his neck.

"And then, earlier today, we found out that the same pharaoh, the one Mike looks like, had a special stone that was connected to this special room in a temple he was building, and other secret stuff that we can't decipher completely. He held these races across the desert to the Atlantic where they gathered rocks or stones or something to bring back to him so he could use them in this room in this temple. It's wild."

"I think they were looking for a certain seashell that is phosphorescent. It was only found on the Atlantic coast of Morocco," said Mike.

"How'd you know that?" asked Jamal.

"A friend of Ike's, a retired tennis player, is from somewhere in Egypt. He told us this story from his childhood about a pharaoh who held these races in search of the shells, and there was something about a room and treasure."

"That's strange," replied Dee. "We've had two men

following us since Athens, and they accosted us in Cyprus asking about a stone. 'Sun Stone,' they called it. They wanted to know if we had it. We had no idea what they were talking about. We're in Egypt now. We saw the pyramids earlier today. We're on our way to Luxor to catch a river cruise for the Valley of the Kings."

"Dee," said Jamal. "You guys have to go visit Amarna. That's the city where this pharaoh ruled and all this stuff happened. It's outside Luxor. Just go look; let me know what you see."

"What would we look for?"

"I don't know for sure. There's supposed to be the remains of a temple. Look it over. I'm fascinated by this thing with the stone, hidden rooms, secret passageways—whatever you can see."

Dee looked to Gina. She nodded. "We'll look," Dee said. "Where is it outside Luxor? I think we have a day before the boat tour begins."

"It's in the desert outside of town. I'm not sure if there are organized tours or not. You'll have to check. I never thought about you going to Luxor. I wasn't sure you'd make it to Egypt."

"You got no faith, Jam."

"You know what I told you about calling me Jam."

Dee laughed. "We miss you guys."

Simultaneously, he and Gina heard the other four sing out, "We miss you too."

51

GATHERING THE FACTS

Dee and Gina got off the phone and laughed about how excited everyone had sounded.

"I hope Jamal can decide," said Gina, "and that Mike gets some energy back. A new house is going to take some effort."

"Yeah, it could. Or he might hire people to do the work. He was a contractor; probably knows how to delegate."

"I imagine he does. But that's nice. I liked it in Key West. I liked Ike's house and the area."

"It was comfortable there. Changing subjects: you okay with this side trip for Jamal?"

Gina nodded. "Yes, I think it might be fun. They found all kinds of fascinating information. I hope it's more than a pile of rocks. Do you think we can get close? In Athens, they wouldn't let us near anything."

"I guess it depends on the size of the site and how it's organized, and if there are tours. Maybe they'll let us look around on our own."

"That would be exciting."

"You ready for bed?" Dee asked.

"I'm still pretty awake. I think I'll read for a while," Gina replied.

Dee brushed his teeth and lay down. Gina shut off all the lights except for a small reading lamp on one wall.

She wanted to check out information on this site they were going to. She hoped that maybe having a little knowledge would make it more interesting. She wouldn't have minded lying down with Dee and getting close, but she wanted to be informed. He always seemed to know everything about everything. Even when he was right, it was annoying.

She was reading general information about Amarna and the pharaoh, Akhenaten, when she saw a related article about ancient Egyptians' fascination with numerology. She started reading the article. It seemed the ancients were intrigued by numbers in general, which contributed to their success in architecture, engineering, mathematics and other fields. But they were most fascinated by the number nine.

The number supposedly represented wisdom and experience, the beginning and the end. The Egyptians also considered the number nine to be perfection or completion. It was thought to be the most powerful and therefore sacred number. The number nine was the last cardinal, single digit number and included all the other cardinal numbers. Nine multiplied by any other single digit number gave an answer that, when the elements of the answer were added together, always totaled back to nine. It is the only number that does that.

There were nine primary Egyptian gods. There were nine months in the cycle of life. The number held a special place in Egyptian mythology and was incorporated into many facets of daily and religious life.

Gina got out the stone. It only had eight sides. Did that mean it wasn't the stone the men were looking for? Could there be some other element that made the total nine? Perhaps the stone itself counted as one, plus the eight sides. It was all very confusing. *Surely this can't be it.* She put the stone away, turned off her phone, stripped off her clothes, and climbed into bed with Dee. He was fast asleep.

———

DEE HAD SET THE ALARM FOR 5 A.M., AND HE HOPPED OUT OF bed when it went off. "You want to get some breakfast?" he asked a still-half-asleep Gina.

"Yeah, I suppose we'd better," she replied while stretching her arms.

Dee stood beside her, admiring the view. "Well, come on then. The train arrives at 6:15."

She got up and slipped into some clothes. "I am hungry."

Dee glanced around the room. "It won't take us long to repack what we have out. We'll have to find out what's available for tours to Amarna once we get off the train."

They made their way to the dining car and, to their surprise, it was about half full. "More early risers than I would have thought," said Dee.

"Everybody gets hungry, and if we all have to get off the train, this is your chance," replied Gina.

They made their way among the tables, and as they headed for an empty one, an Egyptian man's face popped up in front of them from a table they were passing. His eyes got big before he quickly looked down.

Gina made her way to the table and sat. Dee followed her.

"Did you see that?" she asked in a soft voice.

Dee nodded. "Yes, he seemed surprised to see us, or maybe to look up and see anyone so close."

They sat, ordered, and were served in a surprisingly

quick fashion. When they got up to leave, they both noticed that the man with the surprised expression was already gone.

After making their way back to their compartment, they quickly threw everything together and got ready for the day.

———

Standing in the station with their luggage, Dee was trying to decide what approach to take for the excursion to Amarna. There didn't seem to be any organized tour, but the site was open to the public.

"I don't know if the hotel will want to hold our luggage at seven o'clock in the morning," Dee said. "I think we should rent a car and carry it with us. By the time we get back, we should be able to check in. We're only there for tonight, and we board in the morning."

Dee spied a car rental site in the station and turned to Gina. "Over there."

"What about a cab? We could sightsee a bit more," she replied.

"We don't know how long we want to stay, and there may not be a cab back. We could pay him to stay, but then we'd have to leave our luggage in the cab while we wander around. You never know?"

Gina nodded. "Let's check out the car rental. Can we even rent a car?"

"I think so, although it may not be a good idea. Traffic is supposedly frantic in Egypt, but the site may be far enough removed if we can get out of Luxor alive." He grinned at her, and she shook her head in return.

After several minutes of discussion, Dee and Gina decided they would be comfortable renting a car. The route they would follow did not require them to travel extensively within the city limits of Luxor.

"We have a lot here, sir, and another at the Luxor airport. Would you like the vehicle from this lot?" asked the rental attendant.

"Here is fine. Can we return it to either place? Our hotel may be nearer the airport."

"There is a slight surcharge, sir, but yes, you can return the vehicle to the airport, should you need to."

Dee signed all the paperwork and provided all the necessary documentation. They exited the station to the rental lot and waited for the vehicle, a late-model Range Rover in black.

Gina nudged Dee. "We're going to look like mafia or politicians, or maybe the FBI."

Dee smiled at her. "Hopefully, the air conditioning works."

"That would be nice."

The vehicle arrived beside them, and a young man stepped out and moved along without speaking.

Dee and Gina loaded their luggage and got inside. It was an icebox.

"I think it works," quipped Gina.

Dee found the controls and turned them to a warmer setting. Gina pulled out the map the rental agent had given them to direct their way to Amarna.

Dee pulled from the curb, and they were under way.

52

FOLLOWING ALONG

The man went back to his room after eating dinner in the dining car. It had surprised him to see the couple, and he'd been disappointed that neither of them had the stone visible.

He tried to sleep. Several times, he had called the other men who were driving to Luxor. He was supposed to meet them in the morning. At least he would get to sleep comfortably, and he thought perhaps his luck wasn't so bad.

He was surprised to see the couple the next morning. He had not thought they would rise early. Still, they did not seem to have the stone. He'd hoped the woman would wear it.

Making his way from the train and meandering through the station, he saw the couple at the car rental counter but forced himself to keep walking until he found a secluded place to make a call.

"They are renting a car," he exclaimed.

"Surely they are headed to Amarna?"

"Do you want me to rent a car?"

"No, just try to see what type of vehicle they rent. The other two men will follow them more closely, and I will pick you up at the rental location."

The man hung up the phone and made his way to the car lot. He stood just inside the doors, where he could peer out the window and see the couple. They got into a black Range Rover and pulled away.

He stepped outside, and in a few minutes, the other man picked him up. They rode in silence for a few moments.

The driver finally spoke. "Did you see anything in your time on the train?"

"Only them eating, and no evidence of the stone."

"It would behoove us to locate the stone before Amir intervenes. I told him we asked the two men from Spain to assist us in following the couple to Luxor. He and the others will wait there."

"If we could intercept them on the highway, we could strongly inquire as to their intentions in Amarna and the location of the stone."

"I don't disagree, but Amir still hopes for a quiet reacquisition of the stone. I think time is running out."

The driver got on the phone to the car in front of them. "Do you have them in sight?" he asked.

"Yes. There is light traffic, we know the road, and we have them in sight. We will keep you posted if anything changes."

53

LONG LONESOME HIGHWAY

They pulled through the city and found the road to Amarna.

"It looks like it's going to take us a couple of hours. We'd better get a few things for the road before we get too far out of the city," said Dee.

"Yeah, I'd like some water," replied Gina.

They made a quick stop and picked up some supplies, then got back under way.

"We're headed north, aren't we? Back the way we came?" asked Gina.

Dee nodded. "Yes, the site's halfway back to Cairo. If we had known, we might have jumped off the train."

"I don't recall the train stopping."

Dee turned and grinned at her. "It might have been difficult."

They made good time in the Range Rover. There wasn't a lot of traffic on the road, and they left a long dust plume behind themselves, making any visibility in that direction difficult.

"What are we looking for?" asked Gina.

"I'm not sure," replied Dee. "I picked up this pamphlet

and book about the site in the store. Look and see what you think."

He drove on for a few minutes and spoke again as Gina flipped through the pages. "Jamal talked about secret rooms, and tunnels, and the stone thing that is supposedly the key. I guess it depends on what remains of the structure. I'm not sure if it's a temple or a palace or what. Maybe both. I don't know what we're looking for. See if you get any ideas from the book."

They rode along in silence again. The desert slid by them, unchanging and never-ending. The speed of the car seemed indeterminate as the landscape remained constant.

Finally, Gina looked up. "Well, if there was a palace, there isn't one now. The primary surviving structure, other than some tombs, is called the Great Temple of the Aten. It was Akhenaten's primary place of worship for his sun god. It seems to have survived because the builders made most of the other structures were made of mud brick or mud block. Those deteriorate over time and aren't all that architecturally sound. The temple, however, had large components of stone throughout, and it has endured better than the rest of the city. I'm unclear how long the city actually existed, but it appears Akhenaten had it built, and his was a short reign. They abandoned the city after his death. It wasn't around a long time. The temple looks like the best and maybe the only place for us to look."

"That should make it easier. I suggest we take a few pictures, get a good description to share with Jamal, and head back. We need to meet the boat in the morning."

"I'm okay with that if you think Jamal will be happy with it? It seems a shame in a way to come this far and not take more of a look."

Dee glanced toward her quickly and then looked back to

the road. "I thought you might get bored with this and want to get back to the boat."

"Well, I want to, but I also want to satisfy Jamal's request and do a good job. I agree with him that this whole thing is kind of fascinating and gets more intriguing as we go."

Gina didn't share more. She wasn't quite ready to reveal what she was thinking: *This whole thing with the stone—maybe it's the one I have.* Somebody was looking really hard for it. Could she and Dee find a clue? Could they determine if this stone was the stone and the key? But the key to what?

They continued driving, and the time passed slowly.

"It really is halfway back to Cairo," said Gina.

"I wasn't kidding," replied Dee.

"If we spend any time there, do you think we can still make it back to the boat?"

"It might be late, but we have a reservation at the hotel."

They continued on. There had been a few cars in each direction, but that had dwindled to none. The dust plume kept Dee from seeing anything behind him. Ahead lay only open road.

54

ON THE HUNT

The men in the car that trailed the couple where both happy and sad. Happy that they could hide behind the dust plume the car in front of them was creating, but sad that they really couldn't see much because of the dust. They knew they wouldn't lose the couple as there was only one road to Amarna.

They debated dropping back but then feared they would more likely be spotted. It was still early midmorning. They stayed in the dust plume.

The men trailing them in the second car had called several times to check on progress. There wasn't really anything to say, "They are going to Amarna and we are following them."

The men in the first car discussed among themselves what the couple could know. They had trailed them from Greece to Cyprus to Alexandria and now to here. When they had encountered them in Cyprus, they had seemed authentic in not knowing about the stone. But why were they coming here? This was not a major tourist attraction. It was out of the way, and visitation was low. It made little sense to the men. But they were diligent. They wanted to find the stone. Amir would be most unhappy with them and might even try to reduce their claims to the treasure. It was better to find the stone.

They had discussed hijacking the couple and searching them. But they were too well known by the couple. Identification would be easy. Publicity was not what they wanted. The plan was to secure the treasure and slip unnoticed into the world of wealth and privilege.

Back in the second car, the men mostly rode in silence, only chatting occasionally.

"Amir and the rest of the men will wait outside Amarna. The tailing car will drive on past the site, and we will park and observe. They do not know us."

The second man thought, *After this morning and my shocked face, they probably will remember me.*

He replied, "That sounds like a good plan, but I think we should stay out of sight."

The driver turned to look at him briefly. "Is there some reason we should stay out of sight?"

The man hesitated. "None that I know of. It just seems like a good idea."

The driver nodded, momentarily satisfied.

———

AMIR WAS OUTSIDE LUXOR AND HEADED FOR AMARNA. HE was alone in the lead vehicle, a black Range Rover of his own. The rest of his men were behind him in two canopied but open trucks. They were in the dust plume. The convoy streaked down the highway, the men confident of their destiny.

Amir had wanted to intercept the tourists somehow,

preferably alone, but he just hadn't been able to come up with a plan in such a short time. These tourists kept bouncing around never staying in one place long enough to become a target. Perhaps they were smarter than he thought, or maybe, more likely, they were just lucky.

55

TIME IN THE TEMPLE

A couple of hours later, Dee and Gina approached the site. Dee slowed and looked to Gina.

She replied, "The temple appears to be in the middle of the site. It's one of the few visible remaining structures. It should be easy for us to see."

Dee nodded and said, more out loud than to Gina, "I guess we park where we can. I'd prefer to minimize the walk."

"There are signs that indicate the site," Gina answered. "Turn in, and it should be marked to lead us toward the temple."

There were no other cars that Dee could see as he turned into the lot, but it surprised him to see a vehicle speed past them and continue down the road they had been on. The car had apparently been behind him or had appeared from somewhere nearby.

Dee pulled in and parked beside a sign that read *Great Temple of the Aten*.

"This must be the place," noted Gina, setting the book

down and then picking it back up. "I guess I should bring this with us."

They sat in the car for a few moments and looked at the site map. The temple had originally been a lengthy structure that dominated the central city area. There had been gardens and large spaces open to the sun mixed in with altars and adjacent rooms for gathering or living quarters.

Looking out the car windows, Dee and Gina could tell there was a significant portion of the temple still standing. They could see no guards or boundary markers, fences, or barriers of any kind. It appeared the site might be accessible.

They got out slowly. The day's heat had picked up, and the sun was bright overhead. Gina shuddered for just a moment as she climbed from the cold interior of the vehicle out into the bright light of the outdoors. The air was full of dust and sand that blew across them and acted as a curtain to their vision.

Gina got the distinct impression that, as they got closer to the temple, it was going to be like stepping back into the past.

"You ready?" called out Dee.

"What are we looking for again?" she asked.

"Perhaps we'll know it when we see it," he replied.

That's the scary part, she thought. *Maybe we will.*

Dee took her hand, and they walked toward the temple.

They moved slowly along the path that led to one of the temple entrances. As they got closer, they could see again that the doorways and steps weren't closed off.

"It looks like it is accessible," said Dee.

"How safe? I mean, how stable is it, do you think?" she asked.

"Does the guidebook say anything?"

"I didn't see it. Let's stop, and I'll take another look." She continued. "It doesn't say."

"Then let's assume we're allowed to get close and walk

around the perimeter. If we can get inside to see, and there's nothing suspicious underfoot or overhead, we'll look."

"I can't imagine they let people wander around in there. It would be like letting customers on stage with a dancer."

Dee stopped to look at her for a moment. "Yeah, I guess you don't see that very often."

A few moments later, they came to a set of steps that led into the temple. There wasn't much beyond the steps, as the near end of the temple was largely missing. They studied the approach for a moment and decided to move along the perimeter.

From the site map, Gina saw that the principal altar appeared to be on the far end.

"Let's stay around the outside until we get closer to the far end," she whispered to Dee.

"Why are you whispering?" he asked.

"It seemed appropriate. Plus with all this wind and the dust swirls, I had to get close for you to hear. I didn't want to shout in your ear."

Dee nodded, took her free hand, and started walking toward the far end.

"Pictures are going to be difficult with all this dust and sand."

Gina nodded. "Maybe if we get inside, you can get a better shot."

They watched the building closely, stepping among rubble and picking their way toward the far end of the temple.

About two-thirds of the way along the perimeter, they saw steps and a door that led inside a part of the structure that was still standing. They stepped across the loose rock and sand that separated them and mounted the steps.

As soon as they got inside, the wind stopped. They could still hear it, but the dust no longer surrounded them. As they climbed the short set of steps, they saw sunlight coming from the direction they had just traveled.

"There are many open sections of roof," Gina noted. "The book says that the pharaoh wanted everything to be in the presence of the sun. He made use of as much natural lighting as possible."

At the top of the steps, they turned to the right and proceeded into a large room with a vaulted ceiling. There were smaller rooms that adjoined the main room, and they stopped to peer into each area as they passed.

"Are we getting close?" asked Dee.

"It should be any time now, according to the temple layout."

"Is it an altar or a throne or what, exactly?"

"I'm not sure. The book and the brochure called it the primary place of worship for the pharaoh and his family. I'm not sure what that means."

They continued walking and peering slowly in every direction. As they got near the far edge of the large room, they found a couple of dividers on each side and a dais that thrust out into the floor. Atop the dais sat a platform that was probably an altar.

They approached it slowly, and as they climbed the steps, a stone throne came into view in front of a stacked rock wall. Gina stopped.

"I don't know for sure," she said. "But I think this is it."

"It? What?" asked Dee.

"What we're looking for," replied Gina.

Dee stared at her for a moment.

Gina continued, "Jamal was talking about some stone, and some special room, and tunnels, and secrets, and treasure. That looks like a throne to me. If the pharaoh sat there, don't you think he would have commanded everything from that spot?"

"Maybe, but then he could have just sat there and gone down the hall to a secret panel or something."

"Maybe, but I bet he sat there and controlled everyone's fate, including his own."

Gina stepped across the dais and sat in the chair. Nothing happened. She looked around, a little disappointed.

"Did you expect that just sitting down alone would do it?" asked Dee.

"Not really, but it would have been nice."

"Let's assume you are correct for a moment. Look at the chair. Do you see anything that moves, or slides, or pivots?"

Gina stood up and felt all around the chair as Dee moved closer and helped her. They found nothing.

Dee moved over to the wall.

"What are you doing?" Gina asked.

"This wall seems out of place. The room continues, goes deeper down the sides along the dais. It looks like maybe there could be a room on the other side of this."

"Or maybe another entrance?"

Dee examined the wall. It looked and sounded solid when he tapped it. He stepped back by Gina, beside the throne.

"So much for that," she said.

He nodded. "Let's explore the rest of the room." Dee glanced at his watch.

"What time is it?" Gina asked.

"About 11:40," replied Dee.

They stepped down from the dais and explored the rest of the large room. When they got to the far wall, they discovered steps that descended and led to a series of smaller rooms and an open courtyard beyond.

"This is one long building," said Gina.

The sunlight filtered in on them as the sun neared the center of the sky. Gina saw Dee's shadow lengthen.

"Let's go back to the throne for a minute," she said.

Dee nodded, and they started back toward the dais.

When they arrived beside the throne, the sun had come over the lip of the room's ceiling and shone almost directly down on the throne.

Gina looked at Dee. "I have an idea."

56

THE THRONE ROOM

As they stood next to the throne, Gina reached into her purse and removed the jewelry that Angelic had given her. She held it by the chain, and the stone swirled for a few moments before settling. Sunlight reflected through the stone and bounced off the nearby walls.

"What is that?" asked Dee and pointed at the stone.

"It's the piece of costume jewelry that Keno bought in the medina in Morocco. The woman wanted five dollars for it but Keno offered her one, and she took it. I showed this to you on the train."

"Tell me again, how did you get it?"

"When Keno and Mike left for Miami, Keno gave it to Angelic for helping her care for Mike. When Angelic and Jamal left for Spain, Angelic gave it to me to remember them all, a shared memory."

"I just barely recall you showing it to me. I didn't remember that you had it."

"I haven't worn it. We'd been busy hopping around and hiking, and I didn't want to lose it." She paused for a moment. "Also, I had a funny feeling about wearing it, so I just held on to it."

"You think that is the stone those men asked us about?"

"I don't know, but I didn't want to give it up. It meant more to me. It meant our friendship with the others. That was more important to me than wealth. And the feeling developed over time; it wasn't immediate. It just led to here."

"How does it work, what does it do—any thoughts on that?"

"No. I mean, this is just coming together in my mind as we stand here."

She held the stone up in front of her eyes, and Dee saw her lips moving.

She turned to him. "It has eight sides. I was reading the other night, after you went to sleep, that the Egyptians had a fascination with the number nine. They incorporated it in their everyday life, their work, their religion. But this only has eight sides. It's probably not what those men were looking for."

She casually sat on the throne. Dee looked at her.

"I was tired of standing. We've hiked the length of this thing."

He stepped across beside Gina and looked at the stone she still held before her.

Then he looked at the throne again. There at the top, carved into the stone, a round space caught his eye. He ran his hand along the surface, coming to the opening but stopping short of exploring it with his fingers.

Gina noticed him and looked up, but the sunlight was so directly in her eyes that she could hardly see, and she stood up from the seat.

"What?" she asked.

"Hold the stone up here."

She did so, and Dee guided her hand over the top of the throne toward the opening.

"I think the stone will slip right down in there," Dee said.

Gina looked up at him. "Should we do that? What if it won't come out?"

"If it goes in, it should come out."

She was hesitant, almost afraid, but she let Dee guide her hands over the opening, and she slowly lowered the stone into the slot.

It fit perfectly.

They both drew a breath and stepped back. The sunlight caught the stone, refracted the light, and bounced it out in all directions. They turned and marveled at the sight.

"So the Sun King had a thing"— Dee looked at his watch—"at noon. That seems appropriate."

"Look," replied Gina.

Dee turned, and behind them on the stacked stone wall, he saw a pattern of light illuminated.

"Could that be a sign?" she asked.

Dee stepped across to the wall while Gina remained by the throne.

He stood cautiously by the wall, afraid but not knowing of what. *Oh well,* he thought.

He pushed lightly on the first rock, his muscles tense, his knees bent and ready to move. *I've watched too many old movies.*

There was a soft click, and the rock recessed slightly. Dee stood there for a long moment. There was no other sound, and nothing else happened.

After a few seconds, he moved to the next stone and pressed lightly again. That stone also made a soft click and recessed.

Again he stood still, and there was no sound and no activity.

He moved to the third, fourth, fifth, six, and seventh stones, repeating the process. Each time, it was the same.

With only the eighth stone remaining, he turned to Gina. She was watching him, her hand to her mouth.

"What do you think?" he asked.

"I don't know. Maybe you should stop?"

"You said yourself it was a shame to come this far and not take a good look." He smiled at her, turned, and pressed the eighth stone.

Again there was the soft click, which was followed by a louder shudder, almost a groan, but nothing happened. The wall remained in place with the eight stones recessed.

Dee stepped back. "You'd think something would happen."

"Maybe it's been too long? Maybe it doesn't work anymore?" Gina replied.

They both stood and looked for a moment. Dee tapped on the wall elsewhere.

"You know, I was telling you about that Egyptian fascination with the number nine," Gina said. "The stone only had eight sides. Maybe there's one more thing that has to happen?"

"Yeah, maybe there's a lever of a handle or something." Dee looked around the wall. Other than the texture of the block, it was smooth.

Gina, who had been leaning against the throne, glanced over it once more and then turned to assist Dee. Doing so, she caught her foot on the leg of the throne and leaned against it to hold herself up. The throne tilted forward, and there was another screech, and the wall in front of Dee parted.

Gina righted herself, the throne still leaning forward, and crossed over to stand beside Dee.

57

THE HUNT CONTINUES

The men in the first car shot past the turn to the Amarna site. They were happy that their part of the surveillance was over. They were very tired of riding in the dust plume. They would circle back and meet Amir and the others.

They had called the men in the second car and told them the situation. The second car had slowed a bit in order to allow the tourists to get situated and to not arouse their suspicions.

Now, the second car arrived and pulled into the parking lot. They drove until they saw the tourists' Range Rover.

"Just like Amir's," said the one man.

The other grunted. "We'll park further down the lot and come around to the temple from the opposite side. Make it look random."

"There's nobody else here. Why would it matter? What does Amir have in mind?"

Ignoring the other questions, the second man responded, "He'll let us know."

They proceeded cautiously, despite the site appearing to

be empty of any other tourists. Walking slowly along the far side of the temple, the men talked quietly.

"My father and uncle spent their lives on this site looking for the treasure. They never found a thing."

The other man nodded. "My father spent his life looking for the stone. There were rumors occasionally, but nothing ever came of them. There was an incident when I was a small boy. They were making a movie further up the river, and there was a Hollywood star that was playing Cleopatra. She had this huge necklace that her husband had given her. There was talk that her necklace might be the stone. But it was costume jewelry. That's the only instance I remember in my lifetime that there was genuine excitement that we might be close to finding the stone—until now."

They had reached the midway point of the long temple structure and slowed as if to study the site while they looked for the couple.

After several moments, the one man spoke. "I do not see or hear them."

"They may have gone inside. Perhaps they know where to look?"

"How could that be? We have looked for centuries."

"It is a mystery, but we must soon resolve it."

The men continued slowly along the outer wall, looking and listening.

Suddenly, one of their phones rang. Both men nearly jumped out of their skins.

"The phone," said the one. "Answer it quickly."

The other man pulled out his cell and spoke. He listened and nodded for several seconds. Then he said in a quiet voice, "We are beside the temple. We have not yet located them. There is no one else here. We should hear or see them soon. Yes, we will." He hung up.

He exhaled softly and then looked to the other man.

"That was Amir, wanting a progress report. He and the others are still several minutes away. He wants to be notified as soon as we make contact."

The other man returned his sigh and nodded. He waved to the first man. "Then let's go find them."

58

GOING DANCING

The walls slid back and opened to a door-sized space in what had been the center of the wall, right between Dee and Gina. The light from the sun hitting the stone in the throne's head rushed past them and, reaching inside the room, bounced around, glittering and flashing off the walls.

They could see it was a fair-sized room. There were no snakes, no rats, and no 'X' marked a spot. Just a smaller dais in the center of the room, surrounded by an open area that extended to the outer walls. The room itself was lushly decorated. There wasn't a visible pile of treasure, so maybe the room was an inner temple, or a shrine, or family quarters, or maybe the pharaoh's break room, or a harem. Whatever it was, it looked valuable because, despite the lack of a pile of gold objects, gold bars, or precious stones, the room was decorated in gold thread, gold weave, and gold inlays, and had thin sheets of pounded gold on several walls. Embedded ebony, ivory, and jewels were scattered across the other walls, all surrounded by the phosphorescent shells from the Race Across the Sahara. All the walls of the room were at least partially encrusted by the shells with their purple tone. The light refracted all around the room and washed over Dee and Gina.

They stepped inside, with Dee watching to see if the door would close. When it remained open, he stepped a little further inside, following Gina, who seemed instinctively drawn into the room.

Dee realized the door had to stay open for the room to be lit and he relaxed slightly.

"It looks like a giant disco in here," said Gina, holding her arms up and letting the light bounce over them. "Wonder what music they were listening to?"

Dee glanced around the walls, his eyes following the light. "Probably not the Bee Gees."

Gina grimaced at him.

"Let's talk through this," said Dee, looking toward Gina.

She turned to face him.

"It's an event that happens every day at noon, the height of the Sun's power," Dee said. "That makes sense. He placed the stone in the throne's head, which sits at a slight angle. The stone catches the sun at noon, and the light refracts and makes patterns on the wall. The pharaoh traces the pattern on the individual rocks to open the door to the room."

Gina replied, "Yes, but he wouldn't have the light except for a period at midday."

"Which means it should grow darker in here as the day progresses?"

She nodded.

"But as long as some light is coming in the room stays illuminated," Dee continued. "The pattern for the door is refracted from the eight sides of the jewel. It highlights the stacked rock wall behind the throne. If the rocks in the pattern are all pressed, there is a noise like something separating, but the wall doesn't move. It requires one more step, which you figured out."

"'Stumbled onto by accident' is a better way to describe it," Gina replied.

"But still, you found it. Your idea about the Egyptians' great reverence for the number nine turned out to be true. There are eight sides on the stone, and tilting the throne makes the ninth. Moving the throne releases the wall, and it opens to the room inside."

"That sounds about right," replied Gina. "What do you suppose this room really was?"

Dee glanced around again. "We'll probably never know. The truth may be lost to the past."

They moved further around the room, admiring the walls and the ornamentation.

"Jamal said the pharaoh held a race every year around the time of his birthday for the people to collect more shells. There certainly are lots of them." Gina ran her hand lightly across the wall, feeling the texture and the number of shells.

"That's what makes the light bounce so much," said Dee "The high volume of the shells. They're mixed into the wall material, like a component of construction."

They moved around the room, which was mostly vacant, looking for anything else they might see.

"Could it have been a meeting room?" asked Gina.

"Seems reasonable, with that dais," replied Dee. "Perhaps it was some sort of small assembly room."

"A treasury, maybe?"

"Where's the treasure?"

"Someone else took it—a tomb raider or an archeologist."

"That's always possible."

"Could that have been why those men are looking for the stone? They think there's treasure?"

"The components of the room are certainly valuable intrinsically, but even more so archeologically. It doesn't seem like they'd chase an empty room or desecrate these items. But in accounting, we always had a saying, 'Follow the money,' and it always leads to the problem. Maybe they just think there's treasure."

"They're going to be disappointed."

"Yeah, so is Jamal."

They both laughed.

Moving to the last wall, Dee and Gina's attention was captured by two wall hangings in what looked like gold thread and gold weave on a dark material highlighted with colors that still shone brightly.

There were two likenesses hanging side by side. One was of a man, the other of a woman. The man on the hanging was in profile, with his head and shoulders tapering down to a trim waist.

"Who does that look like?" asked Dee, pointing to the man.

Gina turned to look. She had been studying the hanging with the woman.

Gina stared at the man for a moment. "I suppose it's the pharaoh, but it looks like Mike."

Dee nodded.

"But look here," she said, pointing to the hanging of the woman.

Dee turned to see it.

The woman had short dark hair, dark eyes with purple eye shadow, pale skin, and round hips. She wore an open vest, underneath which she was topless and very slight.

Dee turned to look at Gina.

"Who does she look like?" asked Gina.

It took him a second. "Keno. They look like Mike and Keno."

"The resemblance is remarkable," replied Gina.

Dee turned to her. "Could that explain why those men in

the marketplace in Morocco kept staring at Mike? Could they have been part of this group?"

"That would mean they have been after us since we left Spain. How would that be possible?"

Dee turned toward her. "The stone. They were looking for the stone, and we somehow ended up with it."

"But Keno just saw it and bought it. We didn't know."

"Apparently, they somehow did."

They were standing facing one another, contemplating the possibilities, when they heard a sound.

59

CLOSING IN

The two men had been walking along the outside wall of the temple, looking and listening for the tourist couple. So far, they had not seen or heard them.

"They must be inside," said the one man.

"We'll have to backtrack to an entrance."

"Have you been inside there?"

"Not in some time. It's safe enough, just don't go leaning on walls or stepping in holes."

"I've never been in the temple. I've spent most of my time along the perimeter of the city and the tombs looking for the stone. Do we need a light?"

The other man stopped and looked at the one who had just spoken. "It's a temple to the sun. They designed it to provide a great deal of light."

They moved inside the building. The man who had been there before led the way. "Do speak softly, as the acoustics in this closed end are still quite good. Sound will carry a long way. Listen closely for them."

They took another step, and one of the men's phones

rang. "Amir, what lousy timing," he muttered, struggling to reach his phone and answer it.

"Yes, we are inside the temple and tracking them. We've seen nothing so far. You're parked next to them, but the trucks and the men are hidden in the surroundings. Okay, we'll call when we see them or if they flee."

The man hung the phone up. He turned to his associate. "Amir and the bulk of the men are going to remain hidden. He is sending a few men to meet up with us or to remain outside the temple, depending upon our needs. We should wait a moment for them. We can stand and listen."

60

REACH OUT AND TOUCH SOMEONE

Dee and Gina stood still for a moment, straining to first hear and then identify the sound. It was a phone ringing.

Dee whispered, "Someone else is definitely here. Let's go."

He took Gina by the hand, and they quickly exited the room. Gina stopped him as they got to the throne on the dais. "Wait, we want the stone."

Dee glanced quickly around but then nodded. "Let's be quick."

As the throne was leaning forward, Gina placed two fingers on the stone, one on each side, and popped it out of the slot.

Dee looked at her for a moment. "As easy as that."

"Just sitting there taking care of business. The pharaoh was a smart guy. Push the throne back."

Dee looked at the throne. It appeared to be heavy, but Gina had tilted it forward.

There was a commotion at the far end of the room. An older man was yelling. Dee looked up at him and saw something familiar.

"Come on," shouted Gina. She tugged on the throne, and Dee bent to help her. It sat upright easily.

"Simple enough," he said.

"Yeah, well, now we better simply be running."

They took off toward the opposite wall, from where they had come into the room via the exterior steps.

Getting outside, they turned long enough to hear the man still shouting, now sounding closer to them.

They started for the car. Gina stuffed the stone back in her purse and clutched it tightly as she ran. They were careful to try not to lose their footing over the loose sand and rock.

They saw two black Range Rovers parked side by side. There were no other vehicles, and they could see no people.

"Which one is ours?" called Gina.

Dee noted they looked alike. He pulled the key fob from his pocket and clicked it while he ran. The one on the right blinked its lights.

"On the right, we're on the right," he called.

They reached the vehicles, and as Gina went to get in the passenger side, she turned to the other vehicle and tried the door. It opened.

She stuck her head inside as Dee jumped into the driver's seat of their SUV.

"There's a key fob on the console," she called out.

Dee had rolled her window down to yell at her to get in the car, so he heard what she said. "See if it'll start," he called out.

Gina jumped inside, jammed the brake with her foot, and hit the starter. The engine roared to life.

"Follow me," called Dee. "We drive it five or ten miles and dump it. Maybe it'll slow them down." He heard shouting getting nearer and called to Gina, "We got to go."

He slammed the car in reverse and backed out. Gina

followed him. He raced to the exit and, on the spur of the moment, turned north, instead of back south. Gina followed him.

He raced up the road, putting a plume of dust in the air. He saw Gina pull over into the oncoming lane to stay clear of the dust.

At least she can see until she has to get back over, Dee thought.

There was no traffic coming toward him, so Dee wasn't worried for her, and he sped along as fast as the Range Rover would go. They bounded across several small rises but remained surrounded by desert.

Dee couldn't see anything in the mirror, as his dust plume was sizeable. He drove for several miles.

Rounding a slight turn, he could look back far enough to see that there wasn't anyone immediately behind them. He could see no additional plumes of dust in the air.

Crossing over the next rise, Dee slowed the Range Rover, signaled a turnoff, and, as he descended the rise, pulled in behind the dune. Gina followed him.

He opened the door and stepped partially out. When Gina rolled down her window he called to her, "Pull the vehicle further off the road and over closer to the dune, shut it off, and bring the key."

Gina pulled several car lengths further forward, shut the vehicle down, hopped out, and ran toward Dee. She tossed him the key fob as she got close. As Gina got into the vehicle, Dee turned and threw the key fob across the road to the dune on the other side. He got back in the seat and restarted the SUV.

"Time to go," he said. Gina nodded, and they raced across the desert.

61

AHMED RETURNS

The two men stood outside the temple for a few minutes until three of Amir's other men arrived.

The man who had been on the phone with Amir addressed the others. "Let's move inside from a couple different directions. We'll enter here, in the courtyard. You go further down toward the end of the temple, and you go around."

They split up and started in each direction, two groups of two and a single man. The single man's name was Ahmed Alami, and he had helped the tourists change a tire along the road. He felt he would recognize them on sight. He had studied them as he had worked on their car. This was the short, curvy woman with the long dark hair, and one of the men that had spoken the most to him. He had wanted to ask them about the stone on that day, but he had been told not to, only to observe. He'd wanted to tell them what they were getting into and to plead with them to hand the stone over and run away. He would have paid whatever price they had asked. He feared things would soon turn ugly for them if

Amir did not get the stone. All he wanted was to talk with them.

And he knew a shortcut. He had spent a great deal of time in the temple as a child and as a young man. There was a passageway that led underground near the middle of the temple. It was simply too far to walk all the way around.

He entered the passage and came quickly out on the other side of the temple. His new location put him near the far end of the throne room. He approached a short set of steps and entered the temple.

Immediately, he felt the presence of some living thing. The room did not have the stillness and silence of the dead.

He proceeded slowly in the direction of the dais and the throne.

As he crept quietly along, he knew the others would arrive shortly. This might be his only chance to talk to the couple. He eased around the outer wall to where he could better see.

As he gazed up at the throne, he sensed something amiss. He had studied the dais and the throne many times. The wall behind the throne, it was open. There was another room—the treasure.

Ahmed stood motionless for a moment. Then he emitted a cry that came from deep within him. He hadn't meant to make a sound, to alarm them.

Standing there against the wall, Ahmed had been so transfixed that when the couple came running from the room and stopped to set the throne upright, he had only stood frozen. The wall was closing.

He yelled out, "You there, please wait, I must talk to you."

They were already running. He saw the man look at him briefly and thought that he might have recognized him.

Moving quickly, the couple made for the far door. Ahmed

was no young man, and he could not keep up. He turned once as he ran to see the wall coming to a close, and the entrance to the room disappeared. He was heartbroken. *Where are the others?* he thought.

Ahmed got to the steps that led outside, and he saw the couple almost to the vehicles. He stopped to phone the others. They were probably somewhere in the temple, and the tourists would get away. Ahmed knew Amir had led the remaining men around to the far side of the temple, thinking that if the couple ran, that would be the logical direction. He had counted upon the five of them to separate the tourists from their vehicle.

Then Ahmed saw an odd thing. Both vehicles pulled away. Perhaps Amir had stayed in his SUV, and he would secure the couple.

The old man sat on the steps and dialed. He reached the other men in the temple. "They are gone. The couple just fled in their vehicle. Amir appears to be in pursuit in his SUV."

Ahmed listened for a moment. The voice was loud. "That is doubtful. I just spoke to Amir, and he is on the far side of the temple."

Ahmed sighed. "Both vehicles are gone. I watched them pull away. But Amir was right. They knew something about the treasure. When I came into the sanctuary, they were running out of a room that was hidden behind the throne. "

"What are you saying?"

Ahmed repeated, "As I came upon the couple, they were exiting a room that sits behind the throne. The wall had separated, and they were in the room. I saw the door close. I think it's controlled by the throne."

"Stay there; I will tell Amir. We'll come to you."

"Yes, but the door is closed."

"We will find a way to open it."

62

NORTH TO CAIRO

"Why are we going this way?" asked Gina. "Aren't we heading north, toward Cairo?"

Dee nodded as he swerved the vehicle to gain a second of clear rear view. Still, he could see nothing following them from behind.

"I wonder why we don't see them," he said, more to himself than Gina. Then he turned to Gina. "Yes, we are headed north, back to Cairo. I don't think a river cruise is wise at this point. Those guys are serious about the stone, and that"—he pointed at Gina's purse—"appears to be it. We have to lose them and get away."

"Why didn't we just tell them that there was no treasure?"

"I guess we could have, but they would have wanted the stone at the very least. It may be valuable. Is it a diamond or a big piece of quartz or something else?"

"It has eight sides. Diamonds typically have only four unless they're cut or modified in some fashion."

"How do you know diamonds?"

"Silly boy, all girls know diamonds."

Dee looked at her for a moment, and she smiled at him.

"Yeah, and I think quartz has six sides, or more sides than diamonds, anyway, and it's not as hard as a diamond. The stone is probably quartz," said Dee.

"It's pretty hard. I scratched at it."

"With another diamond?"

"No, just a ring guard on another piece of jewelry I have. I think it might be real."

"Do you know what a diamond that size would be worth?"

"No, but I expect it would take a gold bar or two."

Dee grinned at her. "Yeah, and they'd surely kill us for it. Which is why I thought we should run."

"You knew it was a diamond, then?"

"No, I just felt their intensity and their persistence. They want it badly, whatever it's made of."

They were quiet for a few moments. Then Gina spoke again. "So, going back to going north, what is your plan?"

"Our plan," he replied and winked at her. "I'm thinking we drive to Cairo, dump the vehicle at the airport, let the rental company know where it is, maybe throw off the guys following us into thinking we flew out, then grab a ride to the docks and catch the first ship out, wherever it's going."

"That's the plan?"

"It's not in concrete. I'm open to suggestion."

"Actually, I like it. You know I prefer ships. Any idea what the choices might be?"

"Somewhere in the eastern Mediterranean, most likely. From wherever it docks, we can figure out our next location."

"I'm tired of running." She looked at him with a long face.

He reached out, took her hand, and squeezed it. "I am too, but we have to run just a little further, and it'll all be over."

63

ANOTHER BRICK IN THE WALL

The men came running into the sanctuary. Ahmed was sitting on the lowest step of the dais.

"Where?" shouted Amir. "Where is it? Where is the room?"

Ahmed pointed to the wall behind the throne. "There. The wall separates. It seems to have something to do with the throne."

The men hustled up the steps, leaving Ahmed sitting alone. He watched them from below.

They looked all about the throne and ran their hands across it. They tried to shuffle it and tried to lean it forward and back. The throne did not move.

"Are you sure what you saw, old man?" called Amir.

Ahmed rose from the step and nodded as he slowly climbed the stairs. "They appeared to push the throne back, and the wall came together."

Amir pointed to the wall. "Check it."

Several of the men jumped forward and ran their fingers over the wall. It felt seamless and solid.

"There is nothing," called one man.

Amir looked to Ahmed. "How? How did they do it?"

"I do not know the answer."

Amir stood fuming for a moment, then raised a hand and slapped Ahmed across the face. "We had better figure it out. You stay here," he said, pointing at Ahmed, "and you three as well. We'll work on the throne and the wall. All you others, go after the tourists. Take my Rover—the keys are in it—and one truck."

Ahmed and the other man he had told about Amir's SUV looked at one another, but neither spoke up.

64

ON THE RUN

Dee and Gina drove for a while with no other traffic and then looped back onto the main north-south highway, heading straight for Cairo.

"Can you check the GPS for the airport location?" asked Dee.

Gina nodded and went to work. "It looks like we're a little over an hour away from Cairo. The airport is on the northeast side of the city, probably another half hour, depending on traffic. It's another two hours to Port Said. You still want to dump the vehicle?"

"I'd prefer it, just to buy us some cover, some misdirection. We could take a cab, but I'd rather catch a ride at least partway—get out from the airport, try not to leave a trail."

Gina nodded. "Maybe there's a transport area at or around the airport. We could catch a ride on a bus or maybe some kind of truck."

Dee grinned at her. "Good idea. We might lose some time, but it would confuse them in trying to follow us."

"You really think they'll come after us? You haven't seen anything, have you?"

"No, I haven't, and I really can't figure that out. Taking the SUV probably slowed them down a little, and going north may have helped. But would you give up a diamond that size? If that's what it is. It now seems like they've been chasing us all around the Mediterranean. We were oblivious."

"It looked like a five-dollar piece of costume jewelry. How could we have known?"

"Get it out. Hold it up to the light."

Gina reached into her purse and pulled the stone and the chain out. She stretched the chain between her fingers and held the stone aloft. It swirled slowly and caught the light from the windshield. It sparkled and reflected off the dash.

"I don't think that's quartz," said Gina.

Dee nodded. He reached across, squeezed the chain, and ran his fingers along it. "If it were costume, that would be gold plate or gold filled. The color looks real. I got an idea."

Dee pressed the cigarette lighter in the console for it to heat.

"I didn't think cars had lighters anymore," said Gina.

"In America, they only have the insert, for electronic plugs, but you don't get a lighter anymore."

The lighter in the console popped out. Dee pulled it from the slot and handed it to Gina. "Hold it up against the gold. If the gold gets darker, it's plated or filled. If it gets brighter, it's pure."

Gina held the lighter on a portion of the chain. It only took a second, and the gold shone even brighter than it already was.

She turned to Dee. "It looks real."

"Which means the stone is probably real. They will come after us."

Almost an hour and a half later, they saw signs for the airport.

"Look for a long-term parking sign," said Dee.

"We're not going to turn the car in?"

"No, we'll call the company and tell them where it is."

"Will that be all right?"

"They have my credit card. I'm sure they'll make it right."

Gina pointed ahead. "There on the right: *Long-Term Parking*."

They pulled into the lot, finally found a spot on the perimeter, and grabbed their luggage.

"Good thing we're light packers," said Dee.

"How many times have we lost our luggage in the past few months?" replied Gina.

"At least we don't have to do laundry.

We just buy new."

They worked their way toward the exits of the lot. Once they were back out in the street, they headed for the terminal.

"Let's go through the lobby and exit on the ground transportation side. If anybody sees us, we look like we're catching a flight," said Dee.

They passed through the lobby and out to the transportation area. They walked a short way beyond the cabs to where the airport exited into the local traffic. There was an interchange another block away.

Gina pointed. "Let's go there. At least we can sit at the bus stop."

They made their way across to the covered seats and sat for a few moments. Watching traffic pass by, they noticed several transport trucks. There were many business names and locations on the sides.

Gina noticed the box truck first. It had stopped at the corner. The side of the truck read *Port Said Authority*. They could see a young man driver. He had the window rolled down and his hand stuck out on the mirror.

Gina jumped up. She turned toward Dee and quickly unbuttoned the top two buttons on her shirt. Then she turned back and stepped toward the truck. She breathed deeply and waved at the young man, who waved back. Stepping across to his window, she began a conversation with him.

Dee couldn't hear it, but he could see the young man was suddenly paying more attention. He saw Gina turn and point toward him. The young man hesitated, but then Dee saw his face brighten in a smile, and he nodded to Gina.

She turned and waved to Dee. She held out both her hands like she was carrying something. Dee took that to mean *bring the luggage.*

He walked over to the truck with a suitcase in each hand. The young man jerked his thumb toward the other door, and Gina led the way around.

She hopped inside first and slid across to sit next to the boy. He looked down her blouse as far as he could and then looked up and grinned at Dee.

Gina held out her hand toward the boy. "This is Mohammed Abu. He is going to drive us to Port Said."

65

UP AGAINST THE WALL

The men scrambled out of the temple and ran for Amir's SUV. One of them peeled off to get one of the transport trucks.

When they got to the parking lot, it was empty.

"This is not good," said one of the two men who had just returned from Spain. "Amir is going to be most unhappy."

"What do we do?" asked one of the other men in the group.

"I'll call him and tell him. We'll wait for the transport truck and get under way first."

"He's going to be very angry," said the other man who had just returned from Spain.

"That's why we'll be under way when I call and tell him."

———

Inside the temple, Amir was pacing about and berating Ahmed every few moments.

"Why do you not know? Did you not see it?" he shouted.

Ahmed stood silently.

"Tell me again," hissed Amir.

Ahmed moved from where he stood and walked to the throne. He pointed at it.

"The throne was forward, and they pushed it back or lifted it up. The wall"—he pointed behind them—"was open, and it began to close. I did not see what was inside. Surely it was the treasure room. I ran after them but was too far away, and they escaped. I called the others, but they couldn't get here in time. That is all I know."

"But you saw the room?"

"I saw the door."

"Were they carrying anything? Any objects, any treasure?"

Ahmed paused for a moment. "Nothing really. She had a bag, maybe her purse in one hand, and he was holding her other hand, pulling her along. His other hand was empty."

"She must have the stone in her purse since it is not here."

One of the other men spoke. "Could they have left it in the room?"

Amir turned to the man, his voice a snarl. "And why would they lock the stone up with the treasure?"

The man who had spoken looked down and remained silent.

"We need to tell the men chasing them to focus on her purse. Apparently, she does not wear the stone."

Amir's phone rang. He answered quickly. "Yes, tell me."

He stood listening for a moment, his face becoming contorted with rage. "We'll be out in a minute," he snarled, and he flung the phone against the wall.

Amir looked around the group. "We are finished here for now." He pointed at Ahmed. "You come with me. You others, remain and keep watch in case they return. Call me immediately."

One man's eyes wandered to the likely broken phone lying against the wall.

Amir glowered at him. "It appears the tourists have taken my Range Rover as well as their own. No one saw which way they turned from the parking lot. Pursuit is futile. From this point, we'll have to regroup. Surely they will come back for the treasure." He looked at the men who would remain. "Keep a very close watch or suffer the consequences."

They nodded without speaking.

———

THE REMAINING MEN RODE BACK TO LUXOR IN THE TWO transport trucks. Amir and a driver rode in the cab of the first truck, while the two men, just returned from Spain, piloted the second truck. The men from Spain had turned their truck toward Luxor, assuming the tourists would return there.

When the first man had called Amir and told him the news, Amir had told them to wait on him and the others. So they sat patiently beside the road until Amir's truck caught up to them and passed them. They pulled out in the dust plume.

The driver, the second man from Spain, turned to his passenger. "Amir seems to get angrier by the moment. We have waited a long time for this discovery. I would think he would be happier, for himself and for all of us."

The passenger looked at him suspiciously. "One should not speak of such things. Amir is our leader. It is his job to secure the stone and the treasure."

"We are so close," replied the driver.

"Yes, we are, and I think perhaps Amir is now ready to

strike. He has tried to be patient and inconspicuous, but it has not worked." The man paused for a moment before continuing. "We were children together, Amir and I. He has a terrible temper when he is aroused. We keep missing the target, letting these tourists gad about. They clearly have the stone, and they know a secret. I think that will soon come to an end. That is all I have to say about that."

"How could they know?" asked the driver.

The passenger turned and stared at him with stony eyes and then looked away.

66

SITTING ON THE DOCK OF THE BAY

Mohammed dropped them outside the gate of the port. He explained he could not be seen transporting unauthorized passengers. They thanked him, and when Dee went to tip him, Mohammed declined.

"It was my pleasure and my enjoyment," he exclaimed.

Dee and Gina got out of the truck with their luggage and looked about for the cruise line offices. Mohammed had suggested they enter the port and go right on the thoroughfare and they would come to several of the cruise lines.

As they walked in that direction, Dee asked a question. "How did you get him to do that?"

"Do what?" said Gina while turning to smile at him.

"Get him to give us a ride."

"It was easy. You know I told you girls instinctively understand diamonds… well, men instinctively understand cleavage. I know you do. You just about broke your neck the first time we saw each other on the cruise ship. I had that blue thong on, and I thought you were going to choke. Jamal wasn't much better. Angelic and I laughed about that for days."

"That simple, huh?"

"Yep, just sit back and be in charge."

"Did you learn that while you were dancing?"

Gina turned and looked down her nose at him. "What do you think?"

A short time later, they found the offices of a smaller eastern Mediterranean cruise line.

They sat at the desk and asked about what was available immediately.

Gina jumped in and took over. "Egypt just didn't agree with me. I mean, it's beautiful, but I have dust allergies, and the sand and sun were wearing me out. I told him"—pointing at Dee—"that we were just going to move on. I love looking at the pictures, but the climate just didn't work for me."

The woman nodded and replied, "My husband and I were in Germany once, and I had to leave. Just too many trees and flowers and things. Pollen everywhere. What we have immediately—in fact, later this afternoon—is a cruise to Istanbul by way of Haifa. There is a one-day stop there and then on to Istanbul."

Dee and Gina looked at one another. "That'll do," replied Dee.

A few hours later, Dee and Gina found a small portside restaurant. They sat in the shade and watched the ships roll in and out and away again.

"What do you know about Istanbul?" asked Gina.

"It's a former Roman city, once named Constantinople, founded by an Emperor with a similar name. It was conquered by the Muslims in the 1400s, thus the name change. That's about it."

"That's all you got?"

"Afraid so; the well ran dry."

"About time," she said, and she smiled at him.

Dee smiled back at her, not sure if he'd been insulted or not. But he didn't really care. She was amazing.

He thought back on her past. They had met on a slice cruise from Los Angeles to Australia, with stops in Hawaii and Tahiti and a bunch of other islands. They'd been marooned, and she had joined him and their other friends, Jamal and Angelic, and Mike and Keno. They had been through a lot together.

In her former life, she'd been an exotic dancer who'd started out while underage but well developed. She had two brothers and a sister to care for after their mother had died. She had gone to work with what she had once told him were her only assets, and had held her family together until they could be on their own.

Dee couldn't help but admire her determination, her dedication, her persistence, and her common sense. He'd tried to ask her once about how the experience had impacted her, which had been a pretty broad and probably stupid question, but she had come back, in what he now recognized as typical fashion, and replied, "I knew what I had to do. I knew how long I had to do it, and when it was done, I walked away."

They sat quietly for a time, waiting for the moment they could board. When it arrived, they gathered up their suitcases and made their way to the ship. It was larger than a river cruiser but smaller than most of the cruise lines they had been on before. It was in good shape and felt comfortable.

"This is good; I like it," Gina said.

Dee nodded.

"Do you think those men are still after us? How will they find us?"

"I don't know. I guess it's a question of what resources they have. I mean, we had to leave, although they may have thought we'd stick around. If they think there's treasure, they may camp out at the temple. But I think they'll try to find us. They will want the stone. If they can check the airlines and cruise lines, they may catch up with us at some point. Let's see what happens."

"Maybe after we get settled, we could call the others? I'd like to know how they are doing."

"That's a good idea. Let's get unpacked and go up on the pool deck for a few minutes. It'll be dark soon. It's been a long day."

Gina grinned at him. "You just want to see me in that blue thong again."

"It could take my mind off of other things."

"Why do you think I've kept it all this time?" She punched him in the shoulder. "Let's get going."

67

BACK IN THE BLACK

The men arrived back in Luxor. Amir was striding about behind the trucks in front of the men.

He assigned the two from Spain with their task. "Use whatever resources we have to determine airline flights and cruises, maybe also trains. See what you can find. I still think they are hiding somewhere in the area and will be back for the treasure. No one would leave that behind."

"Is it possible they could have gone to get help?" asked one man.

"Interesting thought," replied Amir as he stroked his chin. He looked at the two men he had just assigned the task. "See what you can tell about that. Maybe check on the location of the other couples, if you can find them."

The men nodded in return.

Amir resumed, "For now, pay attention; keep your ears and eyes open; be ready to travel at a moment's notice. We will find them. That is all. You may go."

The men turned to disassemble, but one of them spoke up. "If we find them again, we should just take the stone from them."

The other men stopped and stood to listen to Amir's response.

"And indeed we will, my brother. We will take it by whatever means are necessary. We have waited long enough. Our people are in need. It is our time."

The men disbanded then, talking among themselves, shaking their fists and voicing support for Amir's position.

The two men assigned to find the couple stood to the side and watched the others.

"You were right: Amir's mood has changed."

"Yes, my brother, and I pray we find the tourists quickly, or it may be us he turns upon."

68

RELIVING THE MOMENT

Dee and Gina got situated in their cabin after a few minutes by the pool. Cleaning up for dinner, they tried to decide when to call the others.

"Do you want to eat first or call them?" asked Dee.

"You want to conference them again, if we can?"

Dee nodded.

"Let's try now."

Gina dialed Angelic and got a response on the second ring.

"Hey girl, where are you now?" teased Angelic.

"On a ship. Let me see if I can call Keno."

"Sounds good. I'll get Jamal."

Gina dialed again, and Keno picked up on the first ring.

"Hey, Gina."

In a moment, all three of the women were on the line with the men standing by.

"Hey everybody," said Gina, "Dee and I wanted to tell you what happened to us."

"What?" rang out the other four voices.

"We're on a ship now, headed for Istanbul."

"That was quick," called out Jamal.

"Yeah, but let me explain," Gina said. "Dee and I took the train from Cairo to Luxor after seeing the pyramids at Giza—which were really cool, by the way. You would have loved it, Jamal. Anyway, we took the train overnight to Luxor. We had a day to sightsee before the river cruise started, so we took the tour to Amarna that Jamal told us about. First off, it was halfway back to Cairo."

"I could have told you that," replied Jamal.

"Well, you should have," Gina retorted and then continued, "Anyway, we rented a car, drove to Amarna, and were checking out the great temple." She looked at Dee. He nodded to her. "We found the grand sanctuary, and it had a throne in it tucked back out of the way. I got this crazy idea." She paused.

"And?" chimed Angelic and Keno at nearly the same time.

"And you know that necklace you bought at the medina, Keno?"

"Yes," replied Keno.

"Well, I admired it, and Angelic gave it to me before she and Jamal left. You know those men in Cyprus asked us about a stone, and we didn't realize what they were talking about? I got the necklace out when we were in the temple looking at the throne. Dee got the idea that the stone might fit in the throne's head. I slipped it into a groove that was cut into the throne, and it fit. "

"Seriously?" called out Jamal.

"Yes, it fit, and the sun hit it just right, at noon, and the light flashed all around the room."

"Just like the mural we saw," said Angelic.

"Yes, and it made a pattern on the wall behind the throne. It highlighted eight rocks. Dee pressed them, and they recessed into the wall, and there was this giant click. But nothing happened."

"Nothing happened?" asked Mike, who was now getting drawn into the story.

"Nothing," Gina replied.

Then Dee stepped into the conversation. "Gina figured out the throne had to be tilted forward as the last step, and the wall separated and a door opened to another room."

"How'd you figure that out?" asked Jamal.

"I fell over the throne," replied Gina, laughing.

Dee resumed, "Anyway, we went into the room, and the light from outside was refracting off of all those shells that were embedded in the walls. It was like a giant disco. The room was basically empty except for some really ornate wall decorations and these two tapestries of the pharaoh and the queen, who looked just like Mike and Keno."

"Seriously?" asked Keno.

"Just like you," replied Gina. Then she continued. "We're looking around and we hear a phone, the first sound we've heard since we got to the site. Dee says to run, and we get out of the room, grab the stone, close the door by moving the throne back, and there's this old guy running at us, yelling."

Dee interrupted her. "Jamal, do you remember that man that helped us change the tire in Algeria?"

"Yeah, an old fellow in desert garb."

"It was him."

"That means they'd been following us all that time," said Angelic.

"Probably from the point when we bought the stone," replied Dee.

"That's so strange. But then what happened?" asked Mike.

Gina continued, "We ran back outside. There were two

identical vehicles, ours and someone else's. We took both of them. They left the keys in it. We drove to Cairo and caught the ship for Istanbul."

"Are they still after you?" asked Jamal.

"I think we lost them, but I expect they will try to track us."

"But why?" asked Keno.

"They seem to think the room is full of treasure," replied Dee.

"But we didn't see it," added Gina.

"One thing." It was Dee again. "I think the stone might be real—real gold on the chain and maybe a real diamond."

"You can't be serious," said Mike.

"I bet he's right," said Jamal. "That makes sense with all the tapestries and murals we saw, and everything that Dr. Toussaint told us. That might make sense of why those men in the medina stared at you, Mike: you look like the pharaoh, and we bought the stone before they could. We made them highly suspicious, and they've been following us ever since. That explains the two guys that Col. Sanchez captured fooling around the castle site. He ran them out of the country, but he said his men followed them to the airport, and they caught flights for Cairo. They were part of the group."

"Why did nobody come after us?" asked Mike.

"Maybe they did," said Angelic. "Did you notice anything while you were in Miami?"

"Nothing that I'm aware of," replied Keno.

"Why are you on a ship? Why didn't you fly someplace safe?" asked Jamal.

"We left the vehicle at the airport and caught a ride with a local to the seaport. I thought it might throw them off. This cruise was the first thing available," replied Dee.

"You know they'll keep coming unless you can disappear completely," said Jamal.

"Probably, but on a slow boat to Istanbul, maybe we can lose them. Plus, if they still think there is treasure, they might expect us to try to find it again. They'll think we're still around the area."

"Maybe," replied Jamal.

"Why don't you fly here?" said Keno, "Surely they wouldn't come after you in your own country, and we have the new house, plenty of room."

"Thank you," replied Gina. "Maybe after we get to Istanbul."

"You guys be careful," said Angelic.

"What are you guys doing, Angelic?" asked Gina.

"Jam is finishing up the cataloging, then trying to decide which job he wants to take. We might stay here in Seville or maybe go to Paris."

They finished the call a few minutes later with everyone saying goodbye.

69

———

REALLY

When they got off the call, Jamal and Angelic were stunned.

"That's so hard to believe, Jam," said Angelic. "That stone looked so much like costume jewelry. The chain was too big, and the gold was too shiny. It's hard to believe it could have been real."

"I agree. I mean, I really thought Professor Toussaint was speculating as to what had happened, even with the hieroglyphics and the murals we found. It's been three thousand years."

"But the family, they stayed interested for hundreds of years. They must have thought it was real."

"Yeah, that part bothered me too. I guess I should call Professor Toussaint. She'll be excited to hear all of this."

"But Dee and Gina said they didn't see any treasure. Just an empty, well-decorated room."

"That alone would have enormous historical value. Somebody else probably took the treasure at the time of the Crusades or whenever."

"Wow. I wonder what it was?"

"No way to know. Whatever the pharaoh valued, maybe a big pile of those seashells."

"You better call Professor Toussaint. You can tell Diego in the morning."

70

COMING INTO FOCUS

Mike and Keno sat talking in the living room of Ike's place. The Henderson's hadn't moved out yet, and Mike and Keno had told them not to be in a hurry. They enjoyed being with Ike and Elizabeth and wanted to spend more time with them before undertaking the move.

"That's wild," said Keno, "that the pharaoh and the queen look like us. We ought to go see that."

"Maybe we could just have Jamal send us a picture?" suggested Mike.

Keno grinned at him. "You're comfortable here, are you?"

Mike reached out and squeezed her leg. "I already knew you were my queen."

"Please…" Keno laughed at him.

Ike and Elizabeth came strolling into the room.

"Hey everybody," called Elizabeth.

"We got a story for you," replied Keno.

Ike and Elizabeth quickly sat down opposite Mike and Keno.

"We just got off the phone with Dee and Gina," started Keno.

"And Jamal and Angelic," added Mike.

Keno punched him in the knee. "Don't interrupt. Anyway, it's a wild story."

She went on to recount for them everything that had happened.

Ike and Elizabeth looked at one another for a moment.

Then Elizabeth spoke, "That part where they asked you about anyone following you. Umm… there was a day at the hotel." she looked at Keno. "You were at the hospital with Mike. It looked like someone had gone through our rooms. Nothing was missing. Things were just in different places than we left them. We thought it was the maid service or the fire alarm, but the front desk said it turned out to be a false alarm, and nobody entered the rooms. "

"Whoever wanted to search the room may have triggered the alarm," added Ike.

"Nothing was missing?" asked Keno.

"Nothing that we ever determined," replied Elizabeth.

"I guess they may have followed us too, then," said Mike.

Keno sat silent for a moment. "I guess so. I mean I'm the one who bought the stone, and I wore it a few times. It would have seemed reasonable that I had it. But I gave it to Angelic right before we left."

"Whoever was following you apparently didn't realize that, and from what you told us, they followed Jamal and Angelic, and Dee and Gina as well, at least until they figured out who had the stone," said Ike.

"And I sent Dee and Gina straight to Amarna," sighed Jamal. "No wonder those guys thought Dee and Gina knew something."

71

NEXT STEP

After they ended the call, Dee and Gina sat and talked for a few minutes.

"It's incredible how all those circumstances came together," said Gina.

"Yeah, we walked right into it without even knowing. When did you get an idea about the stone?"

"I didn't, really. I couldn't believe that was what they were after. Once those men in Cyprus questioned us, I considered it, but it just didn't seem possible."

"Well, here we are."

"Yes." She smiled at him. "And there wasn't any treasure, other than the stone. What happens next?"

Dee stood up and paced the room. "We travel overnight to Haifa and spend a day there. Then it's a little over two days to Istanbul."

"Are we going to hang out on the ship or do you have something else in mind?"

"It's a one-day stay. The ship picks up tour groups. For an excursion, we'd have to be back by the afternoon, as the ship will depart that evening." He paused. "I didn't really want to hang out on the ship all day. I thought maybe we should get out and be tourists."

"You don't think it's safer to hide?"

"It could be, but I don't want to be trapped on the ship or in the room. At least if we're out and about, we can run if they see us. I don't think they can catch up that quick."

She nodded. "I hope you're right."

72

BACK ON TRACK

The two men just back from Spain had been busy. They didn't want to feel Amir's wrath.

They had spent the last night tracking routes, schedules, and exits from the country. They had called one of the group members who worked for the state transportation agency. He had pulled the data for them to review.

"The couple hasn't shown up at the temple again and they've not been seen in the area," said one man.

"Yeah, I think they're on the run," replied the other.

"Amir still thinks they will come back."

"I think he is mistaken."

"Are you going to tell him?"

"Not until we find them."

"The men at the temple are growing restless."

"It can't be helped. There's something odd about these tourists. They don't act like treasure hunters."

"How could they have known about the room? Why did they run?"

"They were afraid. We confronted them in Cyprus, but they openly continued on to Amarna. That doesn't seem like the actions of treasure hunters. They would have been more covert."

"Amarna was basically empty until we got there. And they found the treasure room. Our people have been searching for it for thousands of years. They had to have known something."

"Perhaps, but they went on the run. They didn't stay. Maybe there was no treasure."

"Do not speak of that. Amir would surely kill us. You heard what he did to Ahmed."

The other man shook his head. He was the one who had stayed up the longest, until he found the tourists' names: Sanders and Dubulgee. He was grateful. Amir would be pleased. The man didn't want to speak of his thought that if the tourists ran, there was no reason to stay. There was no treasure. It was unthinkable.

"What did he do?" the man interrupted his thoughts to ask.

"He struck Ahmed repeatedly, nearly killed him. He is an old man. That wasn't necessary. Ahmed only saw what he saw."

"I agree, but let us speak of this no more. I shall call Amir and give him the news."

"Since we found them, I suppose he'll send us after them?"

"It is likely. He can't send the others. They have seen them. Yes, it will surely be us."

"I'll tell my wife."

73

ROMAN HOLIDAY

They awoke the next morning. Despite it all, Dee had slept well. It might have been that he was worn out from the excitement of the day before.

Gina rose, yawning. "I tossed and turned all night. I couldn't stop thinking about everything. I think you're right. We should go do something. I'll lose my mind sitting in this room all day."

They ate a quick breakfast and checked on available tours. They were all half-day. At least that would be something.

"There's a tour to Caesarea," said Dee. "It's about a half hour from here. Short ride; it's along the water; should be scenic; there's a large site of Roman ruins."

Gina rolled her eyes at him. "If that's what you want. Along the water?"

"Sitting seaside," he replied.

"Maybe it will be fun."

They boarded the bus shortly afterward and took the brief ride. After arriving at the entrance gates, they got in line with all the other tourists.

They stood and looked out to sea as they moved forward to be paired with a tour guide.

Once started, the guide droned on and on about the site. They were on an avenue that had been recreated as a place for the tour to begin. It was lined with the surviving portions of columns, sat upright, with busts of prominent leaders or figures of interest from the era mounted on the column tops. It was a visual pantheon of Roman figureheads.

Dee had glanced around the grounds several times and among the crowd. So far, he'd seen nothing that looked threatening. He could see Gina doing the same thing but also enjoying the sunshine.

In the distance, they saw an aqueduct leapfrogging its way along the sea.

"How's that work?" asked Gina.

"Even though it appears level to the eye, there's a slight decline in the trough at the top so that the water is gravity-fed," replied Dee.

"That's cool. Must have taken forever to build."

"Yeah. I think it took a while; the builders were clever, but they used lead liners, which eventually made several emperors crazy."

"Really? You're not making that up? Lead does that?"

"Really, yes, lead does that. It made them crazy over time as the lead leached into the water."

They had dropped a little behind their tour group, and they hustled to catch up as the group approached an amphitheater.

Dee moved a little closer to where he could listen to the guide.

What he heard was that once this had been a theater, but the whole thing was basically a reconstruction, and they had left the back wall off to show what both a theater and an amphitheater would look like.

Dee thought, *That's kind of bogus.* He turned to look for Gina to see what she thought, but she wasn't behind him. He glanced around quickly through the crowd, looking for her.

Then he raised his eyes and saw her still standing at the top of the amphitheater, looking out to sea.

"Gina," he called, though he didn't say it very loudly. She looked down at him immediately.

Maybe not so bogus after all. The acoustics are still exceptional, even in a reconstruction, he thought.

He waved to her, and then he saw them.

Two men in desert garb stood just below him on the sand behind the floor of the amphitheater, watching him.

"Run," he called to her, and he saw her take off as he bolted across the floor and jumped to the sand on the far end of the theater, away from the two men.

Dee started down the beach and saw Gina coming from the hillside, running through the streets at an angle to catch up with him.

He looked back and saw the two men jogging after him. Their lack of pace concerned him. Were there more of them?

He raced toward the circus or hippodrome. *Funny, almost,* he thought. *The site of ancient Roman horse and chariot races, and here we are racing toward it.*

Gina came up from the side, and he slowed until she caught up to him.

"Where did they come from?" she panted.

"I don't know. I got to the floor of the amphitheater, and they were standing there on the ground, looking up at me. I wasn't sure at first, but they were watching me so closely, and they looked familiar or similar to the others we saw before. I knew it had to be them."

"They sure got their information fast. What are we going to do? Where are we going?"

They jumped a small wall and ran across the sand, parallel to the sea.

"Right now, we are running across the circus, where the ancient Romans held chariot races."

"It'd be nice to have a chariot about now."

"Yeah," replied Dee as he turned and watched the two men approach the wall. Dee noted that he and Gina were almost halfway across the track.

They turned and sprinted on, and Dee thought, *Here we are racing across the sand where chariots once thundered and crowds roared as participants competed with one another, often to the death. Now it's just sand, sun, silent stone, and us, hoping that this won't end in our death.*

They reached the far end of the circus and climbed over the small retaining wall.

Dee saw a sign that indicated the next structure was a Roman bathhouse.

"Let's go in there." He looked at the sign, which had a diagram of the building. "It's long, and there are several levels. Go to the far end. We'll wait until the men enter this end, and then we'll run down to the beach, near the shoreline, and head back to the bus. Maybe there'll be a cab or something to get us to the ship."

Gina nodded, too winded or scared to speak.

74

THE RUNNING MAN

They had been correct. Amir had told them to go to Haifa and follow the couple, to intercept them if possible and regain the stone. "Do not be shy," had been Amir's words.

While the younger of the two men had been anxious, even eager, to encounter the couple and seize the stone, the older man was troubled. What good would it do them to acquire the stone and be implicated in its theft, or arrested? They would have to be careful. He hoped he could control the younger man's fervor.

They had worked through the night to locate the tourists and then reported the findings to Amir. He had immediately sent them after the couple. The men had made arrangements and flown on a small plane to the Haifa airport. From there, they had gone to the docks.

Again, it had been a simple matter of remaining out of sight and watching for the couple, who had appeared and boarded the tour bus for Caesarea. The men had taken a cab to the site and then worked their way down to the amphitheater.

The older of the two men was still concerned and

confused. He just wanted to talk to the tourists. But they always ran. They were scared. Yet they came out in public and didn't remain hidden on the ship. It made no sense to him. He didn't believe they were treasure hunters, but they seemed to have the stone. He had to talk to them before things got out of hand with Amir.

If they hadn't seen the couple, it would have forced them to purchase tickets and sail to Istanbul. The man hoped they could resolve the issue in Haifa.

The two men could not keep up with Dee and Gina. One was older, and neither of them was a runner. The man appreciated that Amir had sent only the two of them and not a larger force, which would have undoubtedly attracted attention.

As they pursued the couple across the track, the man saw them run into the adjacent building. He watched the building to see if the couple would emerge as he and the other man drew nearer.

Confident that the couple was still within the building, the man slowed to look at the sign and the drawing of the building. It was a bathhouse. There were multiple levels, with many places to hide.

Just as he was about to suggest to the younger man that he remain outside and watched to see if the couple exited, the younger man called to him, "Come on, let's go. We are so close." The younger man bolted inside the building.

The older man would have preferred to enter alone and quietly seek out the couple. But he was afraid to remain outside and let the younger man bull through the building. They did not need a public incident.

He followed the younger man inside.

75

BY THE POOL

Dee stood concealed at the far end of the bathhouse and watched the two men approach from the other side. He waved to Gina, and they slipped along the outside of the building toward the end where the men had just entered. Dee peered around the corner and found both men had gone inside. It had been his fear that one man would remain outside. Dee hoped the men had a few moments to progress into the building and weren't standing at the door watching.

When he saw no one, Dee motioned to Gina to move a few feet back the way they had come. They could then run for the beach unobserved from either end of the building.

They reached the shore after a few moments and turned back toward the site. Running parallel to the race track, they saw Herod's Palace coming up in front of them.

They were about to veer left toward the amphitheater when they heard voices shouting at them. Dee turned to see the two men gaining on them diagonally. He veered back to the right, and Gina followed.

Dee ran along Herod's Palace and, as the men got closer, he ran out on the pool walls. Herod's Palace had originally been enormous. There was little left of it other than a few footers. Near the shore, Herod had installed a freshwater swimming pool that sat right on the sea. It was still plainly visible with the walls defining its shape and size. Dee ran down the right side of the pool.

"Where are we going?" called out Gina, who followed along behind him.

"Keep running," Dee called back.

The two men closed the distance and continued after them.

When Dee reached the end of the pool, he turned and ran along the back wall that faced the sea. Gina followed.

If they could make it to the far side, they could jump to the sand and run for the amphitheater.

The two men following them started down the first side of the pool. As they saw Dee turn onto the opposite side and realized what he would do, the younger of the two men jumped in the pool to cut the couple off.

Dee wasn't sure how deep the pool may have been originally, but it wasn't much more than ankle-to knee-deep now. But it was very rocky and treacherous-looking, likely slick.

When the younger of the two men chasing them jumped into the pool, he immediately slipped and called out as he fell.

The other man stopped.

Dee and Gina continued to run. They jumped from the far wall and ran for the amphitheater.

Dee looked back to see the one man, who must have waded into the pool, helping the fallen man to his feet.

He turned to Gina. "Run for the entrance. Let's get back to the ship."

76

THE SLIPUP

The younger man was only a few feet inside the door of the bathhouse, and the older man called out to him quietly. "Stop, here."

The younger man held up.

"They could easily have been watching us and are waiting for us to go further inside, then they'll run out the other door. Let us stand here for a moment and see if they don't emerge."

"But they may escape if we don't continue to follow them."

"Escape to where? Be patient. We have waited this long."

They stood inside for a moment, the older man watching out the window and the younger man scanning the interior of the building.

"I don't like this."

The older man held up his hand. Then he stepped outside the entrance while staying close to the building. He looked down toward the water, and there they were, running with their backs toward him.

The younger man stuck his head through the door.

The older man waved to him. "Move slowly, and we will walk along the top of the track and then cut across at the palace to trap them."

They executed their plan to perfection, emerging from the hippodrome nearly on top of the couple.

The older man had not anticipated the tourists would run around the pool. They had to get to the exit. Perhaps they could trap the couple by the pool. It would be a great place to talk in private. He knew that if they made it to the far side, the couple could jump and run.

He had just thought to stop and proceed back to the palace side of the structure when the younger man jumped in the pool.

———

THE YOUNGER OF THE TWO MEN SAT IN THE WATER, HIS ankle throbbing. He thought he'd seen a clear spot to land and a path to the other side. He could have cut them off. But he'd hit something, a rock or a patch of gravel, and slipped.

The leg hurt so badly he didn't think he could walk. He looked up, and the older man was wading slowly toward him. The couple had gotten away again.

He looked up toward the site and saw them crossing the amphitheater. He and his partner would have to continue pursuing them to Istanbul.

The older man reached his fallen comrade. "Give me your arm. Can you stand?"

The younger man shook his head.

The older man stooped, placed his arms around the shoulders of his partner, and slowly pushed his way up.

They hobbled from the pool and started toward the amphitheater.

"We will have to sail with them now?" the younger man asked.

"Most certainly," replied the other.

77

BACK IN SIGHT

Dee and Gina caught a cab at the entrance to the site and were taken immediately back to the ship. Afterwards, they cleaned up and stayed in the room.

In the early evening, when they got hungry, Dee offered to go alone and find some takeout or to-go food from the buffet. The ship had departed, and they would be at sea for two and a half days.

He put on khakis and a shirt and wore a ball cap on his head. Moving slowly, he tried to evaluate the surroundings as he went.

There was nothing out of the ordinary, and he saw no sign of the two men or anyone he thought might have accompanied them.

When he returned to the room with food, they ate ravenously.

"What are we going to do?" asked Gina.

"Lie low for a day and see if anyone is on board with us."

"There's not much to do."

"Try to relax, rest up, read, plan. When we get to Istanbul, I think it's time to fly far away."

"Maybe Key West, stay with Mike and Keno or Ike and Elizabeth?"

"Or we could rent our own place. We'll call them tomorrow night and make arrangements."

Gina leaned back on the bed. "Maybe we could take a stroll later this evening, well after dark?"

"Maybe. I don't think it helps at this point to be seen together. They're looking for a couple. A single may not register with them."

"Okay, but do you really think they'd attack us on the ship? I mean, the smartest thing might be to go to dinner and see what we see, or let them see us and hopefully we see them. We're on board a ship. There are a lot of people. "

Dee thought about it for a moment. "So you think the best plan is to take it to them, go on the offensive?"

Gina smiled at him. "We'd at least know where we stand. I don't think I can sit in this cabin for two and a half days."

Dee smiled back at her. "All right, we'll go to the meals but stay close to crowds. We'll see what we see, starting in the morning."

Gina nodded her agreement.

In the morning they did just that, and they saw nothing. They repeated the process at lunch to the same result.

At dinner that night, they again sat at a crowded table and moved around enough to study the passengers. They saw nothing that concerned them. Afterwards, they talked as they strolled the deck, always in sight of another couple or a crew member.

"Maybe when that guy fell they had to stop?" asked Gina.

"Maybe, or maybe it held them up enough that they didn't make the ship, or maybe they didn't plan to take the ship with us. I still think they're out there. I don't see them quitting."

At breakfast the next morning, there were no signs of anyone, nor at lunch. Back in their cabin, Gina announced, "I've got to get out of this room. I want to go sit by the pool. Come with me."

Dee looked up at her. "I'm not sure that's a good idea."

"Come on, just for a little while. I'm about to go crazy in here, and we haven't seen a thing."

"All right," he replied.

She smiled. "Let me show you something."

He shrugged. "Okay."

She took a few minutes, and he noticed she was changing into her swimsuit. It was the blue thong he'd first seen her in on the slice cruise.

When Gina had it on, she bent and reached into her purse. Pulling out the necklace, she slipped it over her head. The stone settled in her cleavage at the bikini's neckline. It sparkled in the sunlight.

"What do you think?" she asked. "It looks good, doesn't it?"

"Yes, it does. Oh, you mean the stone," he added.

She reached across and punched his shoulder. "Get ready." She slipped her cover-up on.

Dee fooled around for a moment and then got into his suit. "I don't think we'll need anything," he said. "We can't stay long."

Gina frowned at him. "Okay."

They started for the pool.

Once they were settled in a couple of deck lounges, Gina went to take her cover-up off and realized she was still wearing the necklace. So she left the cover on and stretched out her legs.

They sat for a while, and Dee ordered them drinks.

"I'm sweating hard. It's good we're not staying long," he said.

Gina nodded. *It is hot,* she thought.

Glancing around the pool she saw no one who seemed out of the ordinary. Mostly it was couples like her and Dee.

Okay, why not? She reached inside the cover-up and pushed the stone more firmly between her breasts. No sense in really flashing it around. She eased the cover-up off and laid back.

Dee saw it in a moment. "Gina, you've still got the stone on," whispered Dee.

"Yeah, I forgot to take it off, and now I don't have anywhere to put it," she replied. "It's mostly hidden."

Dee smiled at her. "Yeah, the stone is, but the chain is pretty visible."

Gina hadn't thought about that.

"Okay, I'll put my cover-up back on."

Dee glanced around the pool quickly, as Gina had done. He had to admit she looked great, and so did the stone, and so did both of them together.

"I suppose a couple of minutes won't hurt. We'll need to leave soon."

PUTTING A SHINE ON IT

The two men hobbled to the entrance of the site and hailed a cab. The older man knew the ship would leave at dusk and that they would have to be back on board by late afternoon. He asked the cab driver, "My friend slipped on the site. Is there a nearby clinic that would be quick to examine him? We need to get back to our cruise ship."

The driver nodded. "There is one on the way; we can stop there, and I can stay, if you like?"

"Yes, thank you," replied the older man.

And so it had been. They had stopped, been examined quickly, and were told that it was a sprain, to use ice, and to stay off of it for a day. Shortly afterward, they were back on the ship.

"There are some shops. I will get a few things for you and some clothes so that we can better blend in on board the ship," said the older man as the younger one struggled to get comfortable.

The older man left the room and went to the shops. He tried to be quick, trying on a few items and leaving them on to minimize being seen in his desert garb. He bought some other things for his younger accomplice. They would only be on the ship for two days.

His most intriguing purchase was a small-brimmed straw fedora and some mirrored glasses. *No one will see me now*, he thought. He paired them with a bright print shirt and, much to his chagrin, some linen shorts and sandals. He looked the part of a tourist as he reviewed himself in the mirror.

He got food for them that evening, and they slept after reporting briefly to Amir that the tourists were still on board the boat and that they would follow along. Amir was not happy.

————

AMIR, BACK IN LUXOR, HAD DECIDED TO HANDLE THE ISSUE himself. He would fly to Istanbul alone and meet the tourists there. If he could coerce them into telling him how they had entered the room, perhaps he would not need the others. There did not appear to have been any booby traps, as the couple had entered the room and left rather quickly. *If that old fool Ahmet had paid better attention or been faster, all this wouldn't have been necessary.*

————

THE FOLLOWING MORNING, AFTER MAKING SURE HIS YOUNGER accomplice was comfortable, the older man went to the pool and parked himself in the shade. He kept his hat and glasses on. He angled his chair where he could see everyone coming or going without moving his head. The biggest issue came later in the day as he grew weary and struggled to stay awake. But he saw nothing.

That night, the younger man still complained of his ankle. The older one suggested he double up on the prescription medication the doctor had issued him at the clinic.

"There is no need for you to be moving about. I have seen nothing. I am perfectly located to see the activity on the ship. They do not appear to be getting out."

"Are we sure they are still on the ship?" the younger man asked.

The idea had occurred to the other man. "I should think so," he replied, although he had little confidence at this point. "I shall look for them again tomorrow, and perhaps they will feel more comfortable and appear."

"If they do, you should just take the stone."

The older man shook his head in agreement as the younger nodded off to sleep, the additional pain medication kicking in for him.

Once the young man was asleep, the older man left the cabin and strolled the decks. He didn't have a plan, but he was looking for one—places to hide, places to observe, more traffic, less traffic. He wasn't sure what he might need, should they reappear. He only knew that time was running out.

The following morning, he parked himself at the pool again. The early hours passed by uneventfully, but then, after lunch, suddenly, there they were.

She had a cover-up on, and he was wearing swim trunks. They had no bag. *That might have been helpful,* he thought. *Perhaps I could have relieved them of it.* Surely the woman carried the stone around with her.

The man sat watching the couple for some time, occasionally swiveling his head so as not to stare or fall asleep.

Late in the afternoon, the woman pulled her cover-up off. The man nearly choked and raised a hand to his mouth to suppress the sound and appear to cough.

The stone was around her neck. He could clearly see the

chain. When she turned in her seat, the man saw the chain disappear into her cleavage. She was wearing the stone. He couldn't quite believe it. After all this time, and his own doubts about whether the couple really had the artifact. Now, them being in the temple, and what Ahmed saw, finally registered with him as being valid, as being a real opportunity. The man squirmed in his chair. He was so close.

He watched the couple for the rest of the afternoon.

79

SUNSET

They ended up staying the rest of the afternoon. The weather was wonderful: high blue sky, good temperature, light breeze. They actually relaxed.

Late in the afternoon, Gina finally said, "I'm hungry. Can we eat casual, outside?"

Dee nodded. "There's an open-air café on the next deck."

They got up, turned their towels in, and started for the restaurant.

Sitting near the rail, they watched the late-afternoon sun across the water. Everything was golden, including the chain on Gina's neck. Dee glanced at the chain and then followed it as far as he could see.

"That really is a beautiful stone. I can see why they wanted it even if there is no treasure."

"Yes, it is," replied Gina, pulling it up slightly. "But we bought it in the medina, across the country. I don't see how that happened. Or even why this stone worked. Could there be another?"

"I wouldn't think so. It fit perfectly in the throne, didn't it?"

Gina nodded.

"Maybe like Jamal said, one of the Crusaders or somebody came to possess it over time, and it moved around. It's hard to know."

They ate as the light grew fainter and the sky lit up from the sun set. They agreed to stay and sit through twilight, then go back to their cabin.

They got up to make their way back to the room.

"Let's walk on the deck for a moment," said Gina. "It's so beautiful right now."

Dee nodded, and they strolled down the deck away from the restaurant.

Dee suddenly realized, "I left my phone on the table. Let me run back and get it. Don't move, okay?"

Gina smiled at him. "I'll be right here." She waved him away.

80

———

THE APPROACH

The man watched the couple until they got up to leave. Then he followed only a few seconds afterward. It was getting late, and people were leaving the pool. He followed along behind and was grateful there were other passengers milling about.

When he saw them take a seat at the café, he waited at the maître d's stand and asked for a table near the window. He could deliberately sit with his back to them and see them in the glass reflection.

As he was about to be seated, he asked the server if he could run to his room for a minute, but ordered a tea and asked for a menu.

"I'll be right back," he said.

The server nodded, and the man hurried to his room. Upon entering, he called to the younger man. "Can you walk?"

The younger man climbed to his feet and shook his head enthusiastically. "Yes, I've been moving around the cabin this afternoon."

"Good. It is time. The couple is on the café deck, and the woman has the stone around her neck. We must get it."

The younger man was visibly excited. "We will not fail," he called as he hobbled toward the door.

The men made their way back to the café area.

"I have a seat," the older man said. "You go on down the deck and keep watch."

The younger man hobbled away.

The older man returned to his seat and ordered dinner.

The couple sat for a long time. The man ate slowly, then ordered dessert, then coffee. He was getting very full when the couple finally rose to leave.

They started down the deck toward where his younger companion was waiting. This concerned the man, but they were close now to finally possessing the stone.

He rose and started behind them. If only his companion would stand on the deck by the rail, they could pen the couple between them.

He sped up his pace as the couple moved around the deck. The lights of the ship had come up as the evening had fallen dark.

81

WAITING AND WATCHING

Gina stood by the rail, watching the evening sky. It was beautiful in this part of the world.

Maybe she had been too hard on Dee. He seemed to genuinely care for her. She'd made him miserable several times, but he'd endured it.

Her mind was drifting along with the stars, and she wasn't paying close attention to the people passing her by.

———

DEE WAS IN A HURRY TO GET BACK TO THE RESTAURANT AND grab his phone. He didn't want to leave Gina alone for long. There didn't seem to be any problems on board the ship, but there was always something. Dee had a feeling that he couldn't put to rest.

He passed several people on the way back to the restaurant. The pleasant evening had brought out several strollers.

Dee slowed a little. This was all too crazy. Surely Gina would be fine for a couple of minutes.

———

GINA NOTICED LITTLE AS A MAN LIMPED UP TO HER. SHE turned and smiled at him. His face was harsh as was his voice. "Where is the stone? Give it to me. I must have it."

Gina gasped and leaned back, but the rail had her penned on one side and the man was standing on the other side. She looked up quickly but did not see Dee returning.

"What are you talking about?" she asked.

"We know you have it. You were seen wearing it earlier today."

"Wearing what? I was at the pool all afternoon."

"And that is where you were seen wearing it. I have no more time; do not make me take it."

He took a step closer.

"I'm going to scream," she stammered.

"Not for long," he replied.

82

WHERE IS HE?

As the man pursued the couple from the café, he saw the male returning toward him. Fortunately, there were other people, and when they passed one another, there was no recognition by the male. The man observed that the male of the couple seemed in a hurry. Maybe he'd forgotten something at the restaurant. It wouldn't take long to recover whatever it was and get back to the woman.

This was their chance. He sped up to get to the woman and his partner. He saw them not far away and ducked into a hallway. He wanted to appear quickly and behind his partner. He popped out another door and found the woman against the rail. His partner stood with his back to the man, blocking him from sight by the woman.

This was perfect. Now for the stone.

———

THE HOBBLING MAN GRABBED GINA'S NECK BEFORE SHE could get a scream out. He had stepped closer while they were talking, and she had nowhere to go.

They struggled. She clawed him, and he squeezed her neck with one hand while tearing at her cover-up with the other. He was going for the necklace, though to the casual observer it might have seemed otherwise.

She tried to knee him, but he had gotten close enough that her blows did not have any strength.

Gina looked up for Dee again, but the passageway beyond her was empty.

The man grabbed the chain and jerked it up so that the stone lodged beneath Gina's chin. She gasped, sputtered, and flayed her arms. *If only I had been paying a little more attention and not let him get so close.*

He had the chain now, and he was forcing it over her head while he continued to choke her. She was getting fainter, trying to breathe, while she struggled.

The man pulled the chain over her head and toward his body. The stone dragged across her throat and bounced off her chin before coming free.

He held it aloft. The stone sparkled in the moonlight, and his eyes grew bright as he pushed Gina against the rail, freeing her from his grasp.

She gasped for a breath, her hands to her neck, but still having presence of mind, she stepped forward and kneed the man in the groin. Only it wasn't a direct hit. She was out of breath and he was a little taller than her, and the glancing blow only caught him partially.

He slung his arm wildly, slapping her in the face. She had ducked but saw his hand coming with the chain in it, and she had taken the slap to re-grab the chain. She caught his palm, bit the back of his hand, and wrenched the chain free.

He lunged at her and, catching her shoulder, pushed her body back into and up the side of the railing. He went to grab the stone from her again, and she pulled it close to her chest, causing her balance to teeter backward.

The man grabbed for her, but it was too late. Her momentum pulled her over the side and him up on the railing as he lost his grip on her.

———

THE SECOND MAN HAD BEEN WATCHING ALL THIS FROM THE shadow of the railing.

It did not look good. His accomplice had lost the chain and the stone. The man had seen it in the girl's hands as she had gone overboard. All was lost. Except they still had to clean up the mess.

He stepped quickly behind his accomplice and kidney punched him hard. The man flinched, and when he did so, the older man pushed the younger one across the rail, and he followed Gina into the sea.

Then the older man slid back into the shadow. Problem solved. If they found them, two dead bodies, they would assume robbery or rape. No questions, case closed, fortune lost. But he could walk away.

Then there was a scream.

He looked quickly. There was a group of older women, and then the man of the couple burst through the throng, took a couple of steps, and dove over the side of the ship.

I've seen it all now, the man thought. *Three dead bodies.*

The women were shrieking, "Man overboard, woman overboard!" Alarms went off, and the man felt the ship slowing, so he slipped away into the night.

83

GONE SWIMMING

Dee sped up again. Something didn't feel right. He was near running when he saw a group of elderly women in front of him and went to slow down. But then he heard their cries of "Overboard," and he burst through the throng.

He saw Gina as she was toppling, and he thought he would carry that image with him for the rest of his life, but then the man went over too, which made little sense. Dee broke through the throng without thinking about it. He went over the side in a graceful dive that arched him away from the ship. It was a long way down, and he had enough time to think of his form and pray that he hit the water correctly.

He did, but he went a long way under, and it took several seconds to reach the top.

He surfaced and called for Gina. He heard a faint cry many yards away and swam for it. The two people had gone over close to one another and were probably near one another in the water.

Dee noticed the ship had slowed, and he hoped it would put out help. The landing had taken some of his wind as well and had smacked him hard even when he had hit properly.

He swam with strong strokes to the area of the sound. When he got to where he thought it was, he found nothing: no sound, no people. He called out twice more. Dee heard only the ship, which appeared to be launching a lifeboat.

He looked around quickly again and then dove under the water and down.

A body hovered just a few feet below the surface. Dee spun it around, already knowing that it was a man. Yes, it was one of the two men who had chased them in Caesarea. His neck was broken, his head at an odd angle. He had not landed well when he'd hit the water.

Dee spun away and dove again. He faced nothing but darkness. He kicked deeper and thought he might have seen movement. He kicked again and felt Gina's leg. He turned her upright, and her head lolled back.

He could mouth breathe to her, but if she had a blockage or had inhaled too much water, that would only make matters worse.

Dee wrapped an arm around her shoulders and kicked for the surface. He had been under for some time, and he had dived deeply. He looked into Gina's face and thought, *Don't you die on me,* remembering once before he had lost a young boy to drowning.

He kept kicking for the surface but felt faint. There wasn't enough ambient light to give him any encouragement, and for just a moment he thought, *At least we're together,* which morphed into, *We're not going to die.*

Dee wasn't sure how far he was or how far he had to go, but with his lungs burning, he breathed into Gina's mouth. It might be the wrong thing, but it might also be the right one to keep her alive.

He leaned forward, exhaled slowly, and felt dizziness overtake him.

84

WAKE UP CALL

Gina woke up. She was in a bed in what looked like an infirmary. She couldn't see anyone else. Then she remembered the struggle, the fall, the water, Dee.

She couldn't see or hear anyone, so she reached for the call button and held it down.

In only seconds, a nurse came running into the room. "What's wrong?" the nurse cried out.

"Dee. Where is Dee?" Gina asked.

The nurse stopped. "Now lie back. You need to rest. I assume you mean the man who saved you?"

Gina nodded, not sure what to say.

"He's in another room."

"He's okay, then?"

"He's alive."

"What are you telling me?" Gina pleaded.

"The doctor will be along shortly now that you are awake. He can explain it better."

The nurse left the room.

Gina sat up in the bed, watching the clock tick: five minutes, ten minutes, fifteen minutes. She was about to ring the call button again when the door opened and a doctor walked into the room. He was an older man who looked as if he should have already been retired.

"How are you?" he asked. "I'm Doctor Roberts, Harlan Roberts. A pleasure to meet you, Ms. Dubulgee."

Gina looked at him. "It's my pleasure too, to meet anyone at this point. What happened?"

"You nearly drowned. A young, strong man, apparently of your acquaintance, saved you. You had taken on water, but he got you to the surface and kept you alive."

Gina looked down, rubbing her fingers together. "How is he?"

The doctor shrugged his shoulders. "Alive, but not as well as you."

"What happened to him?"

"It seems he had an oxygen shortage rather than taking on water. In his struggle to get you both to the top, he nearly asphyxiated."

"You mean he nearly drowned?"

"Yes, that's exactly what I mean. You're a very lucky young lady."

85

LUCKY MAN

The man was now alone in his room. Everything had wrapped up, and the ship would dock soon. There was no evidence, and while he had lost a partner, the stone had also been lost. The man understood that the woman's companion had saved her. *Unbelievable.* He didn't know their exact circumstances at this point but didn't want to arouse curiosity by asking too many questions. He had simply eavesdropped at breakfast and learned what he needed.

He had called Amir the night before, after the accident, and told him the stone was lost. There had been a long silence before Amir responded that now that they knew there was a room, they would determine a way to enter it and claim the treasure.

The man was glad for that but had also been surprised to learn that Amir was in Istanbul already, awaiting him. This news had made the man more than a little nervous.

GINA WAS UP AND ABOUT. THEY HAD RELEASED HER LATER that day after she'd talked to the doctor. She and Dee were still on board the ship, which would be at harbor for another couple of days for cleaning and resupply. They had allowed Dee to stay until either the doctor released him or they were ready to resume.

Most of the passengers were gone, and the ship was quiet. Gina spent most of her time at Dee's side.

As she was sitting there, the doctor—Harlan Roberts, he had said his name was—came in to check on Dee.

"Will he be all right? Will he live?" she asked the doctor.

"That's hard to say," replied the doctor. "He's in a coma. There doesn't seem to be any brain damage, but he just doesn't respond. Mr. Sanders must have been a phenomenal swimmer. The rescuers indicated that he may have been without oxygen for several minutes."

Gina looked at the doctor. She held Dee's hand as she did. "He once told me he could hold his breath for over three minutes. That there were Greek sponge divers that could go nearly twice that long."

The doctor nodded. "I've heard that, although I'd suspect that is under certain nuanced conditions of work and not a rescue attempt. The heart and the lungs can get very amped up in crisis situations."

"So what do you think?" she asked.

"I think he had a really strong reason to live, something he wanted to live for." The doctor looked at Gina and saw a single tear running down her face. He continued, "Would you know anything about that?"

She looked up at him, tears now streaming down her face, but she didn't speak.

"I thought so!" the doctor replied and smiled at her. "He's quite the lucky man."

So she sat with him. For the rest of that day, through the

night and into the next day. She held his hand. She pressed it to her cheek. She whispered under her breath to him, but mostly, she sat.

Late the following morning, he gave a soft sigh and rolled slightly to one side. His eyes fluttered open, but he made no other sound.

Gina suddenly realized she was holding his hand so hard it was turning blue, and she jumped up to press the call button, but he held her firmly. He brought her hand slowly to his lips and kissed her fingers when she tried to speak to him. He nodded and closed his eyes.

She sat there, suddenly knowing that he might be all right, and that he loved her and always had, had nearly given his life for her, and even now, lying there not knowing whether he would live or die, through great effort he had kissed her fingers when he could not speak.

86

NEW KID IN TOWN

The man had left the ship the day before. He had waited as late in the afternoon as possible, but the stewards were escorting everyone ashore. He knew the couple was still in the infirmary, as he'd heard some of the crew members talking about it.

He thought that maybe if he tracked them and could talk to them he might learn something about the treasure room. Anything might help with Amir. Having had the opportunity and lost it was going to make Amir crazy. It was hard to tell who might get hurt.

He had spoken to Amir, who was in Istanbul, but he had not yet met with him. The man wasn't sure why. Amir had told him to stay put and that Amir would call him when it was time to meet.

The man had stayed in the dock area, knowing that the couple would have to disembark the next day as the ship was set to sail the day after that. He stood a good distance from the dock where the ship was harbored and watched the ramp with a monocular.

Little had happened that afternoon. He had cast about

the dock, people-watching, studying the layout, and looking for other places he might stand if he needed to be closer. It was nearing four o'clock.

The couple would have to be leaving soon. He looked again. There they were, on the deck. He pulled back for a moment to catch his breath and removed the monocular from his eye. Something across the dock caught his attention. It was Amir, and he was alone. Standing behind some crates, Amir could see the deck and the ramp, but anyone there could not see him.

The man wondered what was going on. He watched both Amir and the couple as they descended to the dock. Amir maintained his position and did not approach the couple.

As the couple got into a cab, the man watched Amir move into the street and a car pull up for him as well. The man watched both vehicles as they wound their way into the city.

What is Amir up to? Is he going to corner them and talk to them himself? The man doubted Amir would want to do that. There was too much risk.

The man retired to his hotel to wait for Amir to call.

87

OLD HABITS

Dee had been released, and he and Gina left the ship for the hotel. Gina told him they were staying at the Ciragan Palace Kempinski, which was on the water. She had picked it out because she'd thought he'd like it. She had then added that she thought she'd like it too.

As the cab wound through the city, she told him that the hotel was a former Ottoman palace and sat on the edge of the Bosphorus.

"Sounds nice. Do I want to know how much this cost?" he asked and then grinned at her.

"Don't ask, just enjoy," she replied.

After the cab had dropped them off and they had gotten checked into their room, they stood on their balcony overlooking the water.

Dee had his arm around Gina's shoulders, and he looked down at her and said, "This is nice. The view, the room, the company, it's all spectacular."

She smiled up at him. "Yes, it is."

She took a step toward the balcony, turned, and leaned against the railing, which amazed him. She saw him raise his eyes, and she said, "I'm not afraid of the railing, as long as you're here."

He focused his gaze on her eyes.

"I called the others yesterday—Jamal and Angelic, Mike and Keno, Ike and Elizabeth, Diego and Eve. I told them what happened to us and how you nearly died. They are all on their way here. I booked them all suites."

Dee raised a hand to his face and coughed, then muttered, "That's good."

Gina smiled at him. "Yes, it is. They are your friends, and they are concerned about you. Besides, I put it all on my credit card."

He couldn't help but laugh. "It'll be good to see them all, and I'll split it with you."

"Always the Boy Scout," she replied.

"Old habits are the hardest to break."

"And I'm probably only alive today because of it."

He saw a tear in her eye and thought, *This is probably my best chance.*

Dee dropped to one knee and took Gina's hand. "Will you marry me?" he asked.

She grabbed their hands with her free hand and leaned toward him, more tears in her eyes. "I thought you'd never ask." She pulled him to his feet and against her body.

They stood there for a moment, maybe several moments, the night sky sparkling above them and the water shimmering beyond them, alone in their own world.

"Yes," she whispered. "I will most certainly marry you and never let you go."

He hugged her more tightly, and then he spoke. "Well, almost everyone we care about will soon be here. We'd better get busy."

They looked at one another for a moment, and then both said it at the same time: "By the water."

88

TELLING TALES

Amir had finally called and told the man to meet him at the Ciragan Palace Kempinski, and nothing more. The man was confused. That was a luxury resort and former palace. *What is Amir up to? Why does he want me there? I must be cautious.*

————

Amir followed the couple to the hotel. At least they were staying in a nice place. Amir had been there several times in the past. He felt that was an omen and would help him with his plan to "run into" the couple and pump them for information.

He had called his man who had tailed the couple from Egypt. There had been two of them, and now there was only one. Perhaps if he was unneeded after Amir had learned all he wanted to know, there would be none. Amir still believed in the volume and the proximity of the treasure. It would soon be his alone.

————

DEE AND GINA WENT TO WORK ON THE PLANNING. NOT surprisingly, the hotel was fully prepared and had held numerous weddings on the grounds. They dedicated part of their event staff exclusively to planning.

Dee was grateful. He was perfectly willing to hand it over completely to Gina. But she wanted his participation.

They had a day and a half from Dee's proposal before the others arrived. They wanted to have almost everything ready and surprise their guests with the ceremony.

They were crossing the lobby of the hotel the following afternoon when they heard a voice call out, "Dee, Gina."

Turning, they saw Dr. Younes Arazi striding across the lobby.

"Dr. Arazi," said Dee as he turned to shake hands.

Dr. Arazi reached them, shook hands with Dee, and clasped Gina by the shoulder. "It's so wonderful and amazing to see you here," said Dr. Arazi. "How is your friend?"

"The fevers went away. Dr. El Aynaoui couldn't find anything. They just stopped," replied Gina.

"Well, I'm happy they stopped, but I'm sorry to hear he found nothing," replied Dr. Arazi. "Perhaps Mike should have stayed with us." He grinned at them both.

"What are you doing here?" asked Gina.

"A small conference. It is a beautiful facility. Have you been here before?"

"No, Gina picked it out; and yes, it is amazing." Dee was about to consider telling the doctor of their upcoming wedding, but he paused.

"I understand you both have had some fascinating experiences on your travels."

Dee's internal radar went off. He didn't have to look at Gina to sense that hers had too.

"We've just been traveling," replied Dee.

"Italy, Greece, Egypt—those are impressive travels."

"Just seeing the sights," said Gina.

"Let me buy you a drink. I have a few moments; I'd love to hear about it," suggested the doctor.

Dee and Gina glanced quickly at one another, paused for a moment, and then nodded.

"Sounds fun," replied Gina.

Dr. Arazi held out an arm and pointed the way toward one of the hotel bars.

"We'll follow you," answered Dee in return.

89

OBSERVATION

The man had been sitting in the bar looking out into the lobby. He saw Amir call out to the couple, greet them, and chat as friends.

Dr. Younes Amir Arazi was a cunning fellow. He always had been. The man remembered from school that Amir had always gotten the better of anything or anyone he had been involved with. It was how he had become the leader of the group.

They were all descendants of the palace guard from the reign of the pharaoh Akhenaten. They knew there had been a treasure room and a treasure—some had seen it. But over time, the stories lost some details and gained others. Things became distorted, and nothing was ever written down. Now, they were mostly legend.

It had been several generations, and Amarna had been abandoned before the people realized that the treasure was still intact. How did the people know this? King Tut never came for it. He had the wealth of Luxor, Thebes in those days. But he had disowned his father and everything about him.

This development with the couple made the man nervous. If they knew anything, Amir would weasel it out of them. So what was Amir's purpose for him? Why was the man here? He suspected Amir had visions of collecting the treasure only for himself. It was Amir's nature.

The man had been fascinated with the small fedora he had worn on the ship. He had bought another one with a larger brim, which he now wore in the bar. He had half glasses with clear lenses perched on his nose as he looked at the Al-Ahram, Egypt's largest newspaper.

Amir had told him to observe. So he would.

90

BY ANY OTHER NAME

They followed Dr. Arazi into the bar and sat at a small table.

"Let me," said Dr. Arazi, and he ordered them a round of something in Turkish that they couldn't understand. The bartender nodded and scooted away.

The doctor resumed, "Tell me about your travels?"

The couple glanced at each other.

"After we left North Africa, we visited the classical sites in Rome and Athens and went to Egypt," said Gina.

Dr. Arazi nodded without asking questions.

The bartender returned with three glasses of clear liquid. He deposited one with each of them.

"Raki," said Dr. Arazi.

"That's this drink?" asked Dee.

The doctor nodded.

"It looks a little like ouzo."

"It's along those same lines, very potent," replied the doctor. "You'd better be careful," he added with a smile. "It's known to loosen people's tongues." He paused for a moment. "So you went to Egypt?"

"We did," replied Dee. "Stopped in Cairo and saw the pyramids. They were fascinating."

"Yes, I'm sure they were," replied the doctor. "What else did you see?"

"We took the train to Luxor," said Gina. "Then we rented a car and went to Amarna on a day trip."

"Amarna? Really? Not the normal tourist site, if I recall. Anything fascinating?"

"Really not that much left of the site. We poked around the temple a little. That was about it," replied Dee.

Dr. Arazi seemed more interested now, almost intent. He leaned slightly toward them.

"Anything unusual there?"

"We ran across this room. There was a throne in it. We were messing around, and I fell over the throne when Dee called to me. A door opened, and there was another room," answered Gina.

"What did you see?" the doctor asked in an excited voice.

"Nothing," replied Dee. "It was an empty room. I mean, it had a small dais in it, and there were two wall hangings, one of the pharaoh and one of the queen, but otherwise it was empty."

"It was nicely decorated," added Gina. "There was some gold trim and some type of precious stones in the wall. But mostly it was seashells stuck in the wall material. The light reflected off of them and bounced around. It must have been a meeting room or something."

"There was nothing in the room?" whispered Dr. Arazi.

"Nothing," replied Dee.

"And the door just opened for you when you fell over the throne?"

"We had this piece of costume jewelry we'd bought in Tangier, and it was real sparkly," Dee said. "Shame we lost it. There was a cavity in the throne that it fit into, by chance, I guess. We were playing around, but when the sun hit the stone, the light created a pattern on the wall behind the throne. Just for fun, I touched each of the rocks where the light hit. They recessed, but nothing happened. Then Gina fell over the throne and the door opened."

"And you just looked around and left?"

"Well," said Gina, "there was some guy that started yelling at us, probably the guard, because we hadn't seen one until then, and probably weren't supposed to be inside, so we figured we'd better go. It was a long way back to the airport."

Dr. Arazi sat back in his chair. Then he whispered, "That's amazing."

He was thinking, *Could they really have just been tourists? The stone is gone. Maybe another will work.* Everything they had described to him about the room fit the lore he had heard since childhood, except for the fact that there was no treasure. His own men had seen them leave empty-handed and had guarded the site ever since. The couple had not tried to return. It was all unbelievable, unimaginable, after all this time.

He knew from the clinic in Algiers, and their concern for their friend, that they were basically decent people. He did not think them capable of fraud or clever enough for a con.

There was one last thing he thought to try.

"You say this costume jewelry caught the light and made a pattern on the wall?"

"Yes," replied Gina. "It was really wild. The light beams came from the different sides of the stone. There were nine sides, weren't there, Dee?"

Dee paused. "Yeah that's right. I pushed each rock that was highlighted individually."

"And then the throne tilted forward, and the door appeared?"

"Just like that," said Gina.

Dr. Arazi looked at them both and sighed. "That is the most amazing story. Well, I must be going. My meeting will begin soon." He looked at his watch. "I don't want to take any more of your time."

They all rose. He shook hands with Dee and hugged Gina lightly on the shoulders. Then he turned and hurried away.

Gina swiveled to look at Dee. "Yeah," she sighed. "That was amazing. How did he know where we'd been traveling?"

Dee shrugged and smiled.

GET TOGETHER

The man received a call a couple of minutes after Amir left.

"Meet me at the airport as quickly as possible. We have a flight in an hour. We need to get home. There is work to do."

The man was pleased. Apparently, Amir had learned something he thought valuable and still needed help with it. But the man knew now that he would have to be careful in the future. He'd have to keep looking over his shoulder, because Amir would always be there waiting.

***

Everyone arrived the following day. Jamal, Angelic, and Diego were first, just after lunch, followed shortly by Eve Toussaint.

They arrived at the hotel by taxi and were led to their rooms by the bell captain. He provided each of them with Dee and Gina's room number and instructions to call.

Angelic wasted no time. She rang Gina, who picked up quickly.

"Hey, girl. This room—this suite, I should say—is absolutely killer. You are too kind."

"I'm glad you like it. Don't be on the phone; come on up."

Angelic disconnected, and she grabbed Jamal, who was still wandering around the suite. "Get Diego and Eve, and let's go upstairs."

They met at the elevator and rode up to the next floor. They found the room number and knocked. Dee opened up and let them all inside.

Everyone was genuinely happy to see one another and chatted away for the next several hours.

"Mike and Keno and Ike and Elizabeth should be here around dinner. If you all don't mind, let's wait on them to eat. Dee and I have arranged a little treat for us."

Angelic gave her the side-eye. "What are you two up to now?"

"You're just going to have to wait and see," said Dee.

Shortly afterwards, Gina's phone rang again, and this time it was Keno. Gina gave her the same instructions: "Grab everyone and come on up."

In a few minutes, they arrived, and everyone started in again, catching up.

Dee and Gina stood in the center of the room, and everyone got quiet.

"We have a reservation in one of the small dining rooms downstairs. We'll head down in just a minute, but first, Gina has an announcement."

Gina stood silently for a moment, looking at each of the group's faces.

"Dee asked me to marry him, and I said yes."

Angelic and Keno both squealed.

"The wedding is late tomorrow afternoon, down on the beach. You are all our special guests. Now, let's go eat."

***

The next afternoon, the group gathered at the beach. The hotel had wrapped up the final details and provided a Turkish official with the authority to perform the ceremony.

The group was dressed casually and comfortably, as they had not been advised about the wedding beforehand, and while they all indicated they would be happy to purchase formal clothing, Gina had insisted that whatever they had brought with them was perfect.

Dee wore a dark suit, and Gina wore a white dress. There might have been those that thought it inappropriate, but this was a new beginning, and her friends thought she looked beautiful. The dress had slits in the skirt but was not tightly fitted through the body, and had a plunging neckline that was edged in lace with embedded jewels, the biggest of which was enormous and centered in the deepest part of her cleavage. It sparkled like a diamond when it caught the light.

Later that night, after much celebrating and many toasts to their success, and initially breaking up for the evening, the six of them met again in Dee and Gina's room.

"We have really missed all you guys," said Angelic. She sat on the edge of the couch, and Jamal stood behind her with his hands on her shoulders.

"I've got a small announcement as well," he said. "I was offered two jobs, one in Seville and one in Paris, but I've decided I don't want either. Diego and Eve are great friends and I'd enjoy working with either of them. The last few months have been a fabulous experience, but I want to be with my old friends, so I turned them both down."

There were murmurs from the group.

Then Keno spoke up. "We made a decision too." She looked at Mike, and he took her hand. "We closed on a house in Key West. Maybe someday we'll live there, but we want to be with our old friends as well."

Dee raised his glass. "I propose a toast." He paused. "All for one,"

Each of the others raised their glasses and said in unison, "And one for all."

EPILOGUE

Diego and Eve sat at an exclusive restaurant in Istanbul. It was quiet, with soft classical music playing in the background. They could see through a large bay window looking over the Bosphorus.

"It was a beautiful wedding," said Eve. "And it's a beautiful night tonight."

"Yes, it was," replied Diego, "and yes, it is."

"They seemed so well matched. You could tell they were a couple. In fact, you could tell all of them were meant for each other. There's a certain something that well-matched couples have, don't you think, darling?"

"But of course."

"It's really a shame, though, after all we went through with the cataloguing of the Egyptian items and everything Dee and Gina went through."

"What's a shame? It worked out, didn't it?"

"Not really, darling. You see, it was called the Sun Stone for a reason, and as the story goes, it had a special meaning related to the pharaoh's birthday—the month, the day, the time. The stone was the link to those things, based on the timing. There was a rumor that there was a second hidden room inside the first hidden room, and there is where the treasure was kept."

"What?" asked Diego.

"It's hardly valuable information now. The stone is lost," replied Eve. She continued, "You see, the pharaoh was born at night."

"Undoubtedly," replied Diego, arching his eyebrows.

"No, silly, he was literally born at night. So while it is the Sun Stone and its power was directed for Aten, Akhenaten was born at night, and it's the moon's glow on the day and time of his birth that opens the inner door. It's the moon's glow through the stone that reveals the pattern to the treasure. It's the opposite of the power of the sun—it's in the shadow of the moon. Some secrets are void of sunlight." She paused, squeezed his hand knowingly, and smiled. "Sometimes things are best kept hidden."

ENJOY THIS BOOK?

A NOTE FROM AUTHOR LP SNYDER

If you've enjoyed this book, I would be very grateful if you could spend just five minutes leaving a review (it can be as short as you like) on the book's Amazon page and on Goodreads or BookBub.

Thank you very much.

ACKNOWLEDGMENTS

From Author L.P. Snyder

Thanks to all the readers who made my first two books successful. That has encouraged me to try again, and here we are. I hope you enjoy reading the books as much as I enjoy writing them.

I want to thank Vince Conti for the beautiful cover, Elizabeth Mackey for the cover consultation, and Jamie Lee Scott for the amazing travel map. I especially want to thank my editor at Emerald Ink, who helped me pull this book together from a concept to a finished product.

Also, thanks are in order to my friends and fellow authors Kelly Utt and Shannon Brown for their extensive insight, support, and patience, and finally to my wife, Diana. She told me I could do this! So I did. She's also a great beta reader.

ABOUT THE AUTHOR

LP Snyder is a life-long reader who, at the last minute, decided to become a writer. It's been a great experience, and he wonders why it took so long to decide! Having read a little of most genres, LP decided to stick with his favorites—adventure, espionage, and crime thrillers! If you like fast-paced, humorous, action-filled, suspense thrillers, he's your Huckleberry!

Newsletter subscribers receive bonus content, including short stories and extended epilogues. Don't be afraid to ride that train!

Sign up at www.lpsnyder.com.